RESIST

RESIST

EMILY ANN PUTZKE

The White Rose Press

ISBN: 978-0996385428

We will not be silent.
We are your bad conscience.
The White Rose will not
leave you in peace!

PART ONE

a confession

I don't know what possessed me to begin composing this confession. I haven't any doubt the Gestapo will burn it upon finding it, or perhaps it'll rot in the corner of this cell until Stadelheim is finally bombed. Even with this in mind, still I feel inclined to write. What reward could I possibly reap when my literary work (if I'm even qualified to call it that) will almost certainly be destroyed? Perhaps I am addled in the head. But when I feel the urge to pen down my words, I succumb to it. A strange restlessness would take over if I didn't. Anxiety. Insomnia. So I write. I simply cannot relinquish the burning passion.

I suppose the root of this work stems from a strange blend of melancholia, defiance, and a feeling of pride. Not sinful pride, though Lord knows I've battled with that matter my whole life. No. It's not that.

Pride. I'm proud of my actions because I did them in light of my moral, God-given duty. I'm proud of my companions and the work we did together.

Melancholia. It's real and present. How could I not feel it? I would be a liar if I said it didn't course through my veins and ache in my bones.

Defiance. We frightened the Nazis with our words. We wouldn't be here if that weren't true.

When I was a boy, I dreamt of forging my mark into the world. Perhaps I've done that, but not in the way my younger self would ever have contemplated in a million years. Yes, I've forged my way to twenty-four years. I sit in a prison cell, dubbed a treasonous criminal of my homeland. I don't want to be a hero by any means, but I long to be respected. I perceive that the Third Reich will crumble within the year, but suppose it doesn't. My comrades and I will be forever marked as criminals of the state. That is a matter I cannot let rest. That is why I now take this pen in hand to write my story—my confession if you will.

A confession of a broken human being who is far from perfect, but longed to do good in the world. It won't be as poetic, deep, or theological as Augustine's. But it is my story, and if for some heavenly reason it survives, perhaps it'll give you courage.

the piped piper

I must be frank, and not lead you to believe I was entirely innocent and always against National Socialism. I've contemplated beginning this story elsewhere, but that's when my sinful pride flares up in all its grotesque colors.

Do any of us wish to recall our shortcomings? Yet, this story would not be complete without them. It would not be authentic. How easy it would be to say that my father and I got on grandly, that consequently no bitter words were exchanged in our home. As it was, I recall a particularly painful conversation, one that rattled the windows, one that echoed through the house.

In the March of 1933, I joined the Hitler Youth.

The Hitler Youth.

Those words once sent a shock of exhilaration through my veins, causing my boyish energy to flare and my patriotic heart to swell. I would proudly don my Hitler Youth knife with the bright swastika on its handle. I polished the blade every morning. I displayed it to my sisters, brother, friends, and acquaintances with rapture. I knew all the songs, could march as well as any soldier. Hitler was, in a way, my god. At fifteen, I couldn't fathom my father's displeasure towards what I considered my patriotic duty.

I was sitting in the living room. My legs were sprawled out in front of me lazily, and my arms were crossed in a cocky bravado. One eyebrow was raised while my eyes followed Father's form as he paced back and forth in front of me. I was about to receive a tongue lashing, but I didn't care. Father's hands were buried in his pockets, and a cigar was wedged in the corner of his mouth. His mustache twitched. His brown eyes were aflame.

"You listen to me, Hans Scholl." Father cast his dark eyes on me, but I was unassailable, glaring in defiance. "Adolf Hitler is the devil himself."

I laughed then, just to mock his intense conviction.

"What are you talking about? Father," I leaned forward and spoke with my hands, as if he were unable to comprehend my words. "Hitler is *ending* the depression. Our people have jobs again." I was inwardly glowing with what I now identify as arrogance. I thought it was intelligence.

"Yes, Hitler's ending the depression, but he's leading us into war. The wheels of the war industry are turning once again. Hans, my son, just look at the barracks being built, the autobahn. Hitler's leading us right into a total war. He's handing it to us on a silver platter, and the people are dumb enough to take it." Father laughed bitterly, positioning his cigar between his thumb and finger.

I sat up straight, slighted. "Germany is becoming strong again."

"Ah!" Father turned, shaking a finger at me. "Strong. But how. And why? My boy, can you not see where this will all end? Can't you?"

"This is our chance for Germany to prove itself to the world—to prove that we are a great country that deserves to be honored. Hitler is being praised abroad. Look for yourself! Right here in the paper is an interview with Lloyd George." I lifted the paper I had been reading before the confrontation. "George calls Hitler a great leader. He wishes England had a statesman like him."

"Ha! I know more about the Nazis than that Lloyd George

fellow does." Father waved his hand at the paper, his nose wrinkled in disgust. "The Nazis are criminals. They're misusing our people and defiling our country. Mark my words."

"Our people believe in him. They support him." My voice was growing louder. I saw my sisters peek into the room, then disappear hastily.

"Hitler is the Pied Piper, luring the children to perdition with charming tunes on his flute. Don't you remember me reading that story to you, Hans? Don't you see the horrible resemblance? Are you so blind as not to see it?" He hit the back of my head to knock some sense into me.

"You're comparing our Führer to a children's fairy tale?" I couldn't believe what I was hearing. The analogy was entirely immature.

"Because it's true."

"Think what you like. I believe Hitler is going to change Germany."

"Change. Yes, I agree with you there. But what kind of change?"

"He's going to lead us to prosperity. Germany will be respected again."

Father groaned, raking a hand through his thinning brown hair. "Our people are desperate for change. They will listen to any matter of lies, for they have nothing else to grasp onto. They are a hopeless, faithless people."

"What do you have against the Hitler Youth, Father? What is so wrong with serving the Fatherland? I just don't understand your reasoning, and I never will."

"Hitler!" Father sneered. "*Hitler* is what I have against the Hitler Youth! He has no right to defile the Fatherland in this way."

I groaned, burying my head in my hands and ardently wished my father was like my friends' fathers. They supported their sons. They saw hope in the future of Hitler's Germany. Mine was going to get us all into trouble.

"You're so old fashioned! You don't see progress when it's right before you. You're blinding yourself to something good ... something bigger than ourselves. In Hitler's Germany, we must all work together to make the country rise above all the others."

Father's eyes were a concoction of pain and frustration. "You, my son, don't see destruction when it's right before you."

I stood up, nearly eye to eye with my father now. I pulled my shoulders back and held my head high, earnestly wishing my posture would provide me three more inches in height.

"Destruction? Hitler is enriching this country. A flame of pride is burning in every German soul. This is not destruction; this is love for the Fatherland! Why can't you see that?" I was shouting now, intoxicated by anger.

Father placed a firm hand on my shoulder. Our eyes met. "I cannot persuade you against making a terrible decision, one that your sisters and brother will undoubtedly follow. You are the one they look up to. Don't forget that. I pray you will see reason someday, Hans."

I jerked my shoulder free from his grasp, letting father's hand fall to his side. I turned and grabbed my jacket which laid over the back of the sofa.

"Where are you going?"

"To a Hitler Youth meeting, as if you care." I flung my arms through my jacket sleeves with vengeance.

Father took long strides to the window, popping the cigar in his mouth again. He crossed his arms over his chest and fixed his gaze on the Cathedral. I shot him a dagger-like glare as I headed toward the front door. I turned the knob and heard mother's voice.

"He's young, Robert," she said. "He doesn't know what he's doing."

My fists were balled tight. I felt my nails tear through my skin. "I know what I'm doing," I shouted, hostility dripping from every word. "It's you who don't."

despite all powers

Three years passed and with it more hostile remarks between me and my father. By this time, my siblings were all members of various branches within the Hitler Youth. Father was right. They did look up to me.

In the span of those years, the thrill I once felt course through my veins began to turn cold. No, I wouldn't dare tell Father, not after my confident words and my arrogance. It would be entirely too painful and degrading. So I went on, a blind follower. The incessant drills, marching, and speeches drove me to distraction. I couldn't think. When I can't ponder in freedom, I grow moody and elusive.

They took away the books I pored over with rapture— Heine, Remarque, Zweig. They burned their words until only ashes remained. They replaced my repertoire of folk songs from various countries with strictly German marching songs. Songs whose sentiment I couldn't abide.

Germany, awake from your nightmare!
Give foreign Jews no place in your Reich!
We will fight for your resurgence!
Aryan blood shall never perish!

I'm ashamed to say I remember all the words to this particular song. With such a small collection to choose from, these songs were drilled into our minds relentlessly. I was no longer Hans Scholl, the independent thinker. I was becoming whomever they molded me to be. And I had no voice in the matter.

"You were chosen to be the standard-bearer at the Nuremberg rally?" My older sister excitedly fussed around me when I told her. "Hans! That's a wonderful accomplishment!"

I told her that I didn't know why they chose me of all people. Yes, I had been promoted to squad leader, but there were plenty of other boys they could choose from. We were in the kitchen at the time. Mother was scrubbing something in the sink. I was sitting on the counter, fingering my Hitler Youth knife. Inge sat at the table with Elizabeth, Sophie, and Werner, assisting them with their studies.

Mother glanced over her shoulder at me. She smiled, wrinkles forming around her ever-loving and affectionate eyes. "That's obvious, Hans. You're the handsomest boy in the unit."

"The girls will simply faint dead away when you pass by," Elizabeth snickered, her eyes twinkling with mischief.

The tips of my ears burned bright red. I kept my head down, twisting the knife this way and that, watching the light reflect off the smooth blade.

"I think it's more than that," reflected Sophie.

I glanced up, our eyes meeting. She was sixteen now, sporting a boyish haircut that resembled Werner's. Sophie was always such a tomboy, but there was a feminine grace about her and a childlike innocence. A patch of dark hair fell over her brown eyes, and she was smiling.

"It's your conviction. When you are passionate about something, you dive into it with all your energy. You don't hold back."

be good

I was dressed in the Hitler Youth uniform—a brown shirt with a swastika armband and black shorts. I admired the lanyards and emblems pinned to my shoulder. The standard-bearer emblem was my newest pride. The badge with the silver eagle and black swastika outlined by bold red and white gave me the feeling of superiority. I placed my Hitler Youth knife in its sheath and was about to swing open my door when I saw Mother standing outside it, twisting her hands restlessly.

"Mother?"

"Hans." She eyed my uniform with a mother's concern. "Are you all packed?"

"Yes." I stepped back, allowing her to walk in, for she evidently wished to talk or check my bags to make sure I didn't exclusively pack books.

She slowly made her way to my bed, running her fingers across a woolen sweater which lay inside out on my blanket. My school boy clothes were replaced by a uniform. It pained her. I'd be stupid not to see it. She turned her face toward me, forcing a smile. "You look very nice, Hans. Very handsome."

I nodded my thanks, scratching the back of my neck. I didn't care for the look in her eyes when they fell on my armband and the standard-bearer badge. She turned away quickly, setting to work on pulling my sweater sleeves to their rightful place then folding it gently.

"You grew up so fast," she said, her voice heavy with regret.

A dagger pierced my heart. "Yes, but you knew it would happen, Mother. Everyone has to grow up."

"Yes." She opened my bureau drawer and placed the folded sweater inside. "But the Hitler Youth caused it to happen swifter than it needed to be."

"How do you suppose?" I leaned against the open door, arms crossed.

"Hans, you're hardly ever home these days." She began smoothing the wrinkles in my blanket. "The Hitler Youth kept you away from us when you should have been home being a child."

"We can't be children anymore. There's no use for it. If we wish for a greater country and to do our part for the Reich, we have to grow up faster than past generations."

She paused, a hand lingering on the cover of my blanket as she brought it up over the pillows. "I've seen what happens when a generation is forced to grow up too quickly," she said. "Those boys should never have been sent off to fight in a war."

The Great War. Mother always talked about the lost generation with such anguish. When I considered The Great War, I thought of only one thing. The damned Treaty of Versailles.

"Our generation will be different," I said. "We won't be trampled on again."

Mother now moved to my suitcase which lay open on my desk. "You have everything you need?"

"Yes."

"Mind if I just check?"

I shrugged as she peeked into the suitcase. She picked up a book by Stefan Zweig and another by Heinrich Heine, holding them lovingly to her chest. "I'm glad to see you haven't changed too much." She smiled, her eyes lighting up again at last. She set the books down and placed a hand on my shoulder.

"Despite all powers—" she whispered.

"Maintain yourself," I finished the quotation from Goethe.

She kissed my cheek, then patted the side of my face gently. "Be good."

Be good. That's the last thing she said as I slipped out of the room and hurried to the train station. *Be good.*

nuremburg, 1936

I went to Nuremberg with my Hitler Youth unit, bored of the infernal marching and monotony. I was becoming enraged that no originality was allowed. Still a thrill seized me against my better judgement. I could easily crush those seeds of doubt that were beginning to grow when the heady fanfare and excitement encompassed the rally. We were taken by train, bedecked with banners, flags, and soft, leather seats. I was made to feel like an important dignitary. I pushed my feelings aside, convincing myself, *"It's all right. This is what you're supposed to be doing. This is for Germany."*

My eyes swept the vast Zeppelin field in complete awe. I wasn't admiring the bleachers packed full of thousands upon thousands of people as they cheered and shouted. No, I was in awe at the stupidity of it. The lack of diversity. Everyone looked entirely the same. Same uniforms, same banners, same cheers, same speeches. Our Hitler Youth unit marched in unison, not one boy getting too far ahead or behind the others.

"Heil Hitler!" Our chant was lost in the sea of SA, SS, and Hitler Youth. The shouts filled the field and banners rippled in the wind like waves.

Being selected as a standard-banner carrier for the largest rally in Germany was the greatest honor bestowed on a young man. The marching, singing and speeches were meant to enliven our spirits and patriotism for the Fatherland. I raised my right arm in the Nazi salute, joining another chorus of, "Heil Hitler!" The heils roared from the ground, rising like incense to the podium where the Führer stood waving to his people. He was silhouetted against three, stark red Nazi banners.

"I salute you, my banner carriers! You are the hope of the present and the guarantors of our future. You are the standard-bearers of a new history!" The Führer's voice penetrated the crowd, causing us to cheer exuberantly. "We live in exciting times. We make no complaints. We are used to battle, for out of it we came. We will plant our feet firmly in our earth, and no attack will move us. You will stand with me, should such a time come! You will stand before me, at my side, and behind me, holding our flags high! Let our old enemies attempt to rise up once more! They may wave their Soviet flags before us—but our flag will win the battle!"

The band beat its drums as the tune of *Horst Wessel Lied* filled the air.

Clear the streets for the brown battalions,
Clear the streets for the storm division!
Millions are looking upon the swastika full of hope,
The day of freedom and of bread dawns!

We had trained for this day—the day we were to present our unit's banner to the Führer himself. It was evening, and a brisk breeze made our faces ruddy. During a short break from the marching drills, I sank into the grass near my tent, cracking open a book by Zweig. I relished any moments in which I could devour stories. I flipped the pages, fully absorbed until the lighting suddenly changed. I glanced around as a long, dark shadow covered my pages. The senior troop leader was standing above me, one hand on his sheath.

"What are you reading there?" It wasn't a conversational tone. It was stern, as if I were doing something terribly wrong.

"It's *Decisive Moments in History*. One of my favorites since childhood."

He held his hand out. "Let me see it."

I reluctantly handed it to him. It was old and worn, for I had taken it everywhere with me since I was eleven. He flipped it open and leafed through the pages with a scowl. "This is forbidden." He closed the book quickly, tapping it against his palm. "This is trash."

"What?" I stood up, indignant of this accusation against

my favorite piece of literature. "You can't forbid me to read that book."

"Yes, I can." He pointed to the author's name on the cover with a sneer. "Zweig is a Jewish author. It's forbidden to read his work. Listen," he glared at me, "I better not catch you reading this filth ever again, understand?"

I didn't say anything. I couldn't comprehend what he was saying. How would a book make or break the Third Reich? They couldn't simply ban all books written by Jewish authors because they were Jewish, could they? If so, something was internally wrong with this system. That's when I began to realize that we were slowly being denied our human rights.

And the people didn't seem to notice or care.

the banner

That evening I stood with the unit of boys under my command, waiting for the senior Hitler Youth leader to inspect us before the official ceremony. I allowed one of the younger boys to hold the prized banner we'd all made together and to which we had pledged our loyalty. Tired of the swastika banners every group paraded, we wished to distinguish ourselves by creating a banner with mythical beasts and symbols. We were all exceptionally proud of it. The younger boy gripped it tightly with a look of wonder across his face.

We stood for a good fifteen minutes in the parade group, arms behind our backs, eyes forward. I finally spotted the senior leader marching toward us. His steel grey eyes were fixed on our banner.

"What's that?" he yelled, pointing to our banner as it snapped crisply in the wind.

"That is our troop banner," I said. Was he dimwitted?

The senior leader wasn't much older than I, but he demanded respect. He was tall and broad shouldered with unsettling dark eyes.

"You're the troop leader?" He glowered at me, fury blazing in his eyes.

"Yes."

"Then you know that only symbols prescribed in the manual are acceptable. Hand it over."

An aggravated groan traveled through our ranks.

"I said hand it over. Are you deaf?" The senior leader was in the face of the young boy holding the flag, the veins in his neck bulging. He reached out to rip it away from the boy. The boy hesitated, peering from the senior leader to me. His eyes begged me to do something. They didn't have to. My jaw was clenched tight. I took a step forward, breaking up the confrontation. The senior leader straightened before me and crossed his arms.

"Let him keep the flag. They worked so hard on it," I said steadily.

"And disgrace the Hitler Youth? Get him to hand the flag over, or I'll see you stripped of your rank."

"What's so wrong with having a unique flag? It's no crime."

"Yes, it is. The manual clearly states—"

"That's stupid. We're keeping the flag."

The senior leader took a step forward, giving me a firm shove with both hands. I faltered backward for a moment before gaining my footing. What right had they to take our flag away? He threw his fist my way, but I dodged it and cuffed the side of his face. Pain permeated my knuckles, but I was strangely satisfied for a moment when the senior leader lost his footing and tumbled to the ground. His hand clutched the side of his face where blood dripped down his chin.

I rubbed my fist as the boys behind me beamed. But when the senior leader cast those steel eyes on me, I suddenly realized what I had done. Insubordination. I would be stripped of my rank. That much was set in stone. The damage was done. The senior leader was picking himself up, wiping the blood away with the back of his sleeve. "You'll pay for this." His threat lingered in the air long after he had stalked away.

My days as a troop leader were over and so was my fervor for the Hitler Youth. I didn't care anymore.

reconciled

Father and I walked slowly along the Danube river. The silence laid heavy between us. I tossed a pebble, sending it rippling across the clear water. It was brisk that night. I turned my collar up to shield me from the cool breezes. Streaks of coral ripped through the oncoming grey, begging to stay just a little longer. Gravel crunched under my boots. Father said nothing. I cleared my throat as we strolled, wrapped up in tension, hurt, and pain. I had requested we take this walk, but all of the things I had planned to say seemed so petty and dull now. I hadn't very much practice at asking for forgiveness.

"Nice night," I said.

"Mhmm."

I glanced up at the trees, stark and bare against the now grey sky. The colors of day were swept away rapidly.

"Though it's rather cold."

"Mhmm."

I kicked a stone with my boot, scolding myself for being so weak.

"Father, I'm ... I'm really sorry."

"I know you are, son."

"I was so stupid. You warned me, and I didn't listen. I just ... I want to be a part of something bigger than myself. I want to do good."

"You will, Hans. God has plans for you."

I nodded. "I still feel like an idiot."

"Leave the past behind you. Forge forward into a new, fresh start, son. You'll change the world."

I glanced at my father out of the corner of my eye. He was grinning, his hat pushed to the back of his head and his hands buried deep in his pockets. He peered at me, and I smiled in response.

"Thank you."

Father checked his pocket watch, then snapped it shut. "Half past seven. We'll be late for dessert and coffee if we linger long. The girls are having their friends over tonight though Lord knows they pay more attention to you. Perhaps I should keep you out here, so Sophie won't have to deal with friends driven to distraction."

I shoved his shoulder. "That's not true."

"Oh! But it is," he gave me a shove back. I teetered toward the edge of the water. For a moment, it felt like I was taking a walk with my brother. If it were Werner, I'd have thrown him in the Danube. But seeing as it was Father, I thought it best to refrain.

france, 1940

"I swear by God this holy oath. To the leader of the German Reich, Adolf Hitler, total loyalty and obedience."

There are matters in life that rest entirely out of our control, and the only way to get through them is to grit our teeth, beseech God for courage, and go along on our way. I resolved to deal with these matters as courageously as I could—from serving six months in the Reich Labor Service, to being drafted into the Wehrmacht.

I was a half student, half soldier, studying medicine while completing my military service. I wore the field-grey of Hitler's soldiers. I bore the service cap, the army boots. I was, in every outward way, the ideal German soldier of the Third Reich. Only this time, my father wasn't angry with me, for this hadn't been my choice.

During the Battle of France, I was called to active duty as a medic and dispatch rider on the front lines.

War.

I was naive in my conceptions of it. Fresh from my medical books, I was filled with a youthful vigor to strike out on an adventure. Yet in good conscience, I could not contribute to the German war machine. My one consolation was that, as a medic, I would be spared from the fighting. My job was to heal, not harm.

It was spring. The air was heavy with the scent of sulfur, smoke, and death. A year prior that spring day would have held the smells of something entirely different. The French would have been going about their daily routines, shopping, sitting at a cafe, working. Their children would be playing. But the accursed war had stripped it all away, leaving destruction and filth in its wake. German panzers destroyed everything in their paths. The Luftwaffe overtook the country. France was being obliterated.

We were stationed at a hospital in Paris and billeted in occupied homes. I would have preferred a straw mat to the stolen beds. The way our soldiers treated the French made me sick.

One morning I was working in the recovery room. A young German soldier lay on a hospital cot. He had been wounded on the front lines, temporarily patched up at a field hospital there, then rushed to the hospital in Paris for professional treatment. He had a neck wound that the doctors had sewn up without any complications. Doctor Eisenberg was checking over the patient as I began tidying up the room.

"You're going to be discharged today," I said to the soldier. My back was turned as I packed the man's belongings. "Your wife is in the corridor waiting for you. She came all the way to escort you home."

I whipped around when I heard Doctor Eisenberg yell, and my limbs lost all their strength. The soldier was convulsing. The smell of blood overtook the room as it trickled down the man's neck in thick lines, seeping through the cotton of his shirt. He was gasping. His blue eyes were wild.

"Hold him still!" Doctor Eisenberg swiftly worked his gloved hands along the soldier's neck.

I gripped two firm hands on the patient's shoulders as the doctor began tying the jugular vein in his neck to stop the excessive bleeding. His efforts appeared fruitless, for the blood continued to trickle down. I felt the warmth of it on my hands and watched as it trailed down my knuckles. The doctor cursed, then stumbled back. His hands were dripping with blood, and he wiped them on his apron, leaving crimson hand marks on the already stained cloth. The crimson mixed with the yellow and copper blotches, leaving behind yet another trace of war. I felt the soldier's body fall limp under my hands.

"He's dead," the doctor said flatly, no hint of compassion or sadness lacing his words. Just the stark truth.

"What happened?" I stood up, laying the man's head on the pillow. I stared at his glazed over, lifeless eyes then turned away, swallowing a lump in my throat. "He was fine ... he was going home!"

"The wound reopened." Doctor Eisenberg peered at me over his spectacles. "Tell his wife."

"What?" I couldn't imagine going out into the corridor at that moment to tell a young girl that her husband was dead. That he had bled to death. That he died for a corrupt cause and an even more corrupt dictator. I couldn't.

"Go!" The doctor's voice echoed through the empty room, stirring me to action.

"Yes, sir." I wiped off my hands, leaving the blood behind on a cotton cloth before pulling off my white medical coat and tossing it aside. I glanced once more at the corpse, then turned and walked into the corridor, only wishing to get it over with.

I had seen death countless times. I had performed amputations in field hospitals on my own. But I wasn't like the other medical staff. I couldn't become accustomed to it. I couldn't even feign that I wasn't troubled by it. For a split second, I almost wished I were stationed at the field hospital again. One didn't have to confront family members of the deceased there.

A small assembly of women was sitting at the end of the hall. One small woman was especially animated and cheerful. She must be the one, for the other women were somber. I had to tell her. I had to ruin her blissful spirits.

I breathed in deeply before saying, "Frau Dahl?"

The young woman stood up, looking hardly older than my sisters. She had a young, rosy face, and in her hands was a bouquet of flowers which filled the room with the sweet scent of life. The vivid colors were a drastic antithesis to the gloom around us.

"I'm Frau Dahl. I've come to see my husband, Private Josef Dahl. He's supposed to be discharged today. Has there been a delay?"

I looked beyond her, not wishing to meet her eyes. "We tried to save your husband. I'm so sorry." My eyes fell on her face despite my resistance, and I watched with gut wrenching pain as her blissful countenance was swept away, replaced with utter despair.

"No, no, no. You have the wrong patient. There must be more than one Private Dahl in here. My husband is being discharged today. He's coming home!" She laughed nervously.

"He's gone, Frau Dahl."

"No. No, he's not!" She dropped the flowers into a mangled heap on the floor. She was placid for a long moment then suddenly lunged at me, gripping her sharp fingernails into my shoulders. "Go get him right now!" she screeched. I cringed under her grip and attempted to release the woman's nails from my skin. "Please, Frau Dahl! There was nothing we could do."

"How? How did he die?" She stumbled back and fell into a chair, her eyes searching the floor as if she lost something. "He bled to death." I didn't know how to sugar coat the truth, or if I even should.

"Why did he come to this God-forsaken place? Why did he join up? Why was he such a fool?" She was weeping now, but I felt it was safer to keep my distance than attempt to comfort her.

"He did what he thought was right. He was trying to serve and protect the Fatherland," I tentatively placed a hand on her shoulder. "I am truly sorry."

My throat tightened as I turned to escape through a door that led into the alleyway between the hospital and an adjoining building. The wind was brisk that day, carrying ghastly odors on its wings. I fished in my pocket for a cigarette, lit it, then leaned against the hospital wall as I took a drag. I exhaled the smoke into the air, trying to make sense of what was happening around me. The door flew open and out came a fellow medical student, Roland. He nodded to me as he lit his cigarette.

"Taking a break, too?"

"I needed it."

"What happened?"

"A soldier was supposed to go home today, but he died in the recovery room. I was the one assigned to tell his wife."

"Ah, that's hell," Roland said, shaking his head. "But don't worry too much, Scholl. Think of that wine cellar at our château. We'll all be drunk in a few more hours."

"It's not our château."

Roland narrowed his eyes. "What do you mean?"

"We stole someone's home. That was really chivalrous of us, the supposed master race. We're criminals, all of us." Roland pulled the cigarette from his lips, tossing it on the ground. "Shut up, Scholl, before you get in trouble." I challenged his glare. "You live in a nice home, don't you, Roland?"

"I do."

"Let's say that the French were landing an assault against our homeland—"

"They can't even protect *their* homeland, let alone attack the German empire."

"Suppose they did get into Germany, and the first thing they did was march into your home and throw you out. Then they destroy your cities, kill your friends, family, and commit other unspeakable atrocities. Could you still consider them 'the master race' after their actions?"

Roland took a step toward me, grabbing me by the collar and shoving me against the wall. "You better watch your mouth if you want to survive this war, Scholl. I could report you right now."

He released me, but his eyes held a threat in them. "Don't go telling tales when you get home. They won't believe you anyway."

eickemeyer

After serving in France, I was shipped back to Germany and studied medicine at the University of Munich. I would not comply with Roland's threat. I attempted to make the most of my time in Munich by finding out the truth of the crimes our country was committing and beginning a course to oppose it.

That's how I met Manfred Eickemeyer, and that's how he added to my already growing strong opposition toward the Third Reich. We were introduced through a mutual friend, an elderly professor for whom I organized books. Eickemeyer and I soon discovered that we could trust each other with the dangerous topic of war and politics. He arranged a meeting with me one morning to tell me of the Third Reich's behavior in occupied territories.

The heightened wind was brisk and misty. My breath crystallized in the morning fog. My fingers ached to the bone yet I pedaled harder up the steep road, exerting my body with reckless abandon. I attempted to ignore the aching cold in my ears and instead let my eyes wander to the pools of water running off the cobblestone street, taking the filth and debris in their watery clutches. A light rain fell all around me, soaking my collar until it clung to my neck. It ran down my face, smelling like purity. It was purifying the city, at least its exterior. No amount of rainfall could purify its core. I passed a skeleton of a house. The beams were burnt, but the morning shower was cleansing the ashes. I saw a child sitting among the ruins. His soot covered face was situated between two little tanned hands. He peered at me as I rode by, and I promptly back pedaled.

"Where are your parents?" I asked him.

He took in my uniform with wide, russet eyes. "At my aunt's."

"Why aren't you there, too?"

"Thought I'd see if anything was left."

What happened to the land I once loved? My heart stirred in anger to see homes and families destroyed, yet I know it is necessary for the ultimate victory. The Allies wouldn't bomb those who are desperately wishing to be released from the Nazi claw, but they have no way of knowing, for we don't even know the loyalties of each other ... of *ourselves*. How can Allied airmen hundreds of feet above Munich know if we don't even know?

I pedaled on, my grin no longer present. The morning seemed darker, crueler, and an intense despair seized me.

The rain let up as I neared Leopoldstrasse 38, but clouds of grey mist still hovered above the streets. No one was around. The stillness was loud to me. Can silence be deafening? I leaned my bike against the outside of my destination—Eickemeyer's garden house—and simply stared at the door for a long moment. I twisted the excess water from the cuffs of my uniform and combed my fingers through my hair. A cold burst of water dripped down from the roof and trickled down my face, landing on my lips. I wondered if I should save this errand for a day with more sun. But no. Time was of the essence. I had held back long enough.

I rapped on the thick, wooden door, surprised at the noise it made as it echoed through the vacant street. As I waited, I kicked a stone with the side of my boot, watching as it skidded across a murky puddle. I lifted my eyes to the door. No one came. I knocked again, grinding my heel into the gravel. The door creaked open, boisterously at first, then growing quieter as it reached its full width. Eickemeyer stood there, his hair white as a fresh snow and his eyes intense and alert. He was short in stature, donning a pair of spectacles. His dark green knitted sweater bore paint stains along the cuffs. He said my name in an urgent whisper.

"Hans Scholl?"

I nodded. "Good morning, Herr Eickemeyer."

"Morning?" His voice was raspy, as if he had just woken up. "More like the middle of the night."

I glanced at my watch which was smudged with a film of water. It read 5:00 A.M.

"I'm sorry," I apologized. "But this was the only time I could spare."

He grunted something I couldn't hear or comprehend. I stepped into the foyer, wiping my boots on a small, faded red mat. The artist's studio was veiled in dark, grey shadows. Thick blackout curtains hung over the windows, and the floorboards creaked under my boots. The door shut behind me. I heard the lock slide. Eickemeyer pulled the lightbulb chain, the dim glow immediately revealing a homey parlor.

"Would you like coffee or a cigarette?"

I opted with the former. He disappeared into a side room, then reappeared with a tin cup—army issued—filled to the brim with ersatz coffee. I sat down in a high-backed chair, my wet uniform clinging to the wood. The hot coffee relaxed my stiff fingers, and I slowly reclined into the seat. Eickemeyer was clearing his throat as he fished in his coat pocket for a cigarette. I took the opportunity to study his bookshelf to the left of me. I was immediately disappointed in his choice of literature, though it cannot be called literature at all. Painting, sculpting, and architecture instructionals. Perhaps only the mind of an artist could appreciate the thick tomes sitting beside me.

The strike of a match brought my eyes to my host. A small, orange glow hovered beside his wrinkled face as he lit his cigarette. His face reminded me of a map—lines and creases intertwined on tanned skin. His eyes were dull. They brought my mind back to the charred home I had just recently passed—dark, lonely, and stripped of all life. In that moment, I feared. In his eyes were unspoken words of pain and despair. Words I was about to hear. I took a long sip of the coffee, then placed it on the end table beside me. I ran both hands along the arms of the chair, patiently waiting for Eickemeyer to sit. He was pulling back the curtain and gazing outside with a cigarette between his lips.

The silence rang in my ears. I pushed my boot against the floor, just to break the uncomfortable stillness. Eickemeyer glanced over his shoulder at me, as if just recalling that I was sitting there.

"We *did* schedule our meeting for today, didn't we?" I asked uncertainly.

"Of course, and I remembered it. I'm not that old. Not yet."

"War is dangerous to discuss these days," I said.

"Exceptionally. But I trust you. I trust that you can do something about our situation." Eickemeyer's hard gaze was on me.

Could I do something? Could anyone? People must feel it deep in their souls, the desire to do something against the regime. But it rarely grows to be any more than that. A desire. Except, I don't intend to be among them—the dreamers. No. If they allow their dreams to be dormant, I don't see the point in dreaming at all.

"I'm more than ready to do something. I can't sit back any longer."

He leaned forward conspiratorially. "I'll tell you something, Scholl. I was beginning to doubt our young people. They're all stupid, seduced fools. But not you, Scholl. Not you. Perhaps there is some hope for our future after all." He reclined in his seat and stared at the ceiling with a distant look in his sorrowful eyes. "I'll tell you what I've seen on the front."

I watched the man's features intently. Eickemeyer attempted to form words, stopped, then tried again. "I spend a great deal of time in the East, working in construction. My working base is Krakow, which allows me to observe how our soldiers treat people in occupied areas. The SS-Einsatzgruppen," Eickemeyer's voice faltered, and he raked a hand through his white hair. "Their specialty is mass execution. These SS killers are chosen for their ruthlessness."

He stared at me, now speaking with trembling hands.

"Three thousand men who wouldn't think twice about shooting men, women, and children. They simply barge into a village, gather up all the Jews and take away everything these people own, including the clothing off their backs. The Jews are marched to their execution site which is usually a large crater caused by bombings. They're lined up in front of it. Fearful. Pale. Embarrassed by the disregard of their dignity. The SS then release their machine guns on them, and the people tumble back into their graves. The blood ... everywhere ... screams fill the air ..."

If I were some literary genius, perhaps I could explain the way my stomach twisted just then. It reminded me of when my mother would twist a dish cloth after scrubbing dishes. It was as if a cold hand had grabbed my intestines and given them a good wringing. I couldn't say I was incredibly surprised by this lack of human dignity. Hadn't the Nazis rounded up the mentally ill and gassed them all to death? What would stop them from doing this to the Jews ... or anyone they felt inclined to dub "sub-human"?

"You would think a human would feel guilty about these disgusting acts against their fellow man. But no. I'm starting to wonder if the SS are human at all. I saw this happen, Scholl. I saw the terrified, panic stricken faces of the men, women, children, and heard the crying babies." He leaned his wrinkled face into his hands. "I heard the SS joke around after the grave had been filled. They joke about how their fingers hurt from pulling the trigger so many times in a row. They *laugh*. Those bastards laugh as if it is the most humorous thing in the world! What has happened to our country, Scholl? What has happened to our respect for human life?"

Eickemeyer was quiet at length and stared numbly at the floor. "Russians and Poles have been sent to concentration camps for slave labor, which can only mean one thing— torture and death. Slave labor and mass killings. That's what they're doing out there, Scholl. That's what they don't want us to know." Eickemeyer eyed me. "And that's not all."

Must this man go on? And yet, I wanted him to. I needed to know the truth.

"They round up young girls in the occupied areas." Eickemeyer's face drained of color. "They send them to SS brothels."

Suppose we hadn't been so 'fortunate' as to have been

born with pure German blood in our veins? Those would be
my sisters, taken away. And if I tried to save them, I would
be just one more opposer sentenced to torture ... or immediate death. It felt suddenly very cold in the studio. I needed to act.
When he asked if I believed him, I nodded firmly. I would be
a fool not to believe. No, perhaps not a fool. I would be a callous perpetrator, perhaps as vile as the Nazis. They knew the
deeds they committed and did so without remorse. If I knew
what was happening but gave it no heed, I was voluntarily
allowing my people to be devoured by wolves.

gisela

I was home on leave for an entire week. Having just come in
from an evening walk with my father, I tossed my uniform
jacket over the arm of the sofa and caught Mother's stern
glance from across the room. She was knitting, her feet
propped up on a stool. She didn't speak a word, but I caught
her meaning. I picked up my jacket and headed toward the
front closet, hanging it up like I ought to have in the first
place. The rich scent of chocolate drifted through the house,
and I could hear female laughter coming from the brightly lit
kitchen.

"There's cake and coffee in the kitchen, Hans," Mother
said. "Help yourself."

The smell was too intoxicating, so I resolved to hurry into
the kitchen, snatch my share, and leave without conversing
with the girls. If what father told me was true, I didn't wish
to 'distract' Sophie's friends from her. Perhaps I'd pore over
books with Werner.

I entered the kitchen where the sweet smell was stronger
and richer. Inge, Elizabeth, Sophie, and their three friends sat
around the kitchen table, poking their forks into their slices

of chocolate cake. Sophie glanced up when I entered. Her face brightened, and she leaped out of her seat.

"There you are! There's someone I've been dying to introduce to you." Sophie linked her arm through mine and led me to the congregation of girls. Inge and Elizabeth were grinning over their cups of coffee. I recognized the other two girls as friends of my sisters. The third girl I had never seen before. She was small and fair, with golden hair and large, blue eyes. She smiled at me.

"Gisela, this is my *favorite* brother, Hans. Shh, don't tell Werner," Sophie laughed.

"I heard that." Werner came in, glaring at Sophie in mock annoyance. "I thought I was your favorite brother, Sophie."

Sophie smiled sweetly. "Oh, how could I play favorites? You're both dear brothers. Hans is my favorite older brother, you see, and you're my favorite little brother."

"I'm not that little." He sank into a chair next to Elizabeth. "Nearly twenty, you know."

Sophie turned her attention back to Gisela. "Don't mind him. He's moody."

"Am not."

"Are too. Now, Gisela, this is Hans, the brother I told you all about. Hans, this is Gisela Schertling."

My face burned. The brother she told her all about? Why were they talking about me? I grinned cordially, hiding my embarrassment as best as I possibly could.

"It's a pleasure," I said, holding my hand out. Her small, smooth hand clutched mine. I rapidly pulled my hand back, stuffing it in my pocket. I headed toward the counter where the chocolate cake had been desecrated by the girls. My hand was trembling, which I found odd, as I sank the knife into what remained of the dessert. I suddenly felt like a foolish adolescent, shaken over a brief meeting with a girl.

"Sophie's told me so much about you."

A gentle voice caused my head to turn. Gisela was still

looking at me. I balanced the plate on my hand and stared back. How had I suddenly lost my ability to speak?

"Oh, ah, she hasn't told me much about you." I regretted the words immediately. "I mean ... Sophie and I haven't talked in a while. Both of us are occupied with our work right now, you know." I leaned against the counter, praying I hadn't made a blunder. I risked a glance at her. Gisela was grinning down at her plate. The others had begun talking amongst themselves, all but Gisela. The seat beside her was vacant.

"Care to sit?" she asked, as if this were her home and not mine.

I sat down, nervously clearing my throat. No one was paying attention to us now. They were teasing Werner for being so moody, and he was attempting to defend himself against a gaggle of females.

"Sophie told me you're serving with the student company at the University of Munich."

"That's correct." I took a bite of the cake, wondering what had happened to my get-out-without-conversing plan.

"I hope to attend the university."

"Really?" I glanced at her. "Any idea of what you wish to study?"

"Art and art history."

"That's wonderful! Art is important, especially these days. I'm a medical student, but I'm more inclined to litera-ture, art, and music. I enjoy art galleries immensely. You ought to give us a tour sometime and educate us on the paint-ings," I said. I glanced at Gisela's plate. Her cake was half eaten, and she appeared to be uninterested in it.

"Are you going to finish it?"

She seemed confused. "What? The cake?"

I nodded.

She laughed and slid the plate toward me. "Go ahead. So, Sophie hasn't told you *anything* about me?" She folded her arms on the table.

"Oh, perhaps once or twice in a letter. I don't really remember."

"She talks for eons about you."

"How do you know each other?"

"Reich Labor Service. Most of the girls are annoying, and their talk is, well Sophie and I found our conversations much more stimulating. I mean, not our talk of you. We don't always talk about you. I mean stimulating because we talk of literature and art."

Her face was bright red.

I couldn't help but smirk. "Literature is one of my favorite topics to discuss."

"Really?"

"Give me prose, and I'll attempt to place it." I leaned back in my chair.

"Oh ... all right," Gisela tilted her head upward and bit her lip as she pondered. "'Before him he saw two roads, both equally straight; but he did see two; and that terrified him—he who had never in his life known anything but one straight line. And, bitter anguish, these two roads were contradictory.'"

I took a long moment of reflection before answering. "Victor Hugo. That passage parallels the heart of the German people, don't you think?" I could have kicked myself for being so stupid. Not only was it impolite to bring up politics when we barely knew each other, but suppose she was of an entirely different mind than I? It could be not only impolite, but dangerous.

She gazed at me for a long moment. "Go on," she encouraged.

"I don't know if I should."

"Please, tell me what you mean."

I stared at my boots. "In Hitler's Germany, we are presented with two roads. The easy road and the painful road.

Some of us take the easy road, myself included, for why would you risk your safety if you are a decent German citizen who's minding your own business? You can simply close your eyes to the evil your government is committing and pretend you don't notice while they strip away every freedom you possess. Perhaps you'll make it through the war, through the tyrannical government, but at the end of the road, you will be in utter agony. The road that seemed the easiest led to destruction.

"But perhaps you take the painful road instead, the one that causes you to lie wide awake at night in fear. The one that could cut your life short, but would lead to peace and eternal rest. Would you take it? Would you bear the painful road? As you see, just as Hugo writes, 'these two roads were contradictory.'"

I lifted my gaze, attempting to read her expression. She was staring at the wall, her lips pressed tightly together and her hands crossed in front of her. "You are a very profound young man."

She said it so seriously that for some reason I found it humorous. I laughed, which focused her attention on me. I stopped immediately. "Sorry."

"No, it's all right. It's just that you've given me much to think about. Thank you."

"You instigated it."

"Yes, I suppose so." She smiled. "Now you give me prose."

I ran my fingers along the dents in the table as I pondered. After a moment, I looked at her. "All right. 'Hope has two beautiful daughters; their names are Anger and Courage. Anger at the way things are, and Courage to see that they do not remain as they are.'"

"Oh," she said softly. "Is it Augustine?"

I clapped my hands with a wide grin. "Brilliant, Miss Schertling."

We were quiet at length. She finally turned and stared at me. "That quote resembles our political situation. We must hope and take courage in our Heavenly Father. We must be upset and angry at the injustices that surround us. We must have courage to do something about it."

I stared at her.

"My family is very National Socialist inclined, Hans. I suppose you ought to know that."

"But you don't appear to hold the same views."

"No, but what can I do? I must go on as the good, German girl that everyone thinks I am. Something must be done, but I can't do anything."

I folded my arms across the table and stared at the clock hanging above the counter. This was something I had been mulling over ever since I had been drafted. What *can* be done? They have us in their clutches. It's suicide to try to break free. But surely *something*, some kind of underground resistance could be at work, chipping away at the ground beneath the Nazis' feet. If everyone pitched in, the ground would eventually consume them. I thought it best to keep my theoretical thoughts to myself for the time being.

"They have lost all sense of morals and conscience," I said, more to myself than to Gisela. "And they intend to drag everyone else down to the fiery depths with them."

"How can you abide to wear that uniform if you don't agree with what it stands for? Don't you feel like a hypocrite?"

I furrowed my brow in a contemplative manner, but she must have thought me angry, for she gasped and said, "I'm sorry. I didn't mean ... oh, that was entirely impolite. I'm sorry ..."

"Hans! Oh, please, you're not talking politics with Gisela are you?" Elizabeth's voice pulled me from my thoughts. "Are you boring the girl to death?"

"No, it looks as if he's upset her," Inge said. "Gisela, are you all right? You're bright red."

"Leave them be," Sophie jumped into the conversation. "Hans wouldn't say anything to upset Gisela. Now, Lisa, tell us about your trip to the sea side."

The chattering continued on the other side of the table, but I caught Elizabeth giving me a warning glance. *Don't bore the girl to death,* her eyes seemed to say. I didn't think I was boring her to death. Our conversation was anything but dull. It was rather tension filled.

I turned to Gisela who was running her finger along the rim of her coffee cup. "Am I boring you to death?" I asked. "I should be leaving anyway. I've got some reading to do."

"Oh, please, don't go!"

I was half out of my seat when her plea caused me to pause.

"You're not boring me to death in the least, but I'm sorry for my last comment."

I sat back down. "It didn't offend me," I said. "I was just pondering how to answer it."

"I suppose there's nothing you can do about it. I shouldn't have brought it up."

"No, that's not true, Gisela." I turned my chair to face her. "I do feel like a hypocrite, wearing this uniform. I don't agree with anything it stands for, but the men of Germany have no choice but to serve. That doesn't mean we have to submit to them. In fact, being a soldier could be an excellent cover up." What was I doing? How did I know I could trust this girl? Sophie trusted her evidently, but perhaps they didn't talk about politics, and Sophie didn't know this girl's real convictions. I turned away from her. My heart was throbbing. Had I said too much?

"Hans, you look upset. Do … do you not trust me?"

I swallowed and forced a carefree smile. "It's hard to know who to trust these days." I tried to make my words light, but they stabbed her, for her face fell.

"I see."

"I just don't know you very well. I've said entirely too much."

"I understand."

A veil of silence fell over us, and the chattering from the girls seemed distant to me. I groped at something to say.

"'Here is the difference between Christianity and National Socialism," Gisela said. My eyes locked with hers. "'In Christianity, one man died for everyone. In National Socialism, everybody dies for one man.' Hans, I'm not like my parents. Perhaps in public I act like them, but that's not who I really am. I'm just ... scared."

"Of what?"

"I'm scared to choose a side."

"Gisela, if our government is stripping away all our rights, we must obey the moral law of God and not the corrupted one of man. It's as simple as that."

"But it's not that simple." She tore her gaze from me and stared at her hands. "It's not."

"No. It's not simple to carry it out, but it's simple to choose the right course."

"How do I know the right course? My parents and country tell me one thing, and my conscience tells me the other."

I tapped my fingers on the table as I formulated my thoughts. "Are you positive that our country is telling you everything?"

"They say so."

This girl needed to know. Everyone needed to know.

"Gisela, would you like to take a walk down by the Danube? My father and I just returned from there. It's a nice evening, and we'd have plenty of time to talk before it's dark."

She smiled. "Yes, I'd like that."

truth

We strolled parallel to each other along the same worn path my father and I took on evening walks. This pathway reminded me of arguments, debates, and forgiveness. I stuffed my hands in my pockets and hunched my shoulders from a particularly cool breeze coming off the river.

"It's rather chilly," Gisela said.

"Would you like to go inside?"

"No," she said. "I'm fine."

But I noticed she was still shivering. I took off my wool uniform jacket and draped it around her shoulders. "You don't look bad in a Wehrmacht uniform," I smirked.

"Oh," she laughed apprehensively. "What would my sister say about all this ..."

"About all what?" The gravel crunched under my boots.

"Wearing a Wehrmacht jacket and walking with a soldier, unchaperoned." She glanced around with a pale face. "Actually, it appears no one is about on this secluded road." Her face bore anxiety.

I stopped walking, offended that she was questioning my chivalry. Perhaps the jacket had been too forward, but I hadn't meant it as such. I supposed it was too late to take it back. "Gisela, we just came out here to talk about the war in a peaceful place. If you don't wish to—"

"I trust you," she said quickly. "Sophie promised me that I could trust you."

I continued walking, confused by the strange preamble to our conversation. I hadn't thought I was intimidating her. Perhaps she wasn't ready to hear the hard truths of the regime.

"Would you rather talk about this some other time?" I asked.

"No. Please, tell me what's on your mind."

I kicked a stone with the side of my boot and watched as it grazed the top of the water. "Tell me, if you will, your opinion of the Jews."

"The Jews?"

"Yes," I gazed up at the sky, waiting for an answer. "I've been told that they are the reason our country was in such a hopeless state. I've been told that we are the master race, and we must take back our country once more and cleanse it for the sake of future generations."

"I asked what your opinions are. I'm fully aware of the opinions of the Third Reich."

"Well, I haven't given it much thought."

"Perhaps you should."

She tossed an angry glare at me. "Did you come out here to lecture me?"

"No, nothing of the sort." She continued to glare at me. "I mean it!" I held up both hands in surrender.

Gisela stared down at her shoes. "To be honest, I never thought the Jews were bad. I had quite a few Jewish friends growing up."

"And they're not all bad," I said. "Just as not all Germans are Nazis. Gisela, do you know what they're doing to them?"

We ceased walking and stood near the river now, facing each other. She clasped her hands together before her and stared at me, her blue eyes searching my face. "I've heard rumors, but Father said they're not true."

"They are true."

"Now, Hans, we are a civilized nation. The rumors are scandalous. Our country would never do those things. We are … we are the master race."

I turned away from her and watched the water dance over the rocks in a steady flow. "You think we are a civilized, master race, Gisela? Is that what you think?"

"Well, I hope so."

Any delicacy I was going to use with this conversation

completely vanished. I was furious, impassioned and intended to tell her the stark, raw facts. I looked at her, and her eyes widened as I began speaking. "Our so-called civilized nation is raiding towns, gathering up all the Jews and mentally ill ... anyone who resists or whom the Nazis deem 'unworthy' of life. Do you know where they take them?"

Gisela took a step back. "Yes, to labor camps. They are being well fed and cared for." Her voice wavered. "I've seen the films—"

"Propaganda films, you mean. I see that their deception is working, just as they hoped."

"The people look content, Hans." Her tone of voice suggested that she was trying to convince herself more than convince me.

"The death's head insignia on the SS helmets is an obvious sign of what they carry out in those camps. The people are anything *but* content, Gisela."

For the first time, I saw tears glistening in her eyes. They ran down her face in crystal streaks. "If what you say is true, Hans, then surely the Führer doesn't know about this, or he would have stopped it."

"Of course he does. They couldn't be built without his approval. He could easily put an end to the horrors, but he hasn't." I stared at my boots, guilt searing my heart as tears rained down her face. I could hear her breathing deeply, then felt her trembling hand on my arm. I glanced up at her.

"Hans," she said slowly, "is it true?"

"Yes," I whispered. "And there's much more."

Her hand slid from my arm and was at her mouth the next moment. "Why?" Her voice was strangled with tears. "Oh, Hans, why? Why is this happening?"

"Because our 'civilized master race' is anything but. We are a twisted, corrupted race who follows the orders of a demonic beast."

She turned her back to me, and her shoulders heaved as if

she were attempting to hold back the sobs. But I could hear them.

I tentatively set a hand on her arm. "Gisela, I didn't mean to upset you. Maybe we should be getting back."

"You have upset me."

I kicked a stone as hard as a I could. It thunked into the water inside of gliding. "This is not how I usually start conversations with a girl I've just met. I don't know why I've been so frank with you."

She whipped around, and her eyes were red and raw from crying. "I didn't mean *you* have upset me. Your words have. Because if they're true, I don't know what on earth I can do or how I can live in this horrible place."

The fervor tearing through my veins calmed as I watched the evening sunlight reflect off the water, creating faint diamonds on the surface. The trees bent over the river, dipping their overhanging branches into the water. A bird glided by, followed by a cool, gentle breeze. My brow furrowed.

"This place isn't horrible," I said. "The Fatherland is universally known for its divinity."

"How can you say that after all you've just told me?"

"Look around."

She swept her eyes over the river, and then they rested on me.

"Gisela, don't blame our country for what's happening. It's done nothing wrong. It's the people who reside in it who defile the divinity."

"What are you saying?"

"That change must happen within the core of this nation, within the minds and souls of our people. 'The punishment of every disordered mind is its own disorder.'"

"Augustine?"

I nodded with a half-hearted grin. We were silent, watching the clear water move along the rocks. One could forget about the evil for a moment by watching nature. I looked at

Gisela. Her countenance was transfixed with grief. The weight of the world seemed to be on her shoulders. How easy it is to fall into despair.

"'A man should hear a little music, read a little poetry, and see a fine picture every day of his life, in order that worldly cares may not obliterate the sense of the beautiful which God has implanted in the human soul,' according to Goethe. You know, we ought to still have faith that the world is good despite what our eyes see now."

She peered at me, and her wearied visage faded into an almost content smile. *Yes, the world is still good,* her smile seemed to say. *Life is still beautiful.*

"Come on. We better get back to the house," I said. "Everyone will wonder what's happened to us."

matchmaker

"How was your walk?"

"It was fine," I said, squinting into the kitchen light. It was a stark contrast to the dark evening we had just emerged from. Our walk took longer than I anticipated, and by the time we arrived home, everyone was asleep. Sophie was the only one in the kitchen, her finger marking her place in a thick tome. We both suddenly remembered that Gisela was wearing my jacket. She flung it off and stuffed it in my arms.

Sophie smiled while Gisela's face grew red. "Well, Sophie, if you don't mind, I'll be getting ready for bed now."

"Of course. My bedroom is the last door on the left. You can have my bed. I'll fetch a cot from the attic."

Gisela nodded goodnight and then disappeared. I headed for the chocolate cake.

"Want to split this, Sophie?"

"Yes, that's why I didn't eat it all myself."

I grinned as I brought the pan to the table along with two

forks.

"Was it chilly outside?"

I sank my fork into the cake. "Yes, that's why she was wearing my jacket."

"Oh, I see." Sophie took her share and began eating. "Hans, it's evident that Gisela likes you."

I nearly lost my grip on the fork. "What? We talked about the war. We hardly conversed at all about ourselves."

"You like her." Sophie gave me an impish grin.

"Sophie!" I hissed, fearing Gisela might overhear. "I just met her, and like I said, we talked only of war. But why did you introduce me to her? I could have gone to my room and read this evening."

"Because crossed my mind that your personalities are more compatible than yours and Traute's."

I set down my fork and glared at my sister.

"Oh, do you still have feelings for Traute, Hans?"

"No, I don't. We're merely friends now, just as we should have been from the beginning."

"Well then, I was right. You and Gisela are more compatible."

"My little sister, a matchmaker. Well, Sophie, you can stop that right now." My tone was sharper than I intended it to be.

"Oh Hans, you like her!"

"You're ridiculous." I stood up, the chair screeching against the floor. "I better go pack."

She sighed, leaning her chin into her hands. "This week flew by much too quickly. I don't want to return to the RAD and I don't want you to return to Munich. I've missed us all being together like this." Her expression was wistful.

"We just have to get through this, Sophie. We'll all be together again soon. You'll be coming to the university before too long."

She grinned. "I can hardly wait, and Gisela will be there

as well. You're happy to hear that, aren't you?"

I patted her shoulder. "Read the Scriptures tonight and ask for a clean conscience, you wicked cupid."

"Sweet dreams!" Sophie laughed.

alex

It is my firm belief that every human needs at least one friend in whom he can confide. I wouldn't have dared confide in more than a small number, especially with such severed loyalties among neighbors. The most natural people to gravitate to were, of course, my family. I would have confided in them if it weren't such a perilous matter I wished to discuss. Whereas I used to speak freely with anyone, I now kept my confidences to three friends I had made at the university— Alexander Schmorell, Christoph Probst, and Willi Graf. I had a number of other friends, but these three had become my sole confidants.

Alex was the first loyal friend I made. He was like a second brother; he was my 'partner in crime' if you are still thinking of me in criminal terms. We had concocted a plan of action while hiking one brisk February morning in '42. Our boots pounded against the packed dirt, and piles of snow were still present among the thick trees. The winter had been immeasurably long. The sight of spring making its way into being was enough to put a grin on my face. We had all started to wonder if winter would give way to spring, for it didn't seem likely. But it always does. Always. Since the dawn of creation. I don't understand why I doubted that the winter of '42 would be the exception.

We were in civilian clothes. *Glory!* I wore a light jacket and relished the way the spring breeze left ruddy marks on my face. My hands were pocketed, my eyes were heavenward, and I watched the bare branches move gently in the wind. Everything smelled fresh, undefiled. It was an escape from reality, one I was eager to savor even if only for a short interval.

I felt the cold key to Eickemeyer's studio under my fingertips, and after having conversed on various matters, I pulled it out ready to unlock a conversation which would lead to dangerous action, one that couldn't be taken lightly.

"What's that?" Alex asked as we paused to catch our breath. He leaned on a particularly large rock while drinking water from his canteen.

"It's the key to Eickemeyer's studio."

"Eickemeyer?"

"The man who's been enlightening me on the actions of our government. He gave me permission to use his studio."

"Ah," Alex nodded, fishing in his pocket for his pipe. "Yes, you've told me, but what are we waiting for, Hans? Until this blasted war is over? Until fingers are pointed at us for tolerating this regime without even protesting? I'm ashamed of our homeland. Whatever national pride I had has completely vanished."

I was glad to hear such passion. It would cause my flicker of an idea to burn more steadily.

"We're going to do something. Now." I pocketed the key.

"Are we?"

"Herr Eickemeyer is often away in the East. No one occupies his studio while he's gone, except Wilhelm Geyer who happens to be an old friend of mine from Ulm. He's renting the studio and has invited me to come view his work whenever I'd like. He recently told me he'd lend me the key if I'd like to show his work to my friends. Well, I can show you his work, but I have other things in mind for the basement of this studio."

Alex stared, eyebrows furrowed. "Go on."

"We'll purchase a duplicating machine and a typewriter. We'll produce leaflets to educate our people on the horrors our country is committing. We'll distribute them all over Germany! Perhaps we'll even spread them to Austria ... maybe even to the Allies."

That is when my various thoughts fused into one, solid plan. It was a plan I couldn't speak of except in the core of the woods or in a sealed-up basement. I was suddenly feeling overheated, and a thrill coursed through my body.

Alex let out an excited breath. "Brilliant."

"There's only one thing that troubles me," I said, kicking a pile of snow with the tip of my boot.

"Getting caught by the Gestapo?"

Yes, I suppose that should have been on the forefront of my mind, but it wasn't. "No. My little sister, Sophie, is coming to Munich for studies this spring. We're always honest with each other. My entire family is very open. We discuss everything without the hindrance of secrecy, but I can't allow Sophie to become involved in this. It'll be a chore to keep it quiet while around her."

"Have her join us! We'll need all the intelligent, loyal souls we can gather. If she's your sister, I already trust her."

I lost my footing for a split second. I don't often get cross at my friends, but at that moment I sent Alex the harshest glare I could conjure up. "No. I will *not* have her involved with this, Alex. It's too perilous, no matter how important. It must be done, but I'll not have my little sister thrown in this life or death mess, you understand?"

He held up both hands in surrender, as if we were playing war. "Perfectly. But what about Christl and Willi?"

I shrugged. "I feel uneasy about them ... Christl has his wife and boys to think of, and we've just met Willi."

"Willi's a good sort, Hans. I trust him."

"Still, perhaps we should wait to tell them. Let's see if this is something we can effectively carry out first."

"We can effectively carry it out. I won't back down."

I grinned. "Me either."

The wheel was in motion. A wheel that I, myself, had pushed into motion. To run along with it would be lethal.

the white rose

I will forever remember the scent of fresh ink. It intoxicated me, night and day. My arms will forever remember the aching induced by cranking the mimeograph machine. My fingers shall forever bear remnants of black ink. Perhaps if I had been a man destined to live many years, those smells and stains wouldn't have lasted with me. But I will never be an old man.

spring, '42.

I glanced over my shoulder, giving one last cautious glimpse around before turning the key in the door of Eickemeyer's studio. Evening had descended, and the street was veiled in murky, long shadows. My nerves prickled throughout my body. I paused. My over-imaginative mind flew to visions of Gestapo agents or informers hidden in the shadows, watching me—knowing what was in my pocket and what I intended to do with it. I'd hardly get anywhere if I allowed myself to be so paranoid. I turned back towards the door, giving it a silent nudge open.

Tonight was the night.

A shadow caught the corner of my eye, and anxiety gripped its fingers tightly around my throat. My fingers froze on the doorknob as I studied the darkness. *I haven't done anything! They have no cause to arrest me.* Yet, I felt sure that someone was watching me. My eyes focused on a lanky figure calmly gaining the studio.

Alex.

I breathed easier, nodding toward my friend. "Gave me a

start," I whispered as we entered the studio. I shut the door behind us, locking it with trembling fingers. We climbed down the stairs into the basement. I tugged on the lightbulb chain, and the room was immediately cloaked in an eerie glow. My nature loving self would have preferred a window or two, but the stone walls did create an ideal space for an underground resistance. Wilhelm's paintings leaned against the walls haphazardly, and a timeworn bookshelf was home to tubes of paints, brushes, and a variety of paper. Stacks of books lay scattered on various flat surfaces, a result of spending hours reading and composing the evening prior.

"Have a seat."

"Where?" Alex swiped his eyes across the room. "Your precious books have all the good seats."

I grinned and waved my hand toward the chair which was balancing a pile of thick tomes. "Just ask Goethe to kindly move." I ripped off my jacket, tossing it on the stairs. I rolled up my sleeves to my elbows before snatching a cigarette from my pocket.

"Are you all right, Hans?" Alex set a grey typewriter case on the paint stained table and began unlatching the buckles.

"I thought I was all right until you startled me back there."

"Did you really think I was the Gestapo? Hans, how could they even know?"

"Minds have a way of playing tricks on us." I lit my cigarette and exhaled a cloud of smoke into the air. "In a panic I wondered if maybe someone had followed us and heard our plans last evening. But no," I slapped a hand on the cold, stone wall. "No one could have heard through these walls."

"Hans, we won't get caught." Alex's confidence in our mission bolstered my spirits once more.

"No, we won't." I grinned.

Alex ran his hand along the black, polished typewriter. "A real beauty, isn't it?"

I placed my fingers on the heavy typewriter keys with a nod of approval. "We haven't yet considered a title for our leaflets." I glanced at Alex. "It should be something that openly opposes the evil we're going against. Something that reminds our people that there is good in the world after all. Something that speaks of purity and beauty, two things that are on the entirely opposite end of the spectrum from National Socialism."

The basement was still for a long moment. The only sound was the creaking of the chair Alex was leaning his back into. "What could be purer than a white rose?"

I sat up straight, peering across at Alex. "First-rate, Alex. My most sincere compliments to your sharp mind."

"Thank you, thank you." Alex gave a dramatic half bow in his chair. "Now, shall we get to work on the first leaflet of *The White Rose?*"

"Did you bring the supplies?"

Alex opened his satchel, pulling out an address book and envelopes which he set on the table with a broad grin. "What about you?"

I opened my briefcase, withdrawing stamps and paper.

"We're going to need more people, Hans. It'll be suspicious if we purchase too many of the supplies on our own, even by shopping at various establishments."

"We'll worry about that later," I said, setting up the typewriter. "Do you have the stencil?"

"Right here." Alex handed me the bulky, waxed-paper.

I retrieved the handwritten draft from my jacket and laid it beside me on the table. I then placed the stencil in the typewriter. It was a compilation of our long debated over words. Here it was, finally in a coherent form and approved by both parties.

I began typing:

Leaflets of the White Rose

I

Nothing is so unworthy of a civilized nation as allowing itself to be governed without opposition by an irresponsible clique that has yielded to base instinct. It is certain that today every honest German is ashamed of his government. Who among us has any conception of the dimensions of shame that will befall us and our children when one day the veil has fallen from our eyes and the most horrible of crimes—crimes that infinitely outdistance every human measure—reach the light of day?

If the German people are already so corrupted and spiritually crushed that they do not raise a hand, frivolously trusting in a questionable faith in lawful order of history; if they surrender man's highest principle, that which raises him above all other God's creatures, his free will; if they abandon the will to take decisive action and turn the wheel of history and thus subject it to their own rational decision; if they are so devoid of all individuality, have already gone so far along the road toward turning into a spiritless and cowardly mass—then, yes, they deserve their downfall.

Goethe speaks of the Germans as a tragic people, like the Jews and the Greeks, but today it would appear rather that they are a spineless, will-less herd of hangers-on, who now— the marrow sucked out of their bones, robbed of their center of stability—are waiting to be hounded to their destruction.

So it seems—but it is not so. Rather, by means of gradual, treacherous, systematic abuse, the system has put every man into a spiritual prison. Only now, finding himself lying in fetters, has he become aware of his fate. Only a few recognized the threat of ruin, and the reward for their heroic warning was death. We will have more to say about the fate of these persons. If everyone waits until the other man makes a start, the messengers of avenging Nemesis will come steadily closer; then even the last victim will have been cast senselessly into the maw of the insatiable demon. Therefore every individual, conscious of his responsibility as a member of Christian and Western civilization, must defend himself as best he can at this late hour. He must work against the scourges of mankind, against fascism and any similar system of totalitarianism

Offer passive resistance—resistance—wherever you may be, forestall the spread of this atheistic war machine before it is too late, before the last cities, like Cologne, have been reduced to rubble, and before the nation's last young man has given his blood on some battlefield for the hubris of a subhuman. Do not forget that every people deserves the regime it is willing to endure!

From Freidrich Schiller's The Lawgiving of Lycurgus and Solon:

If a state prevents the development of the capacities which reside in man, if it interferes with the progress of the human spirit, then it is reprehensible and injurious, no matter how excellently devised, how perfect in its own way. Its very permanence in that case amounts more to a reproach than to a basis for fame; it becomes a prolonged evil, and the longer it endures, the more harmful it is ...

From Goethe's The Awakening of Epimenides, Act II, Scene 4.

SPIRITS:

Though he who has boldly risen from the abyss
Through an iron will and cunning
May conquer half the world,
Yet to the abyss he must return.
Already a terrible fear has seized him;
In vain he will resist!
And all who still stand with him
Must perish in his fall.

HOPE:
Now I find my good men

Are gathered in the night,
To wait in silence, not to sleep.
And the glorious word of liberty
They whisper and murmur,
Till in unaccustomed strangeness,
On the steps of our temple
Once again in delight they cry:
Freedom! Freedom!

Please make as many copies of this leaflet as you can and
distribute them.

I pushed back my chair, snatching the last page of the stencil from the typewriter with an air of accomplishment. My fingers ached from the seemingly endless typing, but they still had a long night ahead of them. I fished in my pocket for a match, lit it, then held it to the corner of the handwritten paper. I watched as the flame slowly destroyed the evidence.

Alex peered up from where he was addressing envelopes. "Are we ready to begin mimeographing?"

I nodded, taking a few steps to the table which leaned against the wall on the other side of the basement. There sat the mimeograph machine which Alex had managed to obtain. Alex cranked the handle, a redundant chore, while I caught the leaflets and stacked them in a pile. One hundred copies in all, ready to be slipped into the envelopes and mailed throughout Munich.

I shifted from one foot to the other, a proud grin tugging at my lips. "Isn't it thrilling that we're actually *doing* something? I'm not so naive as to think we can actually end the war or destroy Hitler with our words, but we can maim the faith our people have in Hitler and the regime. We can make them weigh and ponder deeply what they are accepting. You realize how dangerous this is, don't you?"

"Of course I do, Hans."

I pulled a bottle of Liebfraumilch wine from behind me, which I had placed on the shelf a few nights previous. I poured two glasses, and we raised them in a toast. "Here's to a new Germany, one where freedom, conscience, and morals will abound. God help us."

into the german night

"Well, here we go," Alex whispered, turning the handle of the studio door. "Are you ready?"

I nodded, patting my briefcase which homed my half of the leaflets. We stepped into the misty, pitch black street. Every window was cloaked in heavy blackout curtains, and the usual street lamps were extinguished. Not a soul stirred as we walked along the damp sidewalk. The only noise was our own heavy breathing and footsteps. We split up once reaching the main street. I glanced over my shoulder as Alex took the road to the right. We nodded to each other, then he melted into the dark shadows.

I was alone now, feeling small amid towering buildings, all of which proudly flew the Nazi flag. When my eyes focused on the stark outline of the swastika, my confidence in my cause was renewed, and it tore through me, prompting me to reach into my coat pocket. I withdrew a stack of addressed leaflets which I slipped into the outgoing mail box. Once my pockets were empty, I kneeled and opened my briefcase. I pulled out a pile of freshly printed leaflets. The top pages were still warm.

My eyes roved for a place to distribute them. I squinted into the murky darkness, tossing leaflets into cars which were parked along the main road. I pinned them up on notice boards and scattered them in alleyways. Perspiration broke out on my forehead even amidst the cool air as I hugged the building to stay in the shadows. The papers flew from my fingers, and my eyes searched the area for any signs of movement. I kept a keen glance on the windows as I tossed leaflets into a nearby telephone booth. Once my pile was gone, I strolled up the road, hands in my pockets, with a grin on my face. I headed back to my apartment, being careful to make my footsteps light, and turned the handle fully before opening and closing the door. I collapsed onto my bed without undressing then glanced at my watch. 3:37 A.M. My eyes were heavy as I drifted to sleep.

traute

My gait was light after emerging from Professor Huber's lecture. I always felt free and self-assured after hearing the man talk of God's goodness and the future of Germany that we would shape. There were only a handful of professors left who dared to speak freely against the evils of the day, for if caught, they were promptly reprimanded by the National Socialist inclined Student Bund. I grinned to myself. The Student Bund was too stupid to interpret Professor Huber's lectures as being anti-Nazi.

"Hans!" My friend Traute, once my girlfriend, saddled up beside me, clutching a paper in her hands. "Did you see this? I found it in my mailbox over the weekend."

I eyed the crisp white paper with the words, *LEAFLET OF THE WHITE ROSE*, typed in a bold black font. I took it in my hands, scanning it as if I'd never read the contents before. All the while my heart was throbbing against my ribs without mercy. I could nearly recite the entire leaflet, but I wasn't about to tell Traute that. She was studying me with her dark, probing eyes.

"Well? What do you make of it?" She asked. "It's already been reported to the Gestapo."

"It has?" My words left my mouth without preamble. My eyes fell to the floor, the only safe place I could rest them while absorbing this information. If Traute saw the panic in my eyes, she'd know the truth. Had it only been the night prior that Alex and I distributed the leaflets? How perilous life could get in a space of twenty-four hours!

"I hear that they're at a loss as to who wrote them," Traute went on. "The leaflets are turning up all over Munich and in bordering towns. They can't track down where they're being produced. I hope the authors stay safe ... whoever they are."

I rapidly sought to recover myself, so I feigned an indifferent air. I sighed, as if annoyed and handed it back to her.

"Ludicrous!" I said, raising my eyes to meet hers. "Who would risk their neck to write something like this?"

Traute folded the leaflet in half, her knowing gaze unsettling me. "Shall we go to a cafe tonight, Hans? Just you and me?"

"What?" I stared at her, my mind still mulling over the Gestapo.

"Don't you want to go out somewhere? We never spend time together anymore."

"No, I can't. I'm sorry." I began heading down the corridor, feeling every student's gaze as a threat.

"Why not, Hans?" Traute hurried to keep pace with me.

I stopped abruptly. The books I clutched underneath my arm slid, and I quickly caught them before they sprawled onto the floor. "Traute, we have agreed to be only friends."

"Yes, I suppose we did." She clutched her books and peered at me. "But Hans, I know you well. I'm worried about you."

"Worried?" I raised an eyebrow. "Why? You don't think I'll pass my exams? I'm studying hard."

"No, it's not that. Can't we get together and talk this over? You're in some sort of danger, I know it."

"I'm in danger of being late for my next lecture." I quickened my pace, waving a hand at her. "We'll talk later."

sophie

Sophie was arriving on the afternoon train to live and study in Munich. After having been separated for so long, I was eager to have my sister near me once more. The Third Reich had split our family into various directions, but we were finally allowed to be reunited.

I was late to pick her up at the station. I glanced nervously at my watch as time ticked on. I was furious with myself for being so thoughtless. If Sophie arrived before me, she would be lost in the crowd without anyone to greet her. It was hardly the best way to welcome my sister to Munich. I shoved my way through the throng that had gathered outside the train station. A few citizens promptly jumped out of my way upon eyeing my uniform. Perhaps the uniform did come in handy occasionally.

I bent my head slightly as a cloud of smoke smothered me. There she was, wading through the crowd and taking everything in with her eyebrows furrowed and her eyes wide. If I didn't know her, I'd think she was angry or upset, but I knew better. Her furrowed brows merely meant she was thinking hard about something.

"Sophie!" I called over the deafening noise around us.

Her eyes roved around until they met with mine. Her face relaxed, brightening into a wide smile. A group of travelers worked its way between us, and I momentarily lost sight of her. Once they had moved, I took the opportunity to rush toward her before anyone else could get in our way. She was carrying a suitcase and a parcel which I immediately suspected was from mother. Sophie dropped her suitcase on the station floor and flung her free arm around my waist.

"Hans!"

I held her close and kissed the top of her head like I used to do when she was small. "It's so good to see you, Sophie." Then, remembering it was her birthday, I glanced at the parcel she was carrying. "I dearly hope there's birthday cake in there."

"Of course! And wine. Mother packed it special for us to share once I arrived."

I smiled, eager for a slice of mother's cake which I had gone without for too long. "How was the train ride?"

I picked up her suitcase and started leading the way through the station. Sophie gripped my jacket sleeve to keep from dissolving into the chaos. "Uneventful. I slept most of the way. I dreamed about wading in a lovely stream we traveled by."

"You don't need to dream about it. We *do* have streams around here. I know that must be hard to believe while being in the heart of the city." I tossed a grin over my shoulder. "I'm so pleased you're here, Sophie. We'll have good times, won't we?"

"I hope so. I'm drained from the RAD and itching to have some fun. Will I enjoy my studies, do you think? I'm rather nervous."

"Yes, I'm confident that you'll enjoy the university. You always were a glutton for knowledge."

Sophie smiled at that comment. "I feel like a baby bird just trying out its wings for the first time," she laughed. "I just pray that I'll fly."

"You will."

We stepped onto the street which now felt wide open compared to the station. "I've organized a birthday party for you tonight at my apartment. It's time for you to meet my friends at long last."

She studied me with her inquisitive eyes for a long moment. I was beginning to feel strangely transparent, as if

Sophie would soon find out about my treasonous business. But she wouldn't. I would see to that.

meet my friends

I stood beside a teetering tower of my medical texts, watching as Sophie gazed up at the French Impressionist paintings pinned all over my walls. It wasn't so unlike my bedroom at home. I was always a great adorer of books, and yet, I let them lie where they might. I was certainly not a great adorer of bookshelves and didn't pretend to be.

"I'm so eager to meet your friends. I feel like I already know them from all your letters." Sophie sat on the edge of my bed, the only clear seating in my apartment. I was attempting to clear off my chairs, but it wasn't an easy feat. I picked up a stack of thick tomes and peered around for a place to set them. Finding none, I set them back down with a heavy sigh.

My friends would just have to stand.

"I'm sure they feel the same way. I've told them all about you." I drummed my fingers on the book covers thoughtfully, wondering how much space was in my closet. I dismissed the thought. There were more books in there.

"Only good things I hope?"

I gave her a mischievous grin. Before Sophie could question me, a rapping sounded at the door. "Come in, Alex."

Alex entered, nearly bumping his head on the door frame. I was still preoccupied with finding seating space, so I made a half-hearted introduction while lifting my blankets to peer under my bed. Suitcases, shoes, a bit of dust—no space whatsoever.

"Sophie, this is my friend from the university, Alexander Schmorell. Alex, this is my little sister, Sophie."

Sophie stood up, extending a hand shyly. She was withdrawn and contemplative before knowing a person, but once you had her friendship, she was lively and cheerful. "I'm pleased to meet you. I've heard so much about you that I rather feel like we're old friends."

"Exactly my feelings. Hans can go on for ages discussing his family back in Ulm. Let's see if I can get the Scholl siblings straight." He scratched his chin thoughtfully. "Inge, Hans, Elizabeth, Sophie, and ... Werner." He glanced from Sophie to me. "Did I get everyone in the correct order?"

"I'm impressed," Sophie grinned.

"Heaven be praised, is that cake?" Alex hurried over to the desk where I was now unpacking the dense cake onto a pile of papers. Mother would have a fit if she knew her cake was being placed on a pile of assignments.

"What would a birthday party be without cake and wine?" Sophie raised a brow.

"It'd be duller than *Mein Kampf.*" I handed Sophie a knife. "Would you slice it? I'm not confident when it comes to culinary matters."

"What on earth do you mean? Don't you remember that time you baked a cake for mother's birthday?"

"Hans *baked?*" Alex's mouth dropped open. "Any more secret talents you haven't shared with your friends, Hans?"

"Inge and Elizabeth refused to help me. I suppose they wished to see me left to my own devices."

"So, I helped him," Sophie said. "But the trouble is, I'm not very good in the kitchen now, let alone when I was twelve."

"Well? How did it turn out?"

I exchanged a glance with Sophie, and we both grinned.

"We had to leave the windows open for two days to allow ventilation throughout our house," I said. "I burned it beyond the scope of imagination."

"But don't worry," Sophie said. "Mother knows how to bake divine cakes." She sunk the blade into the white cake, setting a large slice onto a plate.

"Ah! I heartily approve of the way your sister slices cake." Alex cheered as Sophie handed him the plate.

Another knock sounded at the door, bringing in Christl. He was smoking a pipe and donning a cap which he promptly took off upon entering the room.

"Christl, good to see you." I slapped my friend's shoulder. "Sophie, this is Christoph Probst. How are your boys, Christl?"

"Good as gold. Well, except for Vincent. He's teething. Cries a fit," Christl spoke between the pipe clenched in his teeth. His blue eyes fell on Sophie. "I'm pleased to meet you. You two are the spitting image of each other. Remarkable!"

"Oh, poor girl," I teased. "I'm sorry, Sophie."

"It's a pleasure to meet you, Christl. May I call you Christl?" Sophie gave me a shove in response to my jesting.

"Of course. No one has called me Christoph since I was a child. Say 'Christoph,' and I'll be under the impression that I'm to whitewash the house as punishment for something."

"There's no fear of whitewashing anything. Care for a slice of cake?"

"Sounds splendid."

Sophie set a generous slice on a plate for him. His eyes widened, and he gazed at her in awe. "Is there a war going on? I can hardly tell from such delicacies."

"Our mother is a saint. I don't know how she manages to save enough rations." I glanced at my watch impatiently. "If Willi is any later, he won't get a slice of cake. Three-fourths of it have already vanished before our very eyes. Ah, is that him at the door now?"

Willi strolled in, his round face ruddy from the brisk evening. He wasn't nearly as outgoing as Alex or as laidback as Christl. He was quiet, with pensive eyes. "Willi Graf, it's about time you arrived. Sophie's birthday cake is all but gone." I pointed to what was left of the cake.

Willi nodded toward Sophie. "Happy birthday, Miss Scholl."

"Oh, I'm Sophie. Please call me Sophie. We're all good friends here, and I certainly don't intend to call you Mr. Graf."

Willi grinned. "Sophie, it's a pleasure to meet you."

"How about a game?" Alex asked after he had finished off his cake. He took a long sip of water, wiping his mouth with the back of his sleeve. "We each provide a bit of poetry, and the rest of us must guess who authored it."

"All right. Who'll go first?" I turned toward my sister. "Sophie?"

"This is hardly fair. Hans is so well versed in all the great poets I adore. He'll win on the spot."

"I don't mind," I shrugged.

"Oh, come. Surely there must be a poem even Hans Scholl can't place," Alex reclined in a chair he had cleared off, a pipe wedged in the corner of his mouth.

Sophie was silent for a long moment, strumming her fingers along the desk. "All right. I have one. 'A single fir-tree, lonely, on a northern mountain height, sleeps in a white blanket, draped in snow and ice. His dreams are of a palm tree, who, far in eastern lands, weeps, all alone and silent, among the burning sands.'"

I was about to blurt out the poet, but stopped myself. I really ought to let everyone ponder it a moment and not spoil the fun. Willi's head was bent. Alex peered up at the ceiling. Christl was leaning forward in his seat, and I was grinning like a school boy who just got away with inflicting an antic upon my teacher.

"Heinrich Heine, naturally." I finally let my words break the silence.

"Oh, Hans!" Sophie thrust a book at me, and I dodged it with a gale of laughter.

"Now, may I present one, or are you all angry with me?" I

peered around for an answer.

"Go on," Christl waved a hand at me.

I opened my wallet and pulled out a typewritten page. "This one will surely baffle you. Are you all ready?"

Four heads nodded. I cleared my throat. "'From his dark den there comes a robber to waylay us; He wants to snatch our purses, but finds a better booty; a quarrel over nothing, confused and ignorant rant, a nation's banner torn, a people dull and stupid. Wherever he goes he finds the times are lean and empty, so he can step forth brazenly and play the role of prophet. He boldly plants his foot on the rubbish heap around him and hisses his venal message to an astonished world. Cloaked in deceit and malice, that wraps him like a cloud, he stands before the people, the mightiest in the land. The hands of many helpers of low and high degree, espying their advantage, bring service to his will.

"'They carry forth his message as formerly the angels had done with the five loaves. It rattles on and on! Where once but one man lied, today they come by thousands; and roaring like the storm, his gold draws interest now. It grows to a great harvest, the social order overthrown, the masses live in infamy and laugh at every scurvy deed. It turns out to be true, what first was fabrication: the good have disappeared, the bad come out in crowds! When one day this trouble will melt like winter's ice, the people will recall it like the very Plague itself. They'll raise an effigy of straw; let children on the hearth burn joy from out of sorrow, and light from ancient woe.'"

The room was cast in a spell from the heady words, and no one broke the silence for a long moment.

"That was brilliant." Christl leaned back with a sigh. "I'm sure I don't know who penned it."

Alex slapped his knee. "Let us mimeograph this splendid piece of literature and drop it all over Germany from the sky."

"We'll naturally dedicate it to our great Führer," Willi gleamed.

The room erupted in light-hearted laughter until I finally held a finger to my lips to silence them. "There are other people living in this building, you know."

"You wrote it, I'll wager," Alex pointed a finger at me. "It sounds like something you'd write."

"No, I didn't. It was penned in 1878 by Gottfried Keller. It's terribly ironic that the verses don't have anything to do with Germany. They are about a conflict in Switzerland."

"They suit the current situation of the Fatherland perfectly," Christl said. "Amazing."

"Well," Alex stood up, stretching his arms over his head. "This has been fun, but shouldn't we stroll outdoors now? We could chill the wine in the English Garden. What do you all say to that?"

The outdoors constantly beckoned me, and I could only resist its plea for so long. Sophie must have felt the same way, for she jumped up enthusiastically, a broad smile on her face. "Yes, let's. Hans, bring your guitar, won't you?'"

"All right, though it's been ages since I've played." I snatched my instrument from where it lay in the corner of my room, dusted it off then followed the party outside. The cool spring evening was exhilarating. The full moon battled with the clouds, struggling to bring its light to the world below.

"Do you approve of Hans' choice of friends?" Alex turned to Sophie, as we strolled down the damp road. Flower petals stuck to the brick, and the air smelled musky.

"He couldn't find nicer anywhere in the world."

"Hans, I dearly like your sister." Alex's voice was light, as if he didn't have a care in the world. But I knew better. We all had cares—an extremely perilous one in particular.

We arrived at the English Garden, and I tied a thick string around the bottle of wine, gently placing it in the brisk water of the Isar river. I sank onto the damp grass and ran my fingers along the guitar strings. "It's your birthday, Sophie. What shall we sing?"

"How about *Die Gedanken Sind Frei.*"

"Excellent choice," Christl leaned his back against a tree. "Go on, Hans. Serenade us."

I began to play, the music drifting into the night air where it mingled with the cosmos.

> *Die gedanken sind frei, my thoughts freely flower,*
> *Die gedanken sind frei, my thoughts give me power,*
> *No scholar can map them, no hunter can trap them,*
> *No man can deny, die gedanken sind frei*

s l e e p l e s s   n i g h t

"Did you have a nice birthday?" I wiggled the key into my apartment door knob and shoved it open with my shoulder.

"Finest I've ever had. You really do have such nice friends."

"I had a feeling you'd like them." I set my guitar in the corner near my desk, nodding toward my bed. "You can have my bed. I'll set up a place on the floor."

"Thank you, Hans."

"You should get some sleep. It's been a long day." I wrapped an arm around her shoulder. "Goodnight, Sophie. And happy birthday."

I snatched a few blankets from the top of my closet and spread them on the floor near the door while she prepared for bed. It had been arranged that she would spend the night at my apartment for convenience sake until her permanent room with Frau Berrsche was ready. I was secretly pleased she wouldn't be rooming here, for it would be considerably harder to keep my *White Rose* activities from her if she stayed. I waited until she was tucked in bed to switch off the light. I laid on my back on the hard floor and watched the inky shadows dance on the ceiling. Time passed slowly. I was certain Sophie was fast asleep by now, it being half past two, but I couldn't seem to drift off. Too many thoughts caused me to toss and turn.

"We must get more paper," I whispered into the silence.

"What?" Sophie's voice caused my nerves to stand on end. "Are you still awake, Hans?"

My heart violently twisted. "Forget you heard me, Sophie. I didn't mean to wake you. Go back to sleep."

I would need to be more careful if I was to keep Sophie from knowing.

the second leaflet

In late June of '42, Alex and I had begun composing the second leaflet of *The White Rose*. The sound of pencils writing vigorously against paper and the occasional flip of a page in a book encompassed Eickemeyer's basement while we worked. It was true that he had given me leave to use his studio, but he had no knowledge of what we were carrying out within his walls. Had he known it was the writing of treasonous leaflets, he would have been conflicted, I'm sure. He would encourage me to continue doing something, but perhaps not on his property. So, we said nothing to him regarding it.

I leaned my chin into my hand, tapping the end of the pencil against my lips. "Have you something to show for our ..." I glanced at my watch, "... two hours of political discourse, Alex?"

Alex stopped writing, taking a sip from his glass of water before glancing over his paper. "'It is impossible to engage in intellectual discourse with National Socialist Philosophy, for if there were such an entity, one would have to try by means of analysis and discussion either to prove its validity or to combat it. In actuality, however, we face a totally different situation. At its very inception this movement depended on the deception and betrayal of one's fellow man; even at that time it was inwardly corrupt and could support itself only by constant lies.'"

I reclined in my chair, drumming the pencil along the edge of the table. "Have you ever read *Mein Kampf*, Alex?"

Alex made a nauseated face. "I try to stay away from poorly written literature."

I lifted my paper. "I've written something which will parallel your introduction. I propose this. 'Hitler states in an early edition of 'his' book (a book written in the worst German I have ever read, in spite of the fact that it has been elevated to the position of the Bible in this nation of poets and thinkers)—'"

Alex's attempt at suppressed laughter interrupted my words. "I'm sorry," he smirked. "Go on, go on."

"As I was saying, Hitler states that 'It is unbelievable to what extent one must betray a people in order to rule it.' If at the start this cancerous growth in the nation was not particularly noticeable, it was only because there were still enough forces at work that operated for the good, so that it was kept under control. As it grew larger, however, and finally, in an ultimate spurt of growth, attained ruling power, the tumor broke open, as it were, and infected the whole body. The greater part of its former opponents went into hiding. The German intellectuals fled to their cellars, there, like plants struggling in the dark, away from light and sun, gradually to choke to death.

"'Now the end is at hand. Now it is our task to find one another again, to spread information from person to person, to keep a steady purpose, and to allow ourselves no rest until the last man is persuaded of the urgent need of his struggle against this system. When, thus, a wave of unrest goes through the land, when 'it is in the air,' when many join the cause, then in a great final effort this system can be shaken off. After all, an end in terror is preferable to terror without end.'"

Alex nodded, flipping over the page of his draft. "The atrocities committed against the Jews is of utmost importance. I've written up a piece about that. Shall I read it?" I reclined in my chair. "Yes, by all means."

"'We are not in a position to draw up a final judgment about the meaning of our history, but if this catastrophe can be used to further the public welfare, it will be only by virtue of the fact that we are cleansed by suffering; that we yearn for the light in the midst of deepest night, summon our strength, and finally help in shaking off the yoke which weighs on our world. We do not want to discuss here the question of the Jews, nor do we want in this leaflet to compose a defense or apology. No, only by way of example do we want to cite the fact that since the conquest of Poland three hundred thousand Jews have been murdered in this country in the most bestial way.

"'Here we see the most frightful crime against human dignity, a crime that is unparalleled in the whole of history. For Jews, too, are human beings—no matter what position we take with respect to the Jewish question—and a crime of this dimension has been perpetrated against human beings. Someone may say that the Jews deserve their fate. This assertion would be a monstrous impertinence; but let us assume that someone said this—what position has he then taken toward the fact that the entire Polish aristocratic youth is being annihilated? (May God grant that this program has not yet fully achieved its aim as yet!) All male offspring of the houses of the nobility between the ages of fifteen and twenty were transported to concentration camps in Germany and sentenced to forced labor, and all the girls of this age group were sent to Norway, into the bordellos of the SS!

"'Why do German people behave so apathetically in the face of all these abominable crimes, crimes so unworthy of the human race? Hardly anyone thinks about that. It is accepted as fact and put out of mind. The German people slumber on in their dull, stupid sleep and encourage these fascist criminals; they give them the opportunity to carry on their depredations; and of course they do so. Is this a sign that the Germans are brutalized in their simplest human feelings, that no chord within them cries out at the sight of such deeds, that they have sunk into a fatal consciencelessness from which they will never, never awake? It seems to be so, and will certainly be so, if the German does not at last start up out of his stupor, if he does not protest wherever and whenever he can against this clique of criminal, if he shows no sympathy for these hundreds of thousands of victims. He must evidence not only sympathy; no, much more: a sense of complicity in guilt.'"

"We *must* inflict the people with the sense of guilt." Alex set down his paper. "For if they allow this to go on without making a conscious effort to end it, they are just as guilty as Hitler and the Nazis."

I heartily agreed, but I also knew why no one was doing anything. "They are frightened," I said as I lit my cigarette. "They know the consequences for their actions in this time and day, but they don't consider the consequences their actions will have on their next life where their souls will reside for eternity."

We sat in companionable silence as we resumed our writing. The only sounds were our pencils against paper, the crisp ashes of our cigarettes falling into the ashtray, and the occasional thump of Alex's glass of water as he picked it up and set it down. I broke the stillness with a wave of my paper.

"Listen to this, Alex, and let me in on your thoughts. 'For through his apathetic behavior he gives these evil men the opportunity to act as they do; he tolerates this 'government' which has taken upon itself such an infinitely great burden of guilt; indeed, he himself is to blame for the fact that it came about at all! Each man wants to be exonerated of a guilt of this kind; each one continues on his way with the most placid, the calmest conscience. But he cannot be exonerated; he is guilty, guilty, guilty!

"'It is not too late, however, to do away with this most reprehensible of all miscarriages of government, so as to avoid being burdened with even greater guilt. Now, when in recent years our eyes have been opened, when we know exactly who our adversary is, it is high time to root out this brown horde. Up until the outbreak of the war, the larger part of the German people was blinded; the Nazis did not show themselves in their true aspect. But now, now that we have recognized them for what they are, it must be the sole and first duty, the holiest duty of every German to destroy these beasts.

"'Lao Tzu: If the people are barely aware that the government exists, they are happy. When the government is felt to be oppressive, they are broken. Good fortune, alas!, builds itself upon misery. Good fortune, alas!, is the mask of misery. What will come of this? We cannot foresee the end. Order is upset and turns to disorder, good becomes evil. The people are confused. Is it not so, day in, day out, from the beginning? The wise man is therefore angular, though he does not injure others; he has sharp corners, though he does not harm; he is upright but not gruff. He is clear minded, but he does not try to be brilliant.

"'Whoever undertakes to rule the kingdom and to shape it according to his whim—I foresee that he will fail to reach his goal. That is all. The kingdom is a living being. It cannot be constructed, in truth! He who tries to manipulate it will spoil it, he who tries to put it under his power will lose it.'" I set down my paper. "Do you suppose people have the integrity to pass on our leaflets?"

Alex ran his fingers along the dents in the wood. "Most, I think, will be cowardly, but if we can influence even one person, they can help us make a difference. We could recruit some of our friends to help with distribution. Then we could reach more avenues."

"I feel very unsettled letting anyone else in on the leaflets, Alex. In matters that could end in death, it's best to keep the circle small. I need to protect Sophie, in particular. I've come close to telling, for she has a brilliant mind and would help immensely. But ... I can't." I dropped my cigarette on the floor and extinguished it with the heel of my boot. "It's hard as hell not to tell her."

"You don't think she'll ever find out that you and I wrote them? They're all over Munich by now, Hans. You told me that you two understand each other without needing to utter a word. Won't she recognize your words in the leaflets?"

"I've thought of that, but perhaps she'll be too distracted to think it through clearly. She's still becoming accustomed to the lectures and her new home with Frau Berrsche, not to mention the letters she constantly writes to our family and her boyfriend, Fritz, who's serving on the Eastern Front. Sophie is rather preoccupied. I doubt she'll have the time to decipher me in the leaflets."

"As you say." Alex yawned as he stretched his arms above his head.

"Not sleepy, are you?" I crumpled up the first draft and tossed it at Alex. "We still must mimeograph this leaflet and distribute it. Pry those eyes open."

"Yes, Father." Alex grinned as he lit a match and began burning the evidence of the first draft.

"It's rather funny," I pondered, setting up the mimeograph. "For committing treason against our country, I don't feel quite as nervous as I ought. Should that concern me?"

"Hardly. It'll make it considerably easier to act indifferent to the leaflets when in public."

"How strange it is to criticize our hard work in public. I dubbed it 'ludicrous' while speaking with Traute the other morning."

"Perhaps it is ludicrous," Alex said. "A noble sort of ludicracy."

the secret revealed

I trudged down Franz-Josef-Strasse after a grueling afternoon of medical rounds. Soldiers from the Eastern Front had been arriving in unfathomably mangled conditions. My mind persistently flew to the images of a soldier whose lower jaw was blown to bits and the boy with both legs amputated. One didn't have to be present on the front to be haunted by the groans and cries of the wounded.

The intermittent summer breeze freshened my mind as I continued, desperately seeking beauty amidst the remnants of war. To my right was a flowering cherry tree, radiating with life. It was a drastic contrast to the Nazi banner waving from an office nearby. The flag radiated only one thing—slavery.

My gaze had been fixed above me, watching as the sun unveiled itself from the clouds. When I brought my attention to the street once more, someone was waving to me.

Gisela.

I nearly dropped my briefcase, but gathered my wits about me before I could make a fool out of myself. Gisela was smiling, her entire being beaming. Her blond hair shone like gold in the sunlight, and her eyes were a vivid blue. She was clutching a pile of books to herself.

"Gisela Schertling!" I exclaimed as our footsteps drew closer.

"Hans Scholl!" She laughed, extending a hand. "What a pleasure to see you."

I shook her hand, all the while staring at her in wonder.

"I did tell you I was coming to Munich to study, didn't I?" she asked.

"Oh, yes, of course. I ..."

"You forgot?" she volunteered.

As much as I hated to admit it in front of her, I grinned sheepishly and nodded. "I've been preoccupied lately. I scarcely have time to write home anymore."

"That's understandable, being a student and a medical sergeant. You must be very busy."

We stepped off the street as a parade of students sauntered past. "Have you seen Sophie yet?" I asked.

"Briefly, though neither of us have had much time to talk. Studies are more time consuming than I wagered."

"Are you busy this evening?"

She seemed to weigh my question for a long moment, and then shook her head. "Well, no, actually."

"Sophie and I were going to take the evening off from studying to see a concert. Would you like to join us?"

"Oh, that would be lovely." She rocked on her toes in an air of joyous anticipation. "I'm rooming with Frau Dittmar." She pointed down the street. "The last house on the left."

"We'll be by at seven, then."

"Wonderful! Until then." She smiled a farewell as she hurried past. I didn't move for a long moment. When I glanced back at her, she was peering over her shoulder at me. I turned my head quickly and continued up the street.

Sophie was at my apartment when I arrived, for we often met up after lectures and rounds. I hardly looked at her as I tossed my briefcase on the floor and began discarding my jacket and cap. "Hi, Sophie." I hung my uniform in the closet adjacent to the door. "I just ran into Gisela Schertling. She's going to the concert with us tonight. I hope you don't mind."

No response. I found that odd, for most days she had a

plethora of things to tell me about, ranging from her university lectures, to tales about her new friends, to news from home. I peered over my shoulder at her. "Everything all right?"

She was standing beside my desk, her face frighteningly pale as her eyes were fixed on something in front of her.

I turned toward her, crossing my arms. "Sophie?"

She lifted her eyes toward me, suddenly becoming alert. It was as if she had been in a deep slumber, and someone had just woken her. "Oh, hello, Hans."

Something was extremely wrong.

"How were your lectures?" I sank onto my bed, reclining against the iron uprights.

"Fine, as usual."

Silence consumed us. I studied her from across the room. She was flipping through a book, but I couldn't see the cover. "Sophie, what's going on?"

She reached into her knitted cardigan pocket and handed a paper to me. My throat tightened as I held a leaflet of *The White Rose*. I eyed it, all the while wondering how I was going to get myself out of this. Perhaps she didn't know. I lifted my eyes to meet her steady gaze.

She knew.

"Anti-Nazi leaflets are floating around Munich. Do you know where the leaflets came from?" Her voice was soft. No hint of anger or panic laced her tone.

I examined the leaflet once more with a pensive countenance. "I don't know where they came from. Traute showed me one the other day. It's quite the risk for whoever is writing them." I folded the leaflet into thirds with a shrug.

"So, you *don't* know who wrote them?"

I furrowed my brow. "Why should I know about this, Sophie?"

She viciously snatched the book she had been leafing through and heaved it at me. It slammed against my forearm.

It didn't hurt in the least, but it was an old tome, and I carefully picked it up to inspect the damage. "Sophie Magdalena!" I didn't mean to sound just like my father when he scolded her, but it came out in his tone just the same.

"I read your bookmarked page in *The Lawgiving of Lycurgus and Solon*. That passage you have underlined is the exact same one as is quoted in the first leaflet of *The White Rose*. You, Hans Scholl, wrote the leaflets."

My throat was dry when I tried to swallow. I turned away from her, staring at the book that had given me away instead. Alex was right. It was idiotic of me to think that I could keep something like this from Sophie.

"Admit it, Hans."

I couldn't. Not yet. I was convinced that there must be a way out of this. "I told you that I don't have anything to do with it."

"You're lying to me."

"How would I have time to lead an underground resistance?"

"When you're passionate about something, you find a way." She was standing beside me, one hand on the iron upright. Her eyes bore into me.

Oh, God, she knew.

But it was my last chance of keeping my sister out of this treacherous venture. What on earth could I possibly say to sway her intuition? "Sophie, it's extremely dangerous to find out who's behind matters such as these. Don't worry over it."

"Hans, give up the charade. I know with all my heart that you're behind this. Stop lying to me."

"All right!" I sat up abruptly, not fully believing I had just thrown those words at my sister … that I was telling her the very thing I was attempting to shield her from. But I threw my hands in the air in surrender, too exhausted to keep it from her any longer. "Alex and I wrote the leaflets."

She was silent for a long moment, studying me with her dark, inquisitive eyes. "Why didn't you leave this to people who know what they're doing?" Her voice was strained with emotion. "Why not save yourself? You have a wonderful future ahead of you, Hans!"

I leaped up from the bed and wrapped my arms around her, comforting her like I used to when she was a little girl frightened of the dark. She leaned into my chest, and all I wanted to do was protect my little sister from all of this ... to keep her safe. But I couldn't guarantee that any longer, and Sophie knew that, for she was trembling.

"What hurts me most is that you didn't tell me. We tell each other everything." She pushed away from me, folding her arms across her chest. Her bottom lip quivered. "Don't you trust me?"

"The reason I didn't tell you was out of love for you. How could I, in good conscience, allow my sister to become active in this? Deceiving you was my gift of love. Don't you see that? I don't want anything to happen to you."

"But I don't want anything to happen to you, Hans, if the Gestapo—"

"I know what would happen. It's not a matter of only my own life, but of the thousands upon thousands of innocent souls dying at the hands of the Nazis. It's a matter of saving lives and enlightening our people. Sophie, I long for a clean conscience. I couldn't attain one if I sat back and watched as the destruction rolled on. If everyone waited for the next person to make a start, nothing would be done."

Sophie sank into the desk chair, running both hands through her shoulder length hair. "Then I can do nothing to stop you from this?"

"Nothing. I'm in the thick of it. There's no going back."

She peered up at me, her eyes suddenly aflame with determination. "Then I will join you."

I fixed my sternest gaze on her. "No. Absolutely not."

"I can't sit back now that I know you're deeply involved. It's unthinkable, my abandoning you and you doing this without me. If you're arrested, I couldn't bear to be in safety. Hans, I'm with you, no matter how terrified I feel. I believe in this cause just as strongly as you, and ... and I'm ready to do something."

I perched myself on the edge of the desk, running a hand over my face. What would my parents say if they knew I was about to let Sophie join my treasonous activities? They would want me to protect her at all costs. "As your older brother I—"

"I understand that you only wanted to protect me." She was extremely composed now, no trace of shock present in her countenance. "But I'm determined to join you. You can't stop me, Hans. 'But be ye doers of the word, and not hearers only, deceiving your own selves.' I'm ready to be a doer."

I grinned in spite of myself, and all at once I was giving her my permission. "All right, Sophie. You win."

the concert

I was exceptionally uneasy that evening. My nerves were on edge as I paced the lobby of the concert hall, perspiration dripping down the back of my neck. Sophie and Gisela were chatting and oblivious to my tortured state. At least, I hoped they were. What had I done? How could I have agreed to allow Sophie to join? Was I certifiably insane?

Perhaps I was.

The lights were dim in the velvety theater, and cigarette smoke created a thick haze around us. We were waiting for what seemed like ages for Alex and Willi to arrive. I ceased my pacing and busied my fingers with lighting a cigarette.

"Hans, are you feeling well?" Gisela's voice tore me from my brooding.

I smiled at her. "I'm perfectly fine."

Gisela narrowed her eyes at me, and I glanced at Sophie for assistance. "Brothers," Sophie mused. "One simply can't figure out their state of mind from one minute to the next." That's not the sort of assistance I was hoping for, but I accepted it with an irked glare.

Alex and Willi finally entered through the tall, thick doors, promptly pulling off their hats when they entered the lobby.

"Thought you'd never arrive." I extinguished my cigarette in an ashtray near the door.

"The concert can begin now that I'm here. Go and tell them," Alex grinned.

I wasn't in the mood for humor. "Sophie, why don't you choose the seats?"

Sophie and Gisela, arm in arm, led the way into the theater, Willi following behind them. I lingered behind and grabbed Alex's coat sleeve as he made a move to join them.

"She knows," I whispered.

Alex stared at me, eyes wide. "Who? Sophie?"

I nodded. "I'll bring her by tomorrow."

"Of course." Then Alex smirked. "Didn't I tell you she'd—"

"Shut up."

Alex laughed, but I didn't have the heart to join him.

I sat between Sophie and Willi, leaning my back into the cushioned chair. The musicians' instruments had a bright luster, even more so in the glow of the stage lights. Mozart's D Major was light and pleasurable after a full day of tension. I was mesmerized by the way the bows flew across the violins' strings. The calming serenade enraptured me, so I closed my eyes and drank it in. When I opened them again, I peered to the left of me. Sophie was leaning forward in her seat, taking the concert in with all her might. Gisela, who sat on the other side of Sophie, had her eyes fixed on me. When ours eyes met, she rapidly broke our gaze and fixed her sights on the stage, brushing some hair behind her ears. From the glow of the stage lights, I could see her face beam red. I turned my attention back to the concert, another emotion tossed into my already overstocked supply. I liked her, and that would pose a problem. I didn't have time to like her, nor could I converse with her honestly regarding my work.

Once the concert had ended, Alex proposed that we all head to a coffeehouse to talk over the concert. Everyone heartily agreed. As I sat across from Gisela, I allowed myself to drift away from Alex, Willi, and Sophie's conversation. I looked at my pretty friend.

"Did you enjoy the concert?" I asked.

She nodded, taking a sip of her coffee. "Immensely. I don't have many friends at the university yet, so an outing like this is rare and very enjoyable."

"Ah, don't look too far for friends at the university." I leaned back in my chair, drumming my fingers on the table. The sound of customers chatting created a soft hum behind us.

"Why?"

"Seduced fools, most of them. My group of friends makes a point never to attend Nazi rallies or meetings. Most of the students from the university go willingly."

"Then I hope I can be included in your group of friends."

"Of course. You already are."

She was fingering her coffee cup, keeping her head bent low. "I—I want to apologize for staring at you back there, at the concert."

"It's all right," I smirked.

She was quiet at length. The only sound was her spoon clinking against the cup as she stirred her brew. Then she leaned in, and I lifted my eyes to meet hers.

"We ought to take a walk some evening," she said.

Evenings were now reserved for leaflet production and

distribution, but I couldn't draw attention to myself by refusing a stroll with a beautiful girl. It would be uncharacteristic of me.

"That would be nice, Gisela."

She gave me a broad smile. "I look forward to it."

the third leaflet

"Didn't I tell you that Sophie would find out?" Alex's voice traveled through the basement as we entered the studio the next evening. He was leaning back in a chair, chewing on the end of his pencil. "You two are inseparable."

The studio smelled of fresh paint tonight, a sign that Wilhelm had been there earlier. We had taken to hiding our supplies in the corner of the basement, covered with tarps and papers, or occasionally calling a bookshop friend of mine to hide it in his basement if I felt our base of operations was unsafe.

"She's much too curious for her own good." I pulled out a chair for Sophie as she took in the studio with curious eyes.

"I'd rather be co-conspirators with you two than studying." She tossed a grin at us as she took her seat.

"Ha! Smart girl." Alex passed her a cigarette box.

"Smoke?"

"Not much."

"Well, I know Hans will have one," Alex shoved it toward me. "Me? I'm rather fond of the pipe." "For style?" Sophie smiled.

"Naturally. Makes me appear scholarly, don't you think?"

I laughed as I lit my cigarette. "Continue believing that, Alex."

"What? Isn't it true? Sophie, don't I look intelligent while smoking a pipe?" Alex held his chin high.

Sophie laughed outright, then abruptly covered her mouth

with her hand.

Alex sighed, feigning an offended air. "I hate to tell you this, but you Scholls have no sense of style."

I withdrew a pile of papers from my briefcase and set them on the table. "Just another burden we must bear. Now," I slapped my hand on the papers, "we should get to work. Sophie has agreed to help distribute the leaflets on a broader scale since she enjoys train rides."

"Splendid." Alex nodded his approval toward Sophie.

I turned to my sister. "Alex and I have drafted the third leaflet, which I'd like to read to you. Get comfortable." I motioned toward the cigarettes on the table.

"'All ideal forms of government are utopias. A state cannot be constructed on a purely theoretical basis; rather, it must grow and ripen in the way an individual human being matures but we must not forget that at the starting point of every civilization the state was already there in rudimentary form. The family is as old as man himself, and out of this initial bond, man, endowed with reason, created for himself a state founded on justice, whose highest law was the common good. The state should exist as a parallel to the divine order, and the highest of all utopias, the civitas dei, is the model which in the end it should approximate. Here we will not pass judgment on the many possible forms of the state—democracy, constitutional monarchy, and so on.

"'But one matter needs to be brought out clearly and unambiguously. Every individual human being has a claim to a useful and just state, a state which secures freedom of the individual as well as the good of the whole. For, according to God's will, man is intended to pursue his natural goal, his earthly happiness, in self-reliance and self-chosen activity, freely and independently within the community of life and work of the nation. But our present 'state' is the dictatorship of evil. 'Oh, we've known that for a long time,' I hear you object, 'and it isn't necessary to bring that to our attention again.' But, I ask you, if you know that, why do you not bestir yourselves, why do you allow these men who are in power to rob you step by step, openly and in secret, of one domain of your rights after another, until one day nothing, nothing at all will be left but a mechanized state system presided over by criminals and drunks?

"'Is your spirit already so crushed by abuse that you forget it is your right—or rather, your moral duty—to eliminate this system? But if a man no longer can summon the strength to demand his right, then it is absolutely certain that he will perish. We would deserve to be dispersed through the earth like dust before the wind if we do not muster our powers at this late hour and finally find the courage which up to now we have lacked. Do not hide your cowardice behind a cloak of expediency, for with every new day that you hesitate, failing to oppose this offspring of Hell, your guilt, as in a parabolic curve, grows higher and higher.'"

I began pacing back and forth as I turned the page.

"'Many, perhaps most, of the readers of these leaflets do not see clearly how they can practice an effective opposition. They do not see any avenues open to them. We want to try to show them that everyone is in a position to contribute to the overthrow of this system. It is not possible through solitary withdrawal, in the manner of embittered hermits, to prepare the ground for the overturn of this 'government' or bring about the revolution at the earliest possible moment. No, it can be done only by the cooperation of many convinced, energetic people—people who are agreed as to the means they must use to attain their goal. We have no great number of choices as to these means. The only one available is passive resistance.

"'The meaning and the goal of passive resistance is to topple National Socialism, and in this struggle we must not recoil from any course, any action, whatever its nature. At all points we must oppose National Socialism, wherever it is open to attack. We must soon bring this monster of a state to an end. A victory of fascist Germany in this war would have immeasurable, frightful consequences. The military victory over Bolshevism dare not become the primary concern of the Germans. The defeat of the Nazis must unconditionally be the first order of business, the greater necessity of this latter requirement will be discussed in one of our forthcoming leaflets. And now every convinced opponent of National Socialism must ask himself how he can fight against the present 'state' in the most effective way, how he can strike it the most telling blows. Through passive resistance, without a doubt.

"'We cannot provide each man with the blueprint for his acts; we can only suggest them in general terms, and he alone will find the way of achieving this end: Sabotage in armament plants and war industries, sabotage at all gatherings, rallies, public ceremonies, and organizations of the National Socialist Party. Obstruction of the smooth functioning of the war machine (a machine for war that goes on solely to shore up and perpetuate the National Socialist Party and its dictatorship). Sabotage in all the areas of science and scholarship which further the continuation of the war—whether in universities, technical schools, laboratories, research institutes, or technical bureaus. Sabotage in all cultural institutions which could potentially enhance the 'prestige' of the fascists among the people. Sabotage in all branches of the arts which have even the slightest dependence on National Socialism or render it service. Sabotage in all publications, all newspapers, that are in the pay of the 'government' and that defend its ideology and aid in disseminating the brown lie.

"'Do not give a penny to public drives (even when they are conducted under the pretense of charity), for this is only a disguise. In reality the proceeds aid neither the Red Cross nor the needy. The government does not need this money; it is not financially interested in these money drives. After all, the presses run continuously to manufacture any desired amount of paper currency. But the populace must be kept constantly under tension, the pressure of the bit must not be allowed to slacken! Do not contribute to the collections of metal, textiles, and the like. Try to convince all your acquaintances, including those in the lower social classes, of the senselessness of continuing, of the hopelessness of this war; of our spiritual and economic enslavement at the hands of the National Socialists; of the destruction of all moral and religious values; and urge them to passive resistance! 'Aristotle, Politics: '... and further, it is part of the nature of tyranny to strive to see to it that nothing is kept hidden of that which any subject says or does, but that everywhere he will be spied upon ... and further, to set man against the privileged and the wealthy. Also it is part of these tyrannical measures, to keep the subjects poor, in order to pay the guards and soldiers, and so that they will be occupied with earning their livelihood and will have neither leisure nor opportunity to engage in conspiratorial acts ... Further, to levy such taxes on income as were imposed in Syracuse, for under Dionysius the citizens gladly paid out their whole fortunes in taxes within five years. Also, the tyrant is inclined constantly to ferment wars.'"

I threw the papers on the table with flourish, then ran a hand over my jaw.

Sophie was peering over her wine glass at me. "Alex and I will begin typing and mimeographing the leaflets. I've obtained an address book which you can look through and organize by streets. Once we're finished, we'll divide and distribute them tonight." I fixed my gaze on her. "Are you positive you want to do this, Sophie?" I knew her answer by the fortitude that glistened in her eyes.

"Of course I want to do this, Hans. I'm not backing down, now or ever."

dancing in the rain

The scent of rain hung on the wind as I trekked down Franz-Josef-Strasse. I hunched my shoulders against the damp breeze. The sky was cloaked in dark, inky clouds. I was on break between lectures and medical rounds and had made plans to meet Gisela for a stroll. The weather appeared to be against us. I rapped on her door, glancing to the right of me as the wind accelerated, whipping the Nazi flags violently.

Gisela opened the door, her long overcoat and navy blue hat already on. "Hello, Hans. Did you bring an umbrella?" She gazed past me at the impending storm.

"That would have been clever, but no, I didn't."

She set her eyes back on me. "Well, that's all right. You mentioned that there was a covered bridge near the river. Why don't we picnic in there? That would be rather adventurous." Her eyes danced.

I grinned at the fact that her idea of adventure consisted of having a picnic in a covered bridge amidst a thunderstorm. If she considered that adventurous, what would she think of *The White Rose*?

"All right," I shrugged.

I took a picnic basket from her hands, surprised by the weight of it. "What did you pack in here? Rocks?" I smirked as we hurried down the street.

"The biscuits might as well be. I'm horrible in the kitchen."

"I'm sure everything will be delicious." I tried consoling her, but wasn't certain if I had succeeded. We approached the street corner, entering a bustling area with cars whipping back and forth over the cobblestone road. A glossy, black car slowly drove in front of us, and my eyes met with the surly driver for a split second. My throat went dry.

"Gestapo," Gisela's breath was low, fearful. "I always get

the chills when they drive by."

I turned to her, trying to stop the fear that coursed through me. "Why, did you do something wrong, Gisela Schertling?" I teased.

"Of course not! Don't even jest about such things."

"Then there's no need to fear." Our eyes locked, and she smiled at me.

A surge of droplets began hitting the back of my neck, arms, and head. I linked my arms through Gisela's, leading her toward the Isar river and the covered bridge. The rain picked up in speed, hurling itself against the cobblestone. I relished the feeling of cold rain water trailing down my face. I longed to just stand there, tilt my head up to the torrent of rain and stay until all the inhumanity, all the destruction and war were stripped away by the velocity of the storm. When we reached the bridge, the wooden structure was saturated by the downpour. I lingered outside it.

"Hans, we're getting soaked," Gisela squealed through the wind.

"I rather like it." I ripped off my army cap as another burst of wind wrapped around us.

"What?" She squinted through the rain. She was clutching her hat against her head, and her blue eyes were broad. "Come, the bridge is just a few steps away."

"Isn't the rain refreshing?" I gave her a lopsided grin as I set the basket down. I turned to face her.

She stared at me, a flicker of confusion followed by amusement dancing across her face. "Hans, you do make me smile," she grinned.

"Good. We need more smiling these days." I laced a hand through hers, and then swooped her into a dance as our wet, sodden clothes brushed against each other.

"What on earth are you doing?" Raindrops trailed down her rosy face as she studied me.

"Dancing."

A smile played on her lips. "Oh. Well, this is rather nice."

Our footsteps shuffled against the boardwalk. *Right two, three. Left two, three.* The rain continued battering our heads and soaking our clothing relentlessly.

"What's rather nice?" I asked after a moment. "Dancing or forgetting about the war for one blissful moment?"

"Both. I did nearly forget that there's a war going on."

"But there is, and we're in the thick of it." I brought my gaze down to our feet—my tall, black army boots and her small leather oxfords. "I can't bear the uncertainty of it ... wondering if perhaps I could be killed in the night by a bombing, or if I'll be called to the front again. I feel as though I can't plan for the future. My life is day to day ... no firm plans are in place." I wanted her to know that something could happen to me, and this was why I couldn't become attached to her. But it was entirely too late for that, and I knew it.

"That's dreary talk."

I peered up at her. "I know, but it's how I feel."

The rain dripped between our fingers and traveled down the backs of our hands. "You are a Christian, aren't you, Hans?" she asked.

"Yes."

"Then why are you so worried?" We stopped dancing, and she met my eyes. "Surely you believe God has your life in His hands?"

I breathed deeply, lifting my eyes to the cascade of raindrops pelting down upon my face. "I suppose I've been relying on myself too much lately."

"He will take care of things, Hans. He knows how many hours, days, months, years we have left. Worrying about it won't change the hour fixed for our deaths. Live a good, honest, Godly life, then you won't have any regrets."

I smiled at her, and my heart felt as if a great weight was lifting, slowly but surely. "Shall we continue dancing then?"

"I thought you'd never ask."

alliances

"Sophie, your brother is here to see you." Frau Berrsche, an older woman with a strange persona of refined elegance and extreme gregariousness stood at the foot of the staircase, one pale hand grasping the railing. I was in her parlor studying the bookshelf, disappointed at her meager selection. Her boisterous voice rattled the house, and I cringed as her shout momentarily numbed my ears. She turned to me, her lips and cheeks slathered with blush and lipstick.

"She's been up there all morning writing a reply to that soldier of hers. She's head over heels for that boy."

I raised a brow. "How do you know that, Frau Berrsche?"

"I have eyes. I can read a return address, and I can see the clock tick on after she receives one of those letters. Sophie locks herself in her room for a good two hours." She flopped herself on the sofa. "Do you have a girlfriend?"

I dropped my hand, clearing my throat uncomfortably. She wasn't one for respecting people's privacy, I noticed. I forced a smile. "No, not really ..." I pocketed my hands.

"That's not what Sophie says."

I clenched my jaw. "She talks to you about Gisela, does she?"

Frau Berrsche just grinned in reply.

Presently, Sophie came clambering down the stairs like a rambunctious foal, morning light brightening her face. "Good morning, Hans. No medical rounds today?" She leaned over the railing.

"No work this Saturday. I thought we should have some fun today. Alex, Christl, Willi, and I are going on a hike. Would you like to join us, or are you too busy writing to Fritz?" I glanced from Frau Berrchse to Sophie with a smirk.

"I'm not *always* writing to Fritz, you know," said Sophie.

"You aren't?"

"No, I'm not." She was entirely serious. A reluctant smile overtook her face. "Let me fetch my jacket."

We strolled in companionable silence through the streets of Munich, brushing past civilians who were in a hustle to get somewhere. I studied their faces as they passed. Some were twisted in confusion and fear as they hurried past groups of soldiers lingering in the streets. Others were indifferent. Still others smiled, as if the world didn't have a blemish on it. Cars lashed through the rain puddles left from last evening's downpour. The air was damp and reeked of gasoline. We walked for miles until disappearing out of the city and continuing down a calm, country road. The mountain rose beyond it. Patches of white, misty fog hovered over the rich green leaves.

"We're going to tell them today," I said, breaking the quiet that hung between us.

She turned to me. "But I thought you wished to keep the group small."

"I did." I kicked a stone, watching as it pitched and tumbled a few feet ahead. "But we need help if we want this resistance to grow. The three of us are exhausted. We need help, Sophie."

"You have been looking rather worn out lately," she agreed.

"Willi and Christl need to know what we're doing." I yanked on a piece of tall grass as we walked. "They are the closest friends I have besides you and Alex."

"And Gisela?" Sophie bumped her shoulder into my arm.

"Gisela?"

"She's become a close friend of yours, hasn't she?"

"Perhaps, but I won't be telling her of the leaflets under any circumstances."

"Because you like her."

I didn't argue.

We continued on until reaching the foot of the mountain where a large stone was situated near the entrance of the hiking trail. I could spot Alex's tall form waving a hand. Willi and Christl were sitting on the stone, smoking their pipes. The scent of sweet pine and damp earth clung to the warm breeze.

"There are the Scholls," Alex cheered.

"Sorry we're late." I fixed my collar after the cold burst of a raindrop dripping off an overhanging tree slipped down my neck. "And sorry, but I forgot to pack food."

"Thankfully, my wife anticipated the hunger born of a strenuous hiking excursion and packed us a bundle." Christl held up a satchel with a smirk.

We began our trek by discussing trivial things at first. Then our talk swayed to literature and music. Christl appeared to be holding something in, something he obviously wished to share, for he was grinning and nearly bursting by the time we decided to take a short rest.

"What is it, Christl?" Alex must have noticed too, for he slapped his hand on Christl's shoulder. "You're beaming!"

I braced my foot against a stone and leaned my arms onto my thigh, attempting to catch my breath from the steep incline.

"Herta went to the doctor last week …" Christl began.

"Oh!" Sophie was the first to understand. "Christl, congratulations!"

"On what?" I asked.

Sophie shook her head at me, as if I was a hopeless case.

"Herta is with child, Hans. Honestly, you didn't catch on? And you're all medical students here." She laughed heartily.

I tossed a teasing glare at Sophie. "I was merely concerned for her health. All Christl said was that she went to the doctor. That could mean a countless number of things."

"He wouldn't be so happy about her going to the doctor

unless she was expecting, Hans." Sophie was still grinning at me.

I strode over to where Christl was standing and held out a hand. "I'm happy for you, Christl." A wave of back slapping, hand shaking, and good cheer followed.

"What do you think it'll be? A boy or girl?" Sophie asked.

Christl shrugged as he lit his pipe. "Well, we have two boys. Perhaps I'll have a daughter this time."

"You should name her Sophie." Sophie's eyes danced in amusement.

"We'll consider it. Thank you for your input," Christl laughed.

"Well," I said after a short lull in the conversation. "As long as we're sharing news, I suppose I better get to mine."

Willi, who was perched on a fallen log, grinned. "Let me guess. You are engaged to Miss Schertling?"

Sophie let out a torrent of laughter, which caused the rest of them to join in. All but me. "Of course not!" For some reason unknown, this defensive remark made their gales of laughter even stronger. "Can't we be serious for once?" My voice was lost in their mirth. "I don't see the humor in this at all."

"All right, I apologize," Sophie breathed with a smile. "And I almost wish that were your announcement." Her face suddenly turned stoic. "But I know it's not."

"No, it's not." I glanced at Alex, urging him to go on with it.

Alex understood, for his smile was swept away, and a serious countenance took its place. "Have you all seen the leaflets of *The White Rose*?" he asked them.

"Of course. They're all over Munich." Christl took a long sip of water from his canteen.

"Any idea who wrote them?" I asked, wiping the sweat from my brow with the back of my sleeve.

"No, but the Gestapo is on their trail. I suspect they'll be caught, and we'll know the authors soon."

"What faith you have in us. What cheerful talk you give us, Christl." I glanced at him with a tentative smile.

Christl raised an eyebrow, his visage bearing perplexity. Then his blue eyes widened as he eyed me, Alex, and then Sophie. "Us? Hans, w-what the hell are you talking about?"

"I'd thank you not to swear in front of my little sister." I nodded toward Sophie who had been taking in the entire conversation with her inquiring eyes.

"I apologize. I don't swear ... not often at least. But when I find out that my good friends are the authors of an extremely dangerous leaflet against Hitler, and if caught, would be executed, I have a hell of a time not swearing. Ah!" He placed his head in his hands dejectedly. "I apologize, Sophie."

Willi was hunched over, staring at his dirt encrusted boots. "You three wrote the leaflets of *The White Rose?*" His voice was low, pensive.

"Hans and Alex did," Sophie said. "I found out accidentally, but since then I've been mailing the leaflets and just recently started overseeing the account books. Creating anti-Nazi leaflets is rather expensive these days."

Alex and I let out a stream of laughter at that, but Christl and Willi were silent. Willi's eyes swept over us. I could almost see the wheels turning in his head.

"You realize how dangerous this is?" His voice was calm. Willi was always calm, a trait I respected greatly.

"Perfectly," I replied. "That's why we didn't want to inform anyone outside of me and Alex, but we need help if we wish for these leaflets to be distributed further, and we need funds to produce more. We understand if you two don't want to get involved, you especially Christl. I wouldn't want you to be too deeply involved with your wife, boys and another child to consider, but we are like family, the five of us, and if you're anything like Sophie, you'd be cross at me for not including you, even if I was trying to protect you." I leaned against the coarse, peeling tree bark. It smelled of sweet sap. "We know the consequences. It doesn't deter us."

"My God! I don't know what to say." Christl gazed up at the sky, his eyes searching the heavens. "Our country needs God." I wasn't certain if he was speaking with us anymore or if he was thinking aloud. "It needs respect for human life once again. I'm only worried over what could happen to us as we try to defend it, and I know I shouldn't be."

I wasn't one to quote scripture as a response, but I had held a certain Bible verse close to me since childhood ... a verse that continued to inspire and stir my soul. "'If I have the gift of prophecy and can fathom all mysteries and all knowledge, and if I have a faith that can move mountains, but do not have love, I am nothing.' How am I showing love to my neighbor if I sit back and allow the evil against them to prevail?"

Christl brought his eyes down to earth again. "You're right, but I *can't* endanger my wife or my children."

"No, you can't." I agreed. "But you have ideas, Christl. We are always in desperate need of those, and sharing ideas is safer than acting on them."

"I'll help." Willi's voice turned all heads his way. "I'll help pay for supplies and spread the word of the leaflet on my next trip home." He was fingering the cross around his neck. He peered at me, his blue eyes gleaming with integrity. He meant what he said, and we could always count on his word.

"I'll do what I can," pitched in Christl. "But I won't endanger my family, Hans. I can't."

the fourth leaflet

Be confident. Don't linger. Move quickly.

This is what I told Sophie, Alex, and Willi before they left with their satchels packed full of leaflets. Now I was heeding my own advice as I straightened my collar and moved forward through the crowded train station. It was one thing to distribute them in the cover of darkness, but doing so in broad daylight caused my heart to slam against my chest and my stomach to twist into knots. I approached the train station, thick grey smoke clogging the air. The home guard officers towered over all the passengers, their eyes sharp and alert as they studied papers and passports. I purchased my ticket, then sauntered closer to the train, recalling my own words.

Be confident. Don't linger. Move quickly.

"Papers."

I glanced up. A home guard officer was glowering at me. He had a jagged scar webbed across his jawline and broad shoulders. I reached into my uniform pocket and produced the necessary paperwork, thrusting it into the large, outstretched hand. I watched as he eyed the papers over with a sniff. "Where are you going? Is this trip necessary?"

"My sister lives in Stuttgart. I'm currently on leave and wished to take the opportunity to visit her while I could." The lie came out so smoothly, so effortlessly. I waited, confident that my clear explanation would convince him.

The officer stared at me, his eyes dark. "Ahnenpass."

I immediately withdrew my passport which proved that I was Aryan. He glanced at it, then shoved it back into my hands. "What's in your bag, soldier?"

"Clothes, naturally. I'm spending a few days in Stuttgart."

"How long?"

"Five days."

"What's her name?"

"Whose?"

"Your sister's." The officer's voice raised a notch. This infuriated me. Before the war a person could travel without these idiotic interrogations. One simply purchased a ticket, and that was that. Yet, I complied, not wishing to draw any unnecessary attention to myself. "Inge Scholl." Inge wasn't in Stuttgart as far as I knew, but the officer had no way of knowing. I stared at him, meeting his glare brazenly.

"Does she know you're coming?"

"Of course. May I board now, sir?"

He mumbled something inaudible as he stepped aside. I swiftly boarded, feeling heat rush through my head. I lifted my bag and set it on the overhead baggage rack, then wandered away, hands in my pockets. I found a seat in a separate train car, a safe distance away from the incriminating evidence. That had been Alex's idea, for if the bags were searched, and they found the leaflets, they wouldn't know who the bag belonged to.

I sank down into a seat with a heavy sigh and rubbed my hands together. I tried swallowing, but my throat was dry. I eyed those around me. A middle-aged woman was staring at me over her magazine, then quickly peered down when our eyes met. My skin went cold. I turned my head to watch the city disappear in a cloud of hazy smoke, concluding that I was being paranoid. A long gaze from anyone unnerved me these days, and no wonder for everyone was turning each other in for small offenses. I fingered the cracked leather covering of my seat. The train swayed, and I allowed myself to close my eyes and listen to the glass rattle in the window pane. Visions of the leaflets came to mind. Their words, pounded on the typewriter and multiplied into thousands throughout the night, were imprinted in my brain.

There is an ancient maxim that we repeat to our children: "He who won't listen will have to feel." But a wise child will not burn his fingers the second time on a hot stove. In the past weeks Hitler has choked up successes in Africa and in Russia. In consequence, optimism on the one hand and distress and pessimism on the other have grown within the German people with a rapidity quite inconsistent with traditional German apathy. On all sides one hears among Hitler's opponents—the better segments of the population— exclamations of despair, words of disappointment and discouragement, often ending with the question: "Will Hitler now, after all ...?"

The train slowed as it pulled into the next station. I was forced to wait an agonizing half hour while more civilians and soldiers boarded the train. A mother and her small daughter slid into the seat across from me. I smiled politely, and the child gave me a timid grin, leaning closer into her mother's side. I turned my gaze out the window, watching the home guard board the train behind a group of passengers.

Meanwhile, the German offensive against Egypt has ground to a halt. Rommel has to bide his time in a dangerously exposed position, but the push into the East proceeds. This apparent success has been purchased at the most horrible expense of human life, and so it can no longer be counted an advantage. Therefore, we must warn against all optimism. Neither Hitler nor Goebbels can have counted the dead. In Russia thousands are lost daily. It is the time of the harvest, and the reaper cuts into the ripe grain with wide strokes. Mourning takes up her abode in the country cottages, and there is no one to dry the tears of the mothers. Yet Hitler feeds with lies those people whose most precious belongings he has stolen and whom he has driven to a meaningless death.

"Baggage search."

I leaned my head into the aisle and watched as the officers began to rifle through the newcomers' luggage. I wiped my sweaty palms along my trousers as they began poking at the luggage in the baggage rack. One officer, square jawed and so tall that his blonde hair brushed the top of the ceiling, was making his way up the aisle, his jackboots thumping against the floor.

"What's going on?" I asked. "Not a long hold up, I hope?"

"Just a routine baggage search. If everyone behaves themselves, the train should be on its way shortly."

I leaned back in the chair, looking at the little girl across from me. She was taking the scene in with round, brown eyes. She reminded me of Sophie. The inspection went on for ten minutes, and I spent the time running my finger along the window pane, praying, hoping, pleading that my bag would be overlooked. A storm of officers hurried past, shaking the train car as they marched, then lumbered off the train. I could breathe again as the train gave a jolt forward.

Every word that comes from Hitler's mouth is a lie. When he says peace, he means war, and when he blasphemously uses the name of the Almighty, he means the power of evil, the fallen angel, Satan. His mouth is the foul-smelling maw of Hell, and his might is at bottom accursed. True, we must conduct a struggle against the National Socialist terrorist state with rational means; but whoever today still doubts the reality, the existence of demonic powers, has failed by a wide margin to understand the metaphysical background of this war. Behind the concrete, the visible events, behind all objective, logical considerations, we find the irrational element: The struggle against the demon, against the servants of the Antichrist. Everywhere and at all times demons have been lurking in the dark, waiting for the moment when man is weak; when of his own volition he leaves his place in the order of Creation as founded for him by God in freedom; when he yields to the force of evil, separates himself from the powers of a higher order; and after voluntarily taking the first step, he is driven on to the next and the next at a furiously accelerating rate.

We pulled into Stuttgart, and as soon as the train stopped, I jumped up, nearly bumping my head on the baggage rack as I maneuvered into the aisle. I retrieved my briefcase and stepped off the train, eyeing my surroundings with considerable caution. The vivid reds and russet rays of evening cast down upon the streets, causing a strip of warmth to travel along my face. Moments later it was replaced with the ashen glow of twilight before the darkness began to set in. I strolled along with the small group from the station until reaching the main street where blackout curtains were being drawn over windows as shops were closing their doors.

Everywhere and at all times of greatest trial men have appeared—prophets and saints—who cherished their freedom, who preached the One God and who with His help brought the people to a reversal of their downward course. Man is free, to be sure, but without the true God he is defenseless against the principle of evil. He is a like rudderless ship, at the mercy of the storm, an infant without his mother, a cloud dissolving into thin air.

I reached a quiet alley and began taking out the leaflets from my briefcase, tossing them in the parked cars. I closed the briefcase and continued down the alley, my boots crunching gravel. My heart skipped a beat at the bone chilling sound of jackboots. I hesitantly glanced up and caught the sight of a Schupo coming toward me. I attempted to console myself by reasoning that he was simply walking his beat and knew nothing of my activities. But his gait was swift, and a gun was visible in his belt.

I ask you, you as a Christian wrestling for the preservation of your greatest treasure, whether you hesitate, whether you incline toward intrigue, calculation, or procrastination in the hope that someone else will raise his arm in your defense? Has God not given you the strength, the will to fight? We must attack evil where it is strongest, and it is strongest in the power of Hitler. "So I returned, and considered all the oppressions that are done under the sun: and behold the tears of such as were oppressed, and they had no comforter; and on the side of their oppressors there was power; but they had no comforter. Wherefore I praised the dead which are already dead than the living which are yet alive." Ecclesiastes 4.

"Good evening, soldier," the Schupo said. "Cold spell we're having, isn't it?" He was a jolly sort, more interested in talking about the weather than in searching baggage, so I loosened my clutch on the briefcase with a nod.

"Yes, quite chilly."

We passed without another word. The Schupo was whistling, oblivious to me now.

I took long strides until reaching the end of the alley, then looked over my shoulder. The Schupo was gone, and evening had descended, masking the street in a cloak of inky black. I began pulling out leaflets and slipping them onto benches and the stone wall encircling a fountain in a park nearby.

Novalis: True anarchy is the generative element of religion. Out of the annihilation of every positive element she lifts her gloriously radiant countenance as the founder of a new world ... If Europe were about to awaken again, if a state of states, a teaching of political science were at hand!

*Should hierarchy then... be the principle of the union of
states? Blood will stream over Europe until the nations become aware of the frightful madness which drives them in
circles. And then, struck by celestial music and made gentle,
they approach their former altars all together, hear about
the works of peace, and hold a great celebration of peace
with fervent tears before the smoking altars. Only religion
can reawaken Europe, establish the rights of the peoples,
and install Christianity in new splendor visibly on earth in its
office as guarantor of peace.*

I reached into the inside pocket of my uniform and pulled
out a thick stack of enveloped leaflets which I slipped into
the mailbox. This was to throw the Gestapo off our trail, for
if the leaflets were marked as mailed from various locations,
they couldn't put a finger on the city which was producing
them.

*We wish expressly to point out that The White Rose is not
in the pay of any foreign power. Though we know that National Socialist power must be broken by military means, we
are trying to achieve a renewal from within of the severely
wounded German spirit. This rebirth must be preceded, however, by the clear recognition of all the guilt with which the
German people have burdened themselves, and by an un-
compromising battle against Hitler and his all too many
minions, party members, Quislings, and the like. With total
brutality, the chasm that separates the better portion of the
nation from everything that is opened wide. For Hitler and
his followers there is no punishment on this Earth commen-
surate with their crimes.*

My task was finished. I knew that once I arrived back in
Munich, I'd once again forge into the German night armed
with the dangerous leaflets. But tonight was done, and I

wasn't caught. I wasn't certain how long good fortune could last.

But out of love for coming generations we must make an example after the conclusion of the war, so that no one will ever again have the slightest urge to try a similar action. And do not forget the petty scoundrels in this regime; note their names, so that none will go free! They should not find it possible, having had their part in these abominable crimes, at the last minute to rally to another flag and then act as if nothing had happened! To set you at rest, we add that the addresses of the readers of the White Rose are not recorded in writing. They were picked at random from directories.

We will not be silent. We are your bad conscience. The White Rose will not leave you in peace!

another member

I heard female voices outside my door the next afternoon. I sighed, dropped the pen I had been fingering while gazing out the window, and stood up. I was annoyed that Sophie seemed to have brought along a friend on her visit today. Now we wouldn't be able to discuss *The White Rose* or go over the account books like we planned. I wasn't presentable for company either, having slept all morning and worked all afternoon on medical rounds. My trousers were wrinkled, and my shirt sleeves were haphazardly rolled over my elbows. I pulled my suspenders' straps over my shoulders, then glanced in the mirror. My hair was tousled, but I hadn't the energy to find my Brylcreem. I quickly ran a hand through it and pulled open the door.

Traute stood beside Sophie. I couldn't comprehend why she of all people would be on my doorstep, but I attempted to appear not quite as perplexed as I felt.

"Traute, it's good to see you. Please, come in," I held open the door with one hand. Sophie and Traute entered, and I noted both their expressions. Traute looked fit to be tied; Sophie was pale and wide-eyed.

"Sit down. Can I get you girls something to drink? Or a cigarette?"

"The only thing I want is an answer." Traute fixed her brown eyes on me.

I furrowed my brow and leaned against my desk, clutching the edge with both hands. "Answer to what?"

Traute set her satchel on a chair, withdrawing a paper. She shook out the wrinkles and began to read:

"'So I returned, and considered all the oppressions that are done under the sun: and behold the tears of such as were oppressed, and they had no comforter; and on the side of their oppressors there was power; but they had no comforter. Wherefore I praised the dead which are already dead than the living which are yet alive. Ecclesiastes 4.'" She glanced at me. "I recall drawing your attention to this verse not so long ago, and I find it ironic that it's in this leaflet of *The White Rose* which also reminds me of you."

"That isn't a question, Traute." I hesitantly smiled, willing my features not to betray me. I peered at Sophie, but she was tracing a crack in the floor with the tip of her shoe, unwilling to meet anyone's eyes.

"Are you the author of *The White Rose* leaflets?" Traute dropped the leaflet onto the desk as her eyes bored into mine.

I avoided her gaze. "It's not safe to find out who's responsible in these matters. It only endangers everyone involved."

"That's hardly an answer, Hans Scholl."

"It would be best for you to know as little as possible."

"Hans, I'm not going to turn you in. Is that why you won't tell me? Do you think I'd betray you just because we're no longer in love?" Her cheeks were flushed.

I shook my head, finally meeting her eyes. "Of course not. I'm trying to protect you, just as I tried to protect Sophie, but you two know me far too well." I wandered to the window, peering out to distract myself from the two inquiring faces staring at me. "Are the leaflets so transparent that you could place me as the author?"

"Only because, as you say, I know you so well. Only those of your closest friends may think of you when they read it, but everyone I've talked to is in utter bewilderment over the author. You're safe ... for now."

I watched a Nazi flag on the building across the road ripple in the wind. "You swear you're for us, Traute?"

"Haven't I always been?"

I glanced over my shoulder at her. "Do you wish to help us?"

"Yes, and I already thought over how." She looked first at Sophie, then at me with enthusiasm. I'll take the leaflets on my next trip to Hamburg and show them to my friends. We'll distribute them around the city. I'll be a liaison between Munich and Hamburg."

"Would you?" I felt adrenaline rush through my veins. Knowing we had her confidence caused a plethora of ideas to whirl around in my head. "*The White Rose* could spread all over Germany! We could make connections with other resistance groups and—"

"Slow down, Hans! One step at a time." Traute held up a hand cautiously. "We must take care, for as you are very well aware, this is a matter of life or death for all those involved."

"Of course I know that. That's the exact reason I didn't want you two entangled in it."

"Well, we are now. Your little circle is growing, which means we will all need to be extra careful. I better go. And Hans, your landlady may be watching the comings and goings around here ... be wary of that as well." Traute moved toward the door, stopped, and flashed a grin at me. "'*The*

White Rose will not leave you in peace!' You know how to stir resistance in all of us, Hans."

the reading circle

The Schmorell villa was made available for a night of literature and discussions, a ritual my friends and I enjoyed weekly. Alex's father was of one mind with what our group stood for, though he didn't know to what extent his son was involved. Wine was served, along with flaky biscuits and tea cakes. The reading circle conveniently took place in the spacious library which was bedecked wall to wall with books and a crackling fireplace. It was a small group that evening: only the core members of *The White Rose*, along with Professor Huber and the newest addition to our reading circle, Gisela. The Professor and Gisela were the sole individuals who knew nothing of our part in *The White Rose*.

I was situated comfortably on a cushioned chair, encircled by ancient smelling tomes. I was sipping wine and risking a few glances at Gisela over the rim of my glass. Her hair seemed to glow in the light from the fireplace, and her eyes swept over the large room with curiosity. Our eyes met, and she grinned at me.

As with all our meetings, the conversation always turned to politics after some thoughtful prose or a poem. Gisela instigated it unconsciously by reciting a piece that struck me.

"'But now, for the first time, I see you are a man like me. I thought of your hand-grenades, of your bayonet, of your rifle; now I see your wife and your face and our fellowship. Forgive me, comrade. We always see it too late. Why do they never tell us that you are poor devils like us, that your mothers are just as anxious as ours, and that we have the same fear of death, and the same dying and the same agony—Forgive me, comrade; how could you be my enemy?'"

"Erich Maria Remarque. *All Quiet on the Western Front,*" I said.

"My! You are good at this." Gisela beamed at me.

"It's my father's favorite book, and it is banned by the Nazis." I stood up, churning the piece over in my mind. "Our country lacks humanity and respect for life. If only they could see that all human beings deserve respect, that there is no such thing as a *superior* race. Even if there were such a thing, the Nazis would not be them, for how could someone superior allow the slaughter of innocent human beings? How could they tolerate the concentration camps, the gassing, the mass shootings, the destruction of lives? When this terror is over, are we going to be included with the ones who allowed death to freely reign, or are we going to resist? If we choose the former, then what are we to say when asked 'What did you do about it?' We will have no answer."

Silence wrapped around us. I paused and leaned my arm against the mantle, wondering if I had said too much.

"You speak with such conviction, Hans." Gisela's soft voice caused me to turn. "You inspire me to do something to end this destruction."

I grinned at her. "Well, you got me started on a lecture with that splendid piece from Remarque."

"I have more to recite. Shall we see if you have something to add to my next bit of prose?"

"If you'd like me to lecture again, then yes. What say you all?" I eyed the group.

"Go on, we're enjoying this immensely," Alex said, pipe wedged in the corner of his mouth.

I nodded to Gisela to continue. She bit her lip for a moment, then her eyes brightened. "'God did not create evil. Just as darkness is the absence of light, evil is the absence of God.' Who wrote that?"

"Albert Einstein, another forbidden author," I said. "People tend to believe that God has abandoned us, for how could a loving God allow Hitler and the Nazis to take over? But we are given free will by God. We can either accept his love or reject it. By rejecting it, we're not only corrupting our souls, but hurting those around us. As you recited, 'God did not create evil.' He created goodness, and our sinful nature has led us astray. The only way back to goodness is through God, accepting his gift of love."

"Oh my, I could go on for hours like this," Gisela said.

"I could as well," I smirked.

Gisela and I were in our own world, discussing literature and philosophy as if we'd known each other our entire lives. I couldn't pull myself away from the spell. Was there anyone else in the room but her? I was reminded that there was when Alex's voice broke our momentary silence.

"Well, sadly you cannot, for it is my villa, and I have a striking urge to sing. How about it?" Alex stood up, his tall frame nearly bumping the chandelier.

"But I'd like to discuss Saint Augustine–" I started.

"Grab your guitar my good man!" Alex slapped me on the back.

"Ah, very well. As you say." I retrieved my guitar and ran my fingers along the strings.

change

Change was in the air, threatening my plans and future. It left my heart heavy and my emotions in a tangled mess. I had brooded all night long after hearing the news that threw my life into a whirlwind of uncertainty and obliterated my sense of direction.

Change.

It's a force that no one can evade for long.

I spotted Sophie in the university hallway the following morning, clutching her books to her chest as she hurried on to her next lecture.

"Sophie," I let out a strangled breath as I sought to catch up with her. She paused, turned, and her face went ashen as I surged toward her. By the look on her fear stricken visage, I realized my panic might lead her to believe something had gone wrong with *The White Rose*, so I hurriedly got to the point. "The student medical company just received orders. We're moving to the Eastern Front."

That bit of news did not bring the color back to her face. Her eyes widened, and she gripped my forearm. Her hand was trembling. "Hans, not you too! It's horrible enough to think of Werner out there."

I found the situation that we were all in terribly ironic. Werner was fighting for the Reich as an infantry soldier, while Sophie and I were fighting against it. I knew my brother didn't agree with what he was fighting for, but being conscripted left him little choice.

"I know. I—I didn't take the news well either." I peered down at her. "Walk to my room with me, would you? We need to talk."

The sun beat down on us, making my frantic state consequently worse. The air was heavy, so I unbuttoned my jacket and the top of my white shirt. I licked my dry lips as we trudged on. Sophie said nothing, even as I tried to strike up a light-hearted conversation. Her mind was closed to me, so I finally gave up and consented with mulling over my situation once more. *The White Rose* would have to be put on hold until we returned from the front ... if we returned.

I opened my apartment door without a word and then closed it behind us quietly. I was becoming more aware of my landlady, wondering if she was keeping an eye on my activities. I sank onto my bed, running a hand over my damp forehead. "'Mourning takes up her abode in the country cottages, and there is no one to dry the tears of the mothers. Yet Hitler feeds with lies those people whose most precious belongings he has stolen and whom he has driven to a meaningless death.'" I quoted the fourth leaflet and glanced at my sister.

Sophie sat on my desk, looking wistful and anxious. "I told Werner before he left to promise me that he wouldn't take the life of anyone." She looked down at her shoes. "I hope he's keeping his promise."

"Werner's a good sort, Sophie. Please, don't worry too much."

"But what will happen to *The White Rose?*" Sophie asked.

"I've been thinking about that." I leaned my back against the iron upright. It gnawed at my back uncomfortably, but I didn't have the energy to move. "We'll need to stop production for now. Who knows when we'll be back ... or if—"

"Don't you dare say that," her voice quivered. "You *will* come back." She gazed at me with a lost expression. "It'll be so lonely without you, Alex, and Willi. Will Christl be with you, too?"

"No, he's assigned to a different medical company. I don't know what his orders are." I leafed through a book that was sprawled open on my bed. The pages flew under my fingertips. "I've already begun the logistics for a farewell party at Eickemeyer's studio. I thought it might be nice to have the group all together one last time."

"That would be nice, Hans." Sophie's voice was strained. "It'll be so horrible here without you."

"You should return to Ulm once the semester is over. Nothing is holding you here." I ran a hand over the back of my neck. "When I return, we'll begin where we left off with the leaflets. Only, we'll distribute them further and make more connections with various resistance groups. We'll enlarge our circle, so the leaflets will reach all the corners of Germany and cross borders."

"Do you believe we can do it?" For the first time that day,

I saw enthusiasm in her eyes.

"I hardly ever say things I don't mean."

farewell

I poured a glass of wine for Gisela, who took it with a grateful smile. The studio seemed small tonight with all the bodies coming and going, drinking, eating, laughing, and talking. The blackout curtains were drawn, and the basement door was locked. Wilhelm had opened the studio for the going away party and still had no inkling of what went on in the basement of his rented studio. The table was bedecked with cookies and cakes, fresh biscuits, wine, tea, and brandy. A feast for a war-wearied group. I couldn't yet comprehend that in a week's time I'd be in Russia. It was a dreadful thought to leave my work untouched for an undetermined period. I hadn't come to terms with it yet.

"It's horrible that you have to go to the front," Gisela said, running a finger along the rim of her wine glass.

I took a long sip of wine. The hum of voices was interrupted by occasional bursts of laughter coming from Alex. He was the only one remotely unaffected with being deployed to the Russia. To him, it was going home to be among his own people, the land of his birth. His tall frame towered over the others as he worked his way toward us, pipe fastened between his teeth.

"Gisela, did you come equipped with prose for Hans to place?" Alex asked as he sauntered over to the food table and snatched a handful of cookies.

She blushed, seemingly embarrassed by the question, but then brightened when I said, "I hope you did."

"You have so many people to speak with that I don't want to interrupt your party with a silly little game."

"Please, I enjoy it immensely." I set down my wine glass

and rubbed my hands together.

Gisela's eyes crinkled with mirth. She took a sip of wine, then began. "'To think is easy. To act is hard. But the hardest thing in the world is to act in accordance with your thinking.'"

I considered that it would be polite to at least feign I was pondering who wrote it, but the words left my mouth before I had time. "Goethe."

"You're brilliant," Gisela laughed.

"Hardly." If she knew how idiotic I had been as an adolescent, or how brooding and boyish I could still be on occasion, she wouldn't dub me "brilliant." "I rather like to be nonsensical at times."

"Nonsensical? How do you mean?"

I took the wine glass from her hands and set it on the table.

"What are you doing?" She raised an eyebrow and was genuinely confused.

"We'll dance!" I said, grabbing her hands. "There's far too little dancing these days. Alex," I called over my shoulder, "play us a song."

Alex retrieved his balalaika and began strumming a Russian folk song. The bouncing, light hearted song encompassed the studio, starting off with a slow cadence, then building up momentum into an arousing tune. I pulled Gisela into my arms and swung her about the room, my face already ruddy and sore from smiling. The group had stepped back along the perimeter of the room, laughing, cheering, and clapping along with the music.

My stomach began to ache from the chortling, but what a good feeling it was to have pain from laughter instead of from misery. I sang out of tune as boisterously as I possibly could, which caused Gisela to snort with laughter. We paraded about the room to the toe-tapping music, perspiring from the humidity. The song reached its ending with a bravado of exceptionally fast plucking. Alex's fingers flew over the strings, and I couldn't keep up with them. Gisela and I stopped dancing, leaning into each other for support as we continued beaming and chuckling about nothing in particular, except that we had enjoyed a dance and had forgotten about the war for another blissful minute.

"Oh look, they've finally grown tired," Christl called as Gisela and I stumbled toward the chairs near the bookshelf. Gisela was rosy as she sank down in the seat beside me. We had forgotten to let go of one another's hands. The music had died down, and the mingling began once more. Professor Huber was seated to the left of me. He took the pipe from his mouth and glanced at me conspiratorially. "Did you receive a leaflet of *The White Rose* in the mail?" he asked.

"Yes, I did, Professor."

"As did I," said Gisela. "At last someone is doing something."

I glanced at her, and that's when we both abruptly remembered that we were holding hands. We let go at the same moment.

"They're intelligently written, wouldn't you say?" Alex said. He and Sophie had joined our huddle. He was leaning against the bookshelf, arms crossed. "Must be the work of geniuses."

I lowered my eyes to my boots, lest I should meet his eyes and give the entire operation away with a laugh. A smile tugged at my lips.

"They're bold, I'll give them that," the Professor sighed deeply and leaned against his cane. He wasn't an elderly scholar in the least. He was a middle-aged man, but a limp required him to carry a cane. He stared into the distance with sharp brown eyes, seemingly troubled by something.

"Everything all right, Professor?" I asked.

He shook his head with disgust. "Think of the exquisite architecture that is being destroyed because of Hitler's war—

the museums, the cathedrals, the statues all destroyed and nothing but piles of rubble."

"Not only has Hitler's war caused the destruction of our landmarks, but of our people, our freedom, and our consciences." Sophie was beside Alex, a scowl on her face.

"I find the destruction of humanity more disturbing than the destruction of an art gallery," I added.

Professor Huber nodded. "This war must be shortened whether by sabotage, illegal propaganda, or ... or assassination. We must end this destruction of morals and decency." He shook his pipe vigorously. "I'm encouraged to know someone at last has begun a form of resistance."

We all sat in silence for a moment, the conversations behind us blending into a distortion of noise. Professor Huber glanced at his watch and then stood up. "I must be going. I have a lecture to plan. You'll all be wanting a good time before leaving, and I shouldn't dampen your spirits with political talk." He fixed his eyes on me. "Be sure to write to me on your thoughts of Russia, Hans."

"I will certainly do that, Professor." We shook hands, and the Professor left.

It wasn't long before another visitor joined our party, a friend by the name of Hans Hirzel. He was the brother of Sophie's childhood friend and was visiting Munich from Ulm. He had requested to see me, and I had invited him to meet me at the going away party, finding no other time to spare before leaving for Russia. Hans was bespectacled and pulled at his collar from the overbearing heat. I jumped up, nodding toward Sophie to follow me. "Please excuse us for a moment, Gisela."

Sophie and I strolled across the room. The group had begun to disperse, leaving a few lingering guests to talk amongst themselves and creating a fine setting for three people to conspire.

"Hans," I said, holding out a hand. "What a pleasure to

see you."

He shook my hand firmly. "Hans, Sophie, it's good to see you both."

"What brings you to Munich?" Sophie asked.

"Visiting friends," he said. "I especially wanted to meet up with you two."

"Did you receive my leaflet in the mail?" I asked.

Sophie glanced at me, her eyes widening. "Hans," she cautioned.

I hadn't informed Sophie yet, but when I heard that Hans was coming to Munich, I had decided to ask him a favor that would benefit *The White Rose*. I knew we could trust him, and if we were to broaden our circle, it was vital that we make connections.

He glanced around the room, then took a step forward, speaking in a low whisper. "I immediately suspected it was you after receiving the 'anonymous' leaflet."

"Cigarette?" I asked as I reached in my pocket for a pack.

Hans nodded. "Thanks."

I handed him a cigarette, stuck one between my lips, and withdrew my lighter. "Hans, you're a good sort," I said after a drag. "I wonder if you'd do me a favor while I'm serving on the front."

Sophie had grabbed my arm, looking at me with a million questions on her face.

"What's that?" Hans adjusted his spectacles.

I fished in my jacket pocket and pulled out my wallet. I gave Hans eighty marks. "Can you buy us a duplicating machine? We have big plans for those leaflets when I return."

"Hans, I—"

"Please." I slapped the money in his hand. "Buy it, and keep it hidden until I return."

Hans took the marks, studying me over his spectacles.

"Big plans?"

"*The White Rose* leaflets were a good start, but once we

return we're going to propel forward and broaden our circle. We're going to start a chain reaction throughout Germany and take a bolder stand. Please, get the duplicating machine. I know I can count on you. You've always been a good friend to our family, Hans. Don't you want to end this war?"

"Of course I do."

"Then will you purchase the machine and help us do just that?"

Hans seemed composed now, and he nodded. "Very well. I'll do it."

I clasped my friend on the shoulder with brotherly camaraderie. "Good man."

at the station

The dreaded morning had come. I knew it would, but that hardly made the moment easier to accept. I had woken at 5 o'clock, sat up in bed and stared at the morning shadows moving across the fraying wallpaper while I attempted to rouse myself.

Russia.

What was it like? What would happen to me? Would I ever return to Munich? Would I ever see my sisters, my brother, my parents, or Gisela again? A surge of uncertainty rattled my mind until I forced myself to stumble out of bed. The floorboards creaked under my bare feet as I pulled on my trousers and tugged the suspenders over my shoulders. The apartment was cloaked in grey hues, but I didn't bother switching on a lamp. The lack of light fit my present mood.

I kneeled down, reaching my hand under the bed to withdraw my sturdy ankle-height work boots. With eyes still groggy from slumber, I lifted my foot on a chair and began tucking my trouser legs into the boots, before tossing on my jacket and buttoning it with scorn. I peered down at the eagle emblem, a symbol which invoked patriotism in most. I longed to rip it off and grind it under my boots. I toasted a slice of bread and swallowed a large cup of ersatz coffee, grimacing as it went down. The morning was vanishing much too quickly, and I found myself rushing to get out the door on time.

I trekked down the street toward Frau Berrche's house. Sophie was waiting for me on the front steps, wrapping her knitted sweater around herself and shouldering her satchel of books.

"Good morning," I said.

"There's nothing good about it," she huffed, leaping off the steps and ambling up beside me.

I nodded in agreement. "I considered sleeping in and missing the train, but I suppose that would just get me in considerable trouble with my superiors."

Sophie tossed me an impish grin and studied me with a teasing look in her eyes.

"What?"

She stood on her tiptoes, swiping a hand through my hair. "It's sticking up all over the place," she smirked.

I reached into my bag, retrieved my army cap, and placed it on my head. "There. That'll take care of it."

"Until you take the hat off."

"In that case, I won't take it off."

She laughed as we strolled up the street toward the freight yard. The grass was soaked in dew, and wisps of fog hovered over the brick roads. Sturdy trees, unaffected by the war, lined the iron fence which surrounded the Munich freight yard. There was a group of soldiers mingling beside the tracks, and some leaned against the fence saying goodbye to their families. I caught sight of Christl strolling toward us, his hair smoothed back, pipe in the corner of his mouth. He pocketed one hand and waved with the other.

"I came to say goodbye," he said as his boots thumped

against the brick. "Well, that's only half true. I have a question to ask. Can we sit somewhere?"

I scanned the area and spotted a bench a few feet away near a stout maple tree, a safe distance from the fence. The three of us sat down, shoulders hunched, and heads bent low.

"What will happen to the ..." Christl glanced over his shoulder, then leaned in. "What will happen to your equipment?"

"Traute and I are going to hide them this afternoon," Sophie said.

"I didn't have time. God, they expected us to get here at the crack of dawn." My eyes felt unbearably heavy. All I wanted to do was go home and sleep.

Christl grinned as he slapped me on the shoulder. "Just wait until you're a father someday, Hans. Early mornings will be your new ritual."

I ran my hands over my face. "At least that would be more pleasurable. Holding your child beats being shipped off to war-torn Russia."

I had my doubts that I would return unharmed, but for a blissful moment, I allowed myself to believe that I would come home and someday be a father like Christl. I would hold my child while looking out the window into a hazy morning fog and remember this moment, this lifetime, and pray my son or daughter never has to see an abhorrent regime come to power. In hindsight, I see that it was only a drifting hope, a future that would never be mine.

Christl rubbed his hands together restlessly. "I was worried over what would become of the evidence while you're gone." He eyed us both with an ardent gaze. "Be careful, Scholls."

"You, too." I punched him lightly in the forearm. "Take care of your little family."

"Don't I always?" Christl grinned and turned to Sophie. "Are you staying in Munich, Sophie? If so, Herta would be grateful for your company ... and your help corralling the boys."

"I'm going home to Ulm," she said. "Munich just isn't the same without Hans, and my parents aren't keen on my staying here without him."

Christl nodded. "Well, you two take care of yourselves."

"We'll all be back together again soon, won't we?" Sophie's eyes swept over us anxiously.

"Of course. As soon we return from Russia, our work will begin again." My voice was hushed as I heard shuffling behind us.

Christl sighed. "Hans, I can't get involved."

"I'm not expecting anything from you. I don't want you entangled in this. Just ... pray for us." I smiled, standing up as a comrade approached us. I shook Christl's hand firmly. "Pray for us, Christl," I said for the benefit of whomever was listening. "Who knows what the Eastern Front holds."

"Of course, Hans," Christl said, nodding. "So long."

Sophie and I stood together as Christl strolled away.

"How long can I stay?" Sophie pulled her sweater closer around herself to ward off a cool breeze.

"Train leaves at 7:00." I glanced down at my watch. "About twenty minutes. But family and friends have to stay on this side of the fence."

I stared at her and wondered what had happened to our carefree childhood, a season which seemed to have happened a lifetime ago. Here we were, resisters in a Nazi stronghold, a soldier being shipped to the Eastern Front to tend to the mangled and wounded, a twenty-one-year-old girl who should have been enjoying life, and instead was fearing for it. We had once been young and blissfully innocent. We climbed trees, dashed through fields, hiked mountains until our muscles ached from the exertion. I was her older brother, defending her from antagonizers, carrying her home when she twisted an ankle, laughing at her jokes, encouraging her dreams for the future, teasing her, tormenting her, protecting her.

But now I couldn't.

The antagonizers were infinitely more powerful now. Our once safe world was now in shambles, forcing us to make decisions we never contemplated we'd have to make. It was forcing us to grow up, to fight back. We were different people in a different world.

"I suppose I'll give you a hug then," Sophie said, throwing her arms around my neck. I held her close for a long moment. She laughed.

"What?"

"Someone is coming to say goodbye to you." She pulled back, pointing behind me. I glanced over my shoulder and suddenly lost my breath. Gisela was hurrying up the street, her blonde locks falling over her shoulders carelessly.

"Oh, I'm so glad I didn't miss you!" She stopped a moment to catch her breath. "Why on earth do they send out troops at this ungodly hour?"

"My thoughts exactly," I said, wondering why I couldn't stop grinning at her.

"Please don't look at me like that, Hans. I didn't have time to get ready this morning. Honestly, why couldn't they send you out two hours later?"

I laughed as I stuffed my hands into my pockets. "I'll miss you, Gisela."

"Really?" Her eyes widened. "Good, because I'll miss you rather terribly." Our eyes met for a long moment.

"Scholl!" A voice sliced through the euphoric moment. It was a comrade of mine, Jürgen. "They want all companies to start assembling."

I waved my thanks to him, then turned back to Gisela. "I really should be going," she said. "I just wanted to say a proper goodbye." Gisela held out her gloved hand.

I grasped her hand in mine then pulled her into myself,

giving her a quick embrace. She was stiff for a moment. Then she slowly wrapped her arms around my neck and pecked my cheek. "Be careful out there, Hans."

"I will. Take care of yourself, Gisela." We released each other, and I scratched the back of my neck anxiously. What had I just done? I was taken aback by my boldness and scolded myself for it. My days were fleeting, uncertain, dangerously numbered. I told myself numerous times that it wouldn't be fair to Gisela to encourage a deep relationship. Yet, I'm certain the embrace only sealed what she must have already known. I was hopelessly fond of her.

"I won't be in danger like you." She squeezed my arm. "Come back."

"Of course," I said with certainty, as if the future were something I could control.

I watched her as she hurried down the street, but began to lose sight as she dissolved into the thick morning fog. That's when I suddenly remembered that Sophie was standing beside me. It's rather shameful to note that I was momentarily afraid of my little sister, for I knew she would tease me relentlessly. I chewed on my lip and headed for the gate which led into the freight yard, hoping I could somehow shake that lightheaded feeling.

"That was sweet," Sophie said, galloping up next to me. "I knew you liked her."

I stopped walking, irritation gnawing at me. "Sophie—"

"Don't worry, Hans, it's evident she likes you, too."

"Exactly!" I turned to her. "And if I don't come back from the front ... if I'm arrested or executed when I return ... what then, Sophie?" My tone came out harsher than I intended.

"She'll still love you," was her calm response.

I shook my head in annoyance. "You're not making this any easier."

I strolled into the freight yard while Sophie lingered on

the other side with the family members. I reported to my company and gathered with a few of my comrades: Alex, Willi, and Hubert Furtwängler. Sophie had stepped onto the stone slab and was leaning over the iron fence, looping her satchel around one of the iron spikes.

"Sophie!" Alex cheered, squinting up at her. "Come to see your brothers off?"

I smiled. His statement showed how close our group had become to each other. We were all family in our mind, Alex, Willi, Christl, Sophie and I. We were brothers and sister in arms. Kin.

"Of course. I couldn't let you all leave without wishing you well." Sophie peered down at us.

I heard a sharp click, saw a flash of light, and looked around to see where it came from. Jürgen sauntered over to us, camera positioned in his large hands. "Smile for the camera, would you?"

Sophie adored cameras, for she had been Werner's subject when his favorite pastime was photography. She spread her arms wide with a carefree smile on her face as the camera clicked once more. A high-pitched screech tormented my ears as the troop train pulled into the station, smelling strongly of grease and oil. It loomed over us, casting a dark shadow on the assembling company. All around me comrades began picking up their bags, kissing the hands of their sweethearts through the fence, or giving one last goodbye wave to their family. Sophie and I stared at each other through the thick iron bars. I reached my hand through a gap, and she clutched it in hers. "So long, little Sophie."

"Goodbye, Hans." Her eyes held pools of tears, but I knew her well. She would do her utmost not to spill them until I was gone. "Be careful."

"I will." I stepped back. "Give my love to mother, father, Inge, and Elizabeth."

Sophie nodded firmly, and I saw a single tear trek down

her rosy cheek.

I joined the horde of soldiers boarding the train, glancing one last time at my little sister. "Remember to have a strong spirit—"

Sophie clutched the bars and smiled. "And a gentle heart. I'll remember, but you remember, too."

poland

The train clattered over the tracks, and the swaying caused my eyes to grow heavy. I leaned my head against the window, giving into the lulling movement. I had finally resigned myself to my fate. I was here. There was no going back. Two days of travel had passed and so had countless conversations, chess games, hours of reading, and singing. The train clanged over a bridge. I winced as the force rattled my head.

"Hans! Daydreaming about Gisela, are you?"

"What?" I lifted my head and stared at Alex.

"Did you forget that we're in the middle of a card game? Shall we just wrap it up and declare me the victor?" Alex spoke around his pipe, holding up the cards in his hand.

"Sorry." I tossed my handful of cards at him. I hadn't even noticed I was holding them. "I was caught up in my thoughts."

"Of Gisela?" Alex teased.

I shrugged, turned to the window and let my mind wander as the endless fields of Poland whirled by. Occasionally a scrawny cow or the remnants of a bombed-out home would break up the monotony.

"'From the standpoint of daily life, however, there is one thing we do know: that we are here for the sake of each other—above all for those upon whose smile and well-being our own happiness depends, and also for the countless unknown souls with whose fate we are connected by a bond of sympathy. Many times a day I realize how much my own outer and inner life is built upon the labors of my fellow men, both living and dead, and how earnestly I must exert myself in order to give in return as much as I have received.'" I recited Einstein while keeping my eyes transfixed on the landscape which was now turning into a city.

"Ah, intellectual thoughts, I see," Alex laughed. "Shall we say I won?"

Alex didn't appear the least bit uneasy, and I was envious of that. I couldn't shake the feeling that Poland and Russia were going to leave me haunted ... restless. The train was gradually coming to a halt as Warsaw came into view in the bright afternoon sunlight. I sat up and studied the city, wishing to soak up every detail that I could.

"Do you know how long we have in Warsaw?" I asked Hubert, who was walking down the aisle.

Hubert leaned his arms over the cracked leather seats to converse. "We're staying the night. We've been given leave to walk around the city and enjoy ourselves. Hot as hell out there, so make sure you've got some water on you."

The train came to a violent stop, whipping us all forward. I gripped the bottom of my seat and let out a laugh as Alex's pipe went flying into the aisle.

"Sergeant Scholl, is this yours?"

I looked up, meeting the steely glare of Lieutenant Braun who was holding Alex's pipe in his hand. I raised my arm quickly in a salute. "No, sir. I believe it belongs to Sergeant Schmorell."

Lieutenant Braun handed Alex the pipe with a sharp look. "Unboard."

"Yes, sir." Alex jumped up, banging his head smartly on the top of the baggage car. "Ah!" Alex rubbed the top of his head with a grimace.

I attempted to keep my laughter in check as I unrolled my shirtsleeves and grabbed my jacket off the hook behind me.

But I couldn't mask a smirk, which must have irked Alex, for he gave me a firm shove off the train. I stumbled down the steps with a jesting shout, "You'll pay for that, Schmorell!"

"Are you drunk, Sergeant Scholl?" Lieutenant Braun asked, grabbing my shoulder skeptically.

"No, sir." I stood up straight and dusted off my uniform.

"Then kindly refrain from shouting and stumbling in the street like you're stoned."

I suppressed a grin. "Yes, sir."

My light-hearted mood was stripped away when Alex, Willi, and I took a ramble along the railway toward the city, expecting an easy time with perhaps a shot of vodka or schnapps along the way. What met my eyes instead was human suffering, pain, and despair. We didn't utter a word, but I observed everything with my jaw clenched and eyes open. As we walked further, we passed a mass of Jews being led from the railyard toward the endless cattle cars—men, women, children, and infants. Their faces were frail and etched with exhaustion and fear. They wore tattered rags, caked with mud and waste. Children were thin to the bone, clutching their parents as German soldiers prodded them with the butt of their guns and the Jewish Police with their clubs.

One soldier spat on every single Jew who passed him. Others yelled or cursed at them. Any Jew who stepped out of line or was too weak to walk was grabbed by the collar and shot in the back of the neck. I heard a gunshot every few minutes, each time the sound digging a deeper wound into me. My throat tightened as my eyes met with a little girl who looked no older than five. Her eyes were dark pools of anguish and terror when she saw me. She turned her face into her mother's side to escape my gaze, and I heard her sob, "Mama, don't let him hurt me!"

I glanced down at my uniform with anger tearing at my heart. To her, I was one of the bastards who was involved in the destruction of her life. If only she knew that I'm not like them. I'd never be like them.

I'd die first.

People were visibly perspiring, gazing up at the sun as if convinced it was against them, too. A cry split through the air somewhere up ahead, and I tried to observe what was happening. I could see a soldier's gun glinting in the sunlight as it came up and down in repetition. My eyes flew to the ground where a young woman lay, groaning in agony each time the soldier brought his gun into her. He pounded it into her abdomen, the side of her face, her mouth. A pool of blood formed beneath her body. The soldier attacked her until the groaning stopped, and the girl was dead.

The Jews were being shoved into the cramped cars, so many that they bulged through the doorway, arms reaching out for help. They screamed as the soldiers slammed the metal doors and latched them with indifference.

warsaw

I stepped out of the bar, grateful for the fresh summer wind to revive me. The establishment was packed tightly with soldiers, and it reeked of liquor. The drunk soldiers had grown rowdy, singing repulsive Nazi songs and slurring the words as they bellowed:

> *Sharpen the long knives on the pavement,*
> *Let the knives slip into the Jew's body.*
> *Blood must flow, a whole lot of it,*
> *And we shit on the freedom of this Jew Republic.*

I could still hear them as I strolled down the brick street. Their coarse laughter hung on the wind, and I feared I'd never escape it. I reached into my pocket, fingering the cloth that homed four biscuits as I trailed the brick ghetto wall. My boots ground shards of glass and debris as I took in the somber city around me. How easy it would be for one to fall into despair here. No life. No beauty. Just death, persecution, and hate. I turned the corner, dodging a puddle of water as I hurried up the road toward the ghetto. The lieutenant's words to our company reverberated through my mind:

"Anyone caught throwing food to the swine in the ghetto will be shot dead. Behave yourselves while we're here, and show your patriotism to our Führer by being loyal German soldiers. Don't you dare get soft."

It was a crime to have a conscience. It was a crime to feel an ache in your heart for humans being tortured and starved to death. But I was already a criminal of the state, so I discarded the lieutenant's threat and neared a section of the brick barrier in an alley that curiously wasn't guarded. With a tentative glance around, I turned toward the wall and pulled the biscuits from my pocket. I heard a gasp. My nerves spiked as I glanced down, spotting a child's head and shoulders protruding from the gutter. The girl's face was ashen, her eyes large against her small frame. Two black braids fell across her bony shoulders. She didn't move as her eyes bore into mine. She must have concluded that I was somewhat safe by the absence of a weapon aimed at her.

"Please," she whispered a heart aching plea. "I'll come right back to the ghetto. I'm just so hungry."

I nodded and held out a hand to assist her. Her gaunt hand felt corabselike in mine. "What's your name?"

"Miriam." She held her arms around her stomach, shifting from one foot to the other.

"I'm Hans. I've brought you something."

"What is it?" Her voice was hesitant.

"Food. Would you like it?"

She lifted her eyes in wonder. "Yes, please!"

I reached into my pocket then handed the biscuits to Miriam. She didn't utter a word as she stuffed one into her mouth. I eyed the area once more before continuing our conversation. The street was dank and reeked of human waste. "How old are you?"

"Ten. How old are you?" Her muffled voice made me grin.

"Twenty-three."

"Oh! You're old."

I laughed. "Not *that* old."

"Yes, you're old."

I leaned against the wall, smirking to myself at her perception of old. "All right. I'm old. Are you enjoying the biscuits?"

"I'll only eat one. I have to save the rest for my brother and sisters."

I wished I had brought more. "Is your family all right, Miriam?"

She was silent. For a moment I thought she was about to dart away, but then her tear-stained voice reached my ears.

"They shot Papa. Mama was taken away yesterday, but I hid with my little sisters and brother. Will my Mama come back? Do you know where they took her?"

I closed my eyes as a sharp pain traveled through me. I took a deep breath, blinking away stinging tears. "Your parents must have taught you to have great courage, Miriam. You are far braver than I am." It wasn't an answer to her question, but how could I tell her the truth?

"She's not coming back." It wasn't a question. She knew it to be true. "Are you really a soldier?" she asked, eyeing my uniform. "You can't be. You're nice."

"I'm a medical sergeant," I said.

"I didn't know Germans could be nice."

"Believe it or not, there are some decent ones left." My skin bristled at the sound of intoxicated soldiers marching up the street. "I have to go," I told her. "You better get back inside before they see you."

Miriam was on her knees in an instant, scurrying back into the gutter. "Will you come back tomorrow?" she whispered before disappearing.

"I'll try. Our company is moving out in the morning." I turned and lit a cigarette, stepping onto the street to fall in with the horde of soldiers.

Evening had now descended upon Warsaw, masking the day's cruelty with the cover of darkness. It will someday be brought to light. The inhumanity surely can't remain a secret forever.

moving out

I was pleased to hear that our company would not be moving out until evening. This gave me time to deliver my rations to Miriam. I told no one of this, save for Alex and Willi, who pitched in their own rations for her. With this small feast safely tucked in my pockets, I weaved my way through the city toward the alley.

Screams punctured the air as I neared the ghetto, and my eyes met another deportation. Hundreds of Jews were flooding from the ghetto, flanked by German soldiers. One young soldier, not much older than Werner, had grabbed a girl by her braided hair and dragged her along the broken brick road. Her face was red, her mouth open in a cry that I couldn't hear in the chaos. My mind flew to Miriam. She could be lost among these people, small and helpless. Perhaps she was searching around desperately for a German soldier who was decent, but found none.

The Jews' clothes hung off their emaciated bodies. Gaunt and hollow-eyed, they shuffled toward the railroad. I could scarcely tell the ages of the children, for they were all small and undernourished. I pulled out the rations and began handing them out to the children who passed me. Some hesitated, others snatched it as quickly as they could. Others didn't look at me.

A tiny girl with round, brown eyes pushed through the throng and peered up at me with recognition on her face. "You're the one who gave me food at the wall last night, aren't you?" My eyes burned as she beamed at me, for I knew her fate. I handed her some of my rations. Her small feet were caked with dirt. I could see the bones through her frail skin. An SS officer strode over to me, his tall, black boots pounding against the brick. "

"What the hell are you doing?" he screamed, his spit hitting my face. He turned his attention to Miriam who swiftly hid the rations behind her back and dropped her eyes. The SS officer didn't give me time to utter a word. He wrenched Miriam's arm and yanked her off the ground, his pistol to her neck. She screamed. A sickening shot rang through the air.

I cannot fathom this world's cruelty. All I wanted to do was bring her a scrap of hope and friendship, but the demonic enemy twisted my act of kindness into an atrocity, one I will carry with me until the day I die. I began to wonder if I did the right thing after all, if perhaps I should have minded my own business and stayed away from the ghetto.

I leaned my chin into my palm as I rested on a bench outside the freight yard. I closed my ears to the chatter of the soldiers. Their deep laughter seemed foreign to me now.

"It wasn't your fault, Hans," Willi said.

I stared at the metal railroad tracks. My mind was numb.

"Willi's right." Alex stood over us. "And we mustn't stop performing works of kindness because we're afraid of what could happen. You offered that girl something no one had given her in ages—friendship."

"I just don't understand it." I felt sick to my stomach.

"The lieutenant said anyone giving food to the Jews would

be shot. Why didn't that SS bastard kill me instead?"

"He just wanted to make a scene to scare the others ... warn them not to step out of line or talk to soldiers," Alex said.

The ground began to vibrate violently, and the screeching whistle of the hospital train droned out any more words. Our time in Poland was finished. We were now leaving for Russia.

to russia

I slid my pawn across the chessboard and sat back, anticipating a long lull while Willi thought through every possible move. Whereas I simply moved a piece with reckless abandon, Willi pondered every move with considerable patience.

I didn't mind. I took the time to peer out the window and watch as our rattling transport pushed into Lithuania. A long, clear river snaked through the rolling green hills, and tall pines hemmed a thick forest. A week had passed this way, along with hours of giving into sleep caused by the rhythmic shaking of the train. We were given time to stretch our legs and take in the sun occasionally. As we neared Russia, I raked my gaze across the countryside, spotting remnants of war.

"Work of partisans," Alex stated, pointing out the window. Mangled metal beams of railroad tracks lay sprawled across the trampled grass. Not so long ago a transport much like ours exploded after a partisan set off a bomb which was strapped to the tracks. This was another reminder that my life was in danger. Always. Our men must have restored the rails swiftly, for the damage alongside the road still sent off a burnt mineral stench that sank through the transport and swarmed around us. "And there are the partisans."

Two young men, a boy no older than twelve or thirteen,

and a young woman with long brown hair that blew in the wind swung from sturdy tree branches, ropes cinched around their necks.

It was a warning.

"We're now in the land of the Russian sub-human beasts, or so they tell us," Hubert said, setting down his book. "I don't suppose any of you have been here before?"

"If you count my infancy, then yes." Alex's eyes continued following the words in a book he was devouring.

The rest of us shook our heads, looking at Hubert with curiosity. He was a few years our senior, and I realized I didn't know what he had done before studying with our student company.

"Have you?" Willi asked, moving his rook.

"Yes, in forty-one." He reclined against the seat. He eyed us with an ashen face. "Thank God I was finally transferred to a new company."

We waited for him to go on, to give us yet another reason to despise the Nazis as if there weren't enough reasons. I lowered my gaze to the floorboards, watching the shadows move rapidly.

"We passed Russian women who were working in the fields." He inspected his hands, his face growing red. "Our train stopped briefly. The soldiers jumped out, grabbed the women, and shoved them onto the train. They raped these women, then pushed them off the train with a laugh, and we continued on."

I gritted my teeth as my gut twisted. "Just another example of our 'superior' race honoring Germany." I shook my head with revulsion. "I suppose their superiors did nothing to stop them?"

"They didn't give a damn." Hubert fingered a fraying string on his jacket. "So, don't expect any of the Russian civilians to look upon us with anything but disgust."

"I intend to change the way they perceive all Germans."

Alex tapped the book against his knee.

"How do you plan to do that?" Hubert appeared skeptical.

"A bit of music, vodka, and chivalry."

s t r e n g t h

Another layover prolonged our trip to the Eastern Front. This one, however, restored my strength and resolve to cling to my faith. Alex, Willi, Hubert, another comrade, Dimitri, and I took an entirely different course once reaching the city of Vyazma then most of the men. A Sunday morning layover sent the five of us on a hunt for a church. Dimitri only joined us because he promised his mother he would attend church as regularly as he could. We arrived in time for Divine Liturgy at Church of the Ascension.

Upon entering, my eyes immediately took in the spacious room and vaulted ceiling. A warm dimness enveloped the room, and a calmness passed over me as the candles flickered beneath the altar. The crimson light showered over the sacred paintings around the church and illuminated their gold frames. The women's long hair was pulled back by an array of colorful kerchiefs, while the men donned Kaftans. In the shadowy corner, two women were suckling their babies, a powerful symbol of inexhaustible love. The glow from the candles shone upon their strong-featured faces, and the people sang a hymn of praise.

Jesus my Lord my God my all.
How can I love Thee as I ought?
And how revere this wondrous gift,
So far surpassing hope or thought.

I closed my eyes and savored the moment—a blissful hour of believers united together in fervent prayer. Our hearts seemed to beat in unison, and the outpouring of strong voices stirred my soul. My eyes blurred as I gazed around at the Russian people, a defeated, conquered people who were in the midst of an overpowering war in their homeland. How many of these men and women had lost their fathers, husbands, brothers, nephews, and sons in the fight against us? How many of these hearts had been ripped open in utter agony? Yet, here they were worshiping and giving thanks. What struck me most was their incredible peace.

All at once I felt the urge to laugh, love, to raise my voice in a chorus of praise and joy because when I looked at these people, I knew an angel was hovering over them, stronger than all powers of darkness and defeat. Their faith had sustained them through all that life cruelly threw at them, testing their resolve and tenacity. They came out victorious, I could see that. I longed to attain the same strong faith as they had. I knew life had more to throw at me, more for me to fight through, more struggles, darkness, and obstacles that I would be forced to face.

When we left the church an hour later, I stepped into an overcast afternoon and was immediately drenched by a warm, summer rain. The roads began to sink into oozing ditches of mud, and shelling sounded in the distance.

w e r n e r

I dropped my knapsack on the wooden floorboards, hunching over to keep my head from hitting the ceiling of our dugout. We had just split up with Willi and Hubert as our company had been divided to various sectors on the front. Alex was already making himself comfortable in the cramped dugout we were to share with four or five other medics from our student company. The walls were made of thick logs and sand padding. A radio sat on a shelf-like split in the wall playing *Lili Marlene*. It reeked of sweat, and flies buzzed around our faces. I reached into my pocket and withdrew a soiled letter, eyeing over the contents once more.

"What's that?" Alex asked.

"Letter from my mother. Coincidentally, Werner was assigned to the same sector as us. He's only a few miles from here." I nodded in a vague direction.

"No kidding?" Alex shook his head with a grin. "Well, isn't Russia small?"

"He received permission to visit us. I got a telegram saying he's coming this afternoon."

"Well!" Alex got to his knees and began rummaging through his bag.

"What are you doing?"

Alex pulled a full bottle of vodka from his knapsack, holding it up as if it were an Olympic medal. "What better way to start our visit in Russia than with a little vodka?"

This brought the attention of the other five upon us. "Hey, Schmorell, we're pals, right? So be a chum and send some of that my way."

A rapping sounded on the dugout door, followed by a staff sergeant barging in and bringing the jesting to a halt. The stark sunlight silhouetted his frame in the doorway.

"Sergeant Scholl?" He eyed us.

"Yes, sir?" I was still hunched against the ceiling.

"A Private Werner Scholl is here to see you."

Alex and I emerged from the dugout, squinting into the sunlight. The horizon was layered with various hues of green, and thin trees waved their leafy branches against the endless expanse of blue sky. Our horses grazed in a war-torn pasture, and all around us, soldiers were loafing around, telling jokes, sleeping, or lying on their backs to take in the sun.

My brother stood beside his chestnut horse, one hand wrapped around the reins, the other stuffed in his pocket. His tuft of brown hair was mussed from the ride. He lifted his hand in greeting as a boyish smile overtook his smooth, round face. I waved back as Werner handed the reins to a soldier nearby.

"How are you doing, Has?" I asked, now taking in the picture of my brother in the grey uniform with the eagle emblem and sturdy black boots. Neither of us wanted to be here. Neither of us wanted this uniform, yet, here we were.

Hitler's soldiers.

"Fine, if you'd stop calling me Has. I haven't been called that since I was a kid." Werner punched my arm good naturedly.

"Oh, so sorry. You are a soldier now, Has. I nearly forgot." I smirked as Werner punched my arm again, not holding back this time.

"Imagine you two being in the *same* sector on the *same* front at the *same* exact time. Unfathomable." Alex shook his head in disbelief as he fingered the bottle of vodka.

"Alex!" Werner held out a hand. "It's been far too long. It's good to see you."

Alex shook his hand, the vodka bottle clearly visible to the entire camp. I shoved him. "That'll get confiscated, you know."

Alex swiftly stuffed it in his trouser pocket with a cautious glance around. "I forgot I was holding it."

"What are you planning on using that for?" Werner asked, folding both arms over his chest.

"Hans and I are on a quest to change the way the Russians perceive Germans as a whole." Alex continued eyeing the camp.

"So, you're using *vodka*?" Werner appeared amused.

"Well, not just vodka. But it can't hurt, right?" I said, stuffing both hands in my pockets.

"No, I suppose not," Werner shrugged. "I'd be happy to join you on this quest of yours."

"Because of the vodka?" I studied him with suspicion.

His face broke into a wide grin. "Of course because of the vodka, stupid."

"The army's had a bad influence on you, Has. What would Mother say?"

A wave of fear passed over his face for a split second. "You won't tell her, will you?"

"I guess we can keep this between us." I grinned as Werner's face relaxed.

"Well, let me get my balalaika, and we'll find some Russians to impress." Alex ran back to the dugout, then led us toward a wooded area where trees were rich green and untouched by the war ... for now. Dust billowed around our boots as we followed him.

the russians

"You're sure these people will let us into their houses?" Werner asked as we approached a cottage on the outskirts of the war-torn Gzhatsk. We had tuned out the sounds of the Russian artillery in the distance. Alex was carrying his balalaika, and the vodka was safely tucked in his pocket.

"Not entirely, but I tend to think so. After all, we come in peace, and I am one of them."

"Have you looked at your uniform lately?" I asked.

"I'll explain everything to them. You two just mind that you don't look too intimidating, all right?" Alex cleared his throat, then rapped on the splintered door of the broken-down home. We could hear panicked whispers coming from within. No one came. Alex knocked once more, handing me the bottle of vodka. "You look less formidable that way," he explained.

The door slowly creaked open, and our eyes met with a young boy and girl. They were brother and sister; I could see the resemblance in their dark, curly hair and pensive brown eyes. A voice sounded behind them, but I couldn't understand what was said, for the woman had a thick Russian accent. The handful of Russian phrases Alex had taught me weren't helping in this situation.

"What's going on?" I whispered, but Alex was stepping into the house, his boots thumping against the packed earthen floor, and speaking Russian before the door could be slammed in his face. I risked a glance into the house which was only one large room with blankets hanging from the ceiling as dividers. A man and woman were pleading with Alex, fear evident in their eyes and in their desperate voices. Whatever Alex was able to convey to them brought relief to their faces, and they allowed us inside. The family stayed close to each other's sides, taking in the presence of three Germans who claimed to come in peace. I was sure they didn't quite believe that *could* be true.

Alex was all good cheer as he motioned for me to hand the patriarch the bottle of vodka. He continued talking to them, pointing to his balalaika. The man and women nodded, small smiles creeping across their faces. Alex sat crossed legged on the floor like a schoolboy, Werner and I following his lead. The quiet cottage suddenly became alive with the sound of the instrument, gently at first as Alex ran his fingers along the strings. Then the song picked up speed, and I watched, always in awe of how fast Alex's fingers could pluck the strings. It was a lively tune that seemed to awaken the dark, gloomy cottage into a place of joy.

The boy and girl started dancing, timidly at first. They laughed as they whirled each other around in circles. The father was opening the vodka while the mother gazed on, smiling for what could have been the first time in months. The little girl with two messy braids suddenly thrust her thin face before me, her eyes bright as they searched my face. I looked at Alex to interpret, as if it wasn't evident that she wished to dance with me.

Alex chuckled as his fingers instinctively played the song. "Dance, Hans! Dance!"

I stood up, Werner's boyish laughter in my wake, as the girl pulled me into a dance. The music was wildly fast—faster than I had ever heard Alex play. I desperately tried to keep up with her fast leg kicks and jumps. Alex and Werner's faces were red from laughter as I jumped, kicked, and spun in circles with a girl half my height. I was out of breath, my legs bogged down by army boots. They didn't lift as easily as the little girl's bare feet. But I had to admit that it was a jolly time, and the dance was freeing me of all my worries and cares, for my biggest concern at the moment was trying keep up with her.

When Alex's fingers were calloused from playing, and the vodka was gone, we left, hoping we had changed the minds of the Russian family who had come to think all Germans were savage beasts.

the prisoner

I closed my journal, tucking the pencil in the spine. The dugout was dark, save for the carbide lamp casting shadows on the walls. I lit my cigarette and leaned my back against the cool wall, squinting against the clouds of smoke coming from the other men. Some were composing letters. Others simply loafed or told crude jokes. The Russians were attacking north and south of us, but they always withdrew at night. The casualties on our side had varying degrees of injuries. Some had shrapnel wounds that had resulted in amputations. Others had been severely burned. One man lost both hands in an explosion.

"I hear that the partisans are active around here," the red headed boy named Otto said. He was reclining against a crate, a cigarette between his teeth.

"How do you know that?" I asked, flicking ashes on the floor.

"Met up with a dispatch rider yesterday. He said that in his sector the partisans blew up forty-eight trains in one week. Lot of our boys died."

Alex tossed a used cigarette at me. "If only Hitler could be here to witness such grand, victorious times on the front."

"It doesn't seem right that the Führer has never been to the front, and yet he talks as if he can somehow identify with us." I tucked my journal into my back pocket.

"Wait, wait! I've got a joke," Otto said, grinning between his cigarette. "Hitler came to visit the boys on the front lines, which I know is hard to imagine, but try to picture it anyway. He asked a private what his final wish would be if suddenly a Russian shell landed near him. 'I would wish that my Führer were standing beside me,' replied the private."

Suppressed laughter filled the cramped dugout, and a sense of elation filled me. At last I was starting to see evidence that we were not alone in our opposition to Hitler. Perhaps the confidence and loyalty these men once had for the Führer were beginning to erode.

"You'll get in trouble telling jokes like that." Dominic was an older soldier with worry lines etched around his dark eyes. "Watch your mouth. Didn't you hear what happened to that company commander just south of here? Arrested by the Field Police and shot dead by a firing squad for expressing his political beliefs too freely." The mood changed, and Otto suddenly ceased chuckling.

I stood up, dusting the dirt off my trousers. "I don't hear any more shooting. I'm going for a walk. Maybe I'll listen to Vladislav sing." No one seemed to hear me. They were each in their own worlds now. Were they pondering good and evil? No. Most likely thinking about their next meal.

I climbed out of the dugout, and the bright sun warmed my face. Not a single cloud hung in the clear blue sky. But as my eyes swept over the camp, I knew that the calm atmosphere was only a charade. Less than thirty miles from here, war was ripping away life after life, leaving mangled bodies, ashes, and burned structures in its wake. I headed toward the stable where one of our Russian prisoners, Vladislav, worked. When I needed to clear my head, I sat on a crate in the stable and listened to him sing. He had become a friend of ours, though he didn't speak any German except, *Nein,* which earned him a beating after he said it in response to an order from our superior officer. Vladislav didn't even understand what the word meant.

When I first met him, I was sitting on the stone steps outside our makeshift hospital—a deserted Russian school—and was smoking with Alex, Otto, and Dimitri. We were listening to the machine gun fire on the opposite side of the field.

"Think something's going to happen now?" Dimitri had asked, squinting across the field of sunflowers swaying in the warm wind.

"With that little bit of machine gun fire? Don't hold your breath." Otto ground his cigarette under his boot heel.

"I see someone coming toward us." Alex held his hand over his eyes to block the sun. "I think it's a Russian."

I followed his gaze out into the field and spotted a young man trudging through the flowers. It was a drastic contrast—a soldier with soot covering his boyish face, his clothes singed from an explosion, and his gait weary among the cheerful, waving sunflowers. Otto snatched a rifle that was leaning against the school and clicked off the safety. He closed one eye and aimed.

"Let him go, Otto. He doesn't even have a weapon." I tossed my cigarette onto the grass and stood up.

Otto didn't listen and pulled the trigger. *Click.* Nothing happened. The three of us grinned as Otto threw the rifle down with a scowl. His face now matched the color of his hair. "Damn thing's not loaded."

Dimitri burst out laughing. "Thought you'd be a hero for killing the first Russian on our campaign? Trying to get an Iron Cross?"

"I was just trying to do my job." Otto gave the rifle a kick. I looked up and noticed that the Russian was close now, eyeing us tentatively. I shoved Dimitri who was still laughing. "Shut up. He thinks we're all insane."

"We *are* insane. Why make him believe otherwise?"

I saw his point.

By now the Russian boy was only a few steps away, his cap in his hands. His face was round and smooth, his tousled hair light-brown. "Had enough, Ivan?" Dimitri asked, slapping him on the shoulder.

An officer put him to work in the stables after that, and we had good times with Vladislav. Even Otto was glad the rifle didn't have bullets in it after all.

Now I heard fierce shouting ahead and placed it without a second thought. It was Private Ackermann, a young soldier who thought it was his duty in life to inflict torment on Russians, Jews, and anyone else he deemed below him. Ackermann was braced against the stable for support as he kicked his boot into Vladislav's abdomen, screaming profanity with each gut wrenching blow. His eyes were wild with hate as Vladislav gasped for breath, cowering into a fetal position among the dirt and sharp edged stones.

I ripped off my cap in anger and gained the ground between us in a split second. I grabbed Ackermann's arm in a death grip, yanking him away from Vladislav. He reeked of sweaty wool.

"What do you think you're doing?" I stared evenly at him, disgusted with the gleam of wickedness in his eyes.

"He's a prisoner of war, sergeant. I'm treating him like one." Ackermann hacked up a wad of saliva and discharged it at Vladislav.

"And what exactly did he do to earn this?" I nodded toward Vladislav who was clutching his stomach, his eyes closed to ward off the pain.

"Dammit, Sergeant! He's a filthy, stupid bastard of an Ivan."

"Do you have no decency or respect left at all, Private? Have you stooped so low?" Ackermann glowered at me, no sign of remorse in his grim countenance. "Get out of here." I shoved him away, watching his retreating form until he resumed his post near headquarters.

There had been other soldiers witnessing this, I noted, but they did nothing ... said nothing. I kneeled next to Vladislav, checking to see how much damage Ackermann had inflicted. The young man's face was smeared with earth and blood. His trembling hands were still clutched around his middle. He turned his eyes to me, thanked me in Russian, then slowly stood and stumbled off into the stable.

i scorn the fatherland

There is nothing quite like abandoning yourself to a ride in an endless field, listening to the horse's hooves thud against the ground rhythmically, and breathing in the damp, morning air. My worries seemed to part from me, carried off on a warm breeze. Coral rays of sunrise hung like ribbons against the misty blue sky. Along the horizon, birch trees swayed against the heavens, and I could nearly forget about the death and destruction we were forced to live among. But the abhorrent stench of gangrene that encompassed the hospital was not a smell I could easily escape from, even in this vast field.

Eyeing a stream up ahead, I pulled on the reins and brought the horse to a slow trot. I dismounted and tied the reins around a stout tree as the horse drank from the bubbling stream. The sound of Russian fliers buzzed above me, and I squinted up into the sky, spotting the star on the tail of a Il-yushin Il-2 as it disappeared over the thick woods to my right. I took an aimless stroll around, soaking in the beauty of the sunrise setting the sky on fire with its rose and amber hues. I turned my eyes to the billowing grass which seemed to be bowing to the heavenly show above it. It was then that I noticed the grass was charred and trampled in areas. I strained my eyes as the sun shed light on a form.

It was a body.

My boots crunched the dead grass as I neared the body. The Russian soldier lay with his face in the dirt, his arms spread out above him, as if he had dived into the grass for cover. His right hand was missing three fingers. The other hand was completely gone. Shrapnel was strewn around him, and I concluded that a grenade had ended his life. His legs had been blown off at the shins, leaving two stumps of shattered bone, dark blood, and tattered cloth. Droplets of dew ran down his hair, puddling in the dirt beside him. I leaned down and pushed his shoulder, giving him a roll over, so I could see his face. It was cemented in earth and his own blood. His grey eyes stared blankly at the sky. His ashen lips were cracked. My stomach wavered. No matter how many deaths I had seen, no matter how many wounded I had cared for, the sight always made my gut twist, and an uncomfortable chill crawl along my spine.

I couldn't allow myself the time to brood over the young soldier robbed of his youth. He needed a proper burial. I set to work ripping through the earth with the butt of my pistol. It gave way easily as it was drenched with the breath of morning. The stench of decaying flesh, sickeningly sweet, clung to the breeze. I lifted my head, the scent so strong that I felt weak and lightheaded. Just inches in front of me lay the torn off legs, rotting in the grass. The boots were still on his feet. I stood up, running a hand over the back my neck and gasping for clean air. But now I couldn't escape it. It was as if the air was impregnated with death, casting a horrible spell on anyone who entered its realm. I rolled the soldier into the grave, then picked up the legs and placed them beside him. Using both hands, I filled the grave with earth, watching as it covered his glassy eyes. I wondered how old he was ... if his family was still alive. Perhaps he was even related to the little girl I danced with the other evening.

In less than one month, I had seen enough to make me scorn the Fatherland, its Führer, and the German people who allowed this persecution and death to go on. I ripped off my cap with a groan as I stared at the grave of the young man whose people were in agony because my country dubbed them sub-human and declared that civilization ended at the eastern borders of Germany. I recalled the Jews being taken away to their deaths, children starving. And just the other day, I caught Ackermann beating a Russian woman with the butt of his gun. Ackermann swore at her for getting blood on his boots. Was this what the Führer meant when he said Germany would be respected by all? How can anyone respect us when we don't respect human life?

I rode on again, breathing deeply. The smell wouldn't leave me. I had been detailed to travel by horseback to German positions and inoculate the men against cholera, and I set my mind on the mission ahead, trying to forget the grave. To the left of me lay the carbonized skeleton of an exploded tank among a patch of daisies that danced under the wind's gentle fingertips. I shook my head at the irony.

I slowed the horse as I neared a railroad bed where a group of women were working with picks, repairing the tracks which the Russians had destroyed. I yanked on the horse's reins, peering closer. They were dark haired women, each branded with a Star of David on their thin jackets. A wisp of a girl, with arms so thin I thought they might snap under the strain, stared at me as I approached them. She had hollow, ebony eyes that bore into me as she lifted the burdensome pick, a tool meant for a healthy man to use, not an emaciated child. Her face was pensive, her dry lips drawn tightly together. Two disheveled braids tumbled over her shoulders. I reached into my pocket and withdrew my iron rations—dried fruit, nuts, and chocolate. I dismounted and made my way over to the girl. My boots thumped against the gravel, causing the women to glance up in fearful anticipation. The girl was glaring at me as she leaned against her pick, her eyes daring me to step any closer.

"Here." I held out my rations to her. "I want you to have this."

She narrowed her eyes as I held the packet of rations in my palm. "I don't want anything from you." Her voice was high and delicate, but her intentions strong as she grabbed the rations from my hand and threw them into the gravel, spitting on it for good measure. My heart constricted. Again the uniform was defining me. I let out a long breath, trying to understand what this little girl must have been through. She was separated from her family and forced to work among women she didn't know, to restore a supply route for her enemy. Was her family still alive? When was the last time she had eaten? Her childhood was stripped away from her, replaced by war, starvation, and persecution. She had every right to scorn me.

I picked up the rations, giving it a good dusting off. That's when I eyed a vibrant blue flower along the tracks. I snapped the stem then laid it atop the rations which I left at the girl's bare feet. They were hardened in dried mud and sliced open from sharp-edged rocks.

"I'm sorry. I only wished to give you some pleasure." I smiled softly at her, then headed back toward where I had left my horse tethered to a lone tree. I sunk my hands in my pockets, then risked a glance over my shoulder. The little girl was leaning over and picking up the gifts I had left at her feet. I grinned and felt a burst of elation rise in me as she tucked the flower behind her ear with a small smile. It was moment's like these that made me thankful to be serving in Russia, if only to bring a smile to a lonely and oppressed child's face.

a toast to russia

In the autumn of '42, we learned that we were being sent back to Munich for further studies. Part of me was thrilled at the idea of returning to my underground work. The other part felt an ache of sorrow at leaving behind the Russians with this unfathomable mess. Otto, Dimitri, Alex, and I were taking a ramble through the countryside, all needing to clear our heads after the recent news. I gazed around at the expanse of land before us—the dirt roads that curved around crimson, yellow, and russet patches of trees, and the wooden fences that perimetered the farmyards. Daylight was fading, casting inky shadows across the fields.

"I've become attached to these people." Alex snatched a leaf from an overhanging tree and began tearing it to shreds. The pieces cascaded down to the path, disappearing into the dusk. "I feel at home among them. I'll miss the children. I … I wonder what will become of them."

"They thought we'd be repulsed by the 'sub humans.' They didn't wager that we'd fall in love with Russia. It's rather ironic." I swatted a fly as it hummed around my ear.

"I'll never remove the Russian soil from my boots," Alex said with sincerity, his chin high and a pipe wedged in the corner of his mouth. "I don't want to leave."

"You're acting like a little kid, Schmorell." Otto gave Alex a jesting shove.

"And we have business to attend to back in Munich." I slapped Alex on the shoulder. "God is with these people, Alex."

He nodded, ripped off his cap and gave his head a violent scratch. Lice had overtaken the dugout last week and left no man free from their wrath. "Well, if we must leave, we might as well make a grand farewell."

"How about a toast to Russia down at the tavern," Dimitri proposed. "Schnapps and the like."

I grinned. "Schnapps it is."

We continued conversing about the Russians and what we would do once we arrived in Germany as we strolled. When we reached the local tavern—an establishment that was recently repaired with incredible speed after a bombing—it was swarming with intoxicated soldiers. The door was wide open, and the scent of liquor and cigarettes drifted into the night air. The room was hazy with smoke, and every table was occupied by men in uniform, empty glasses scattered across the surfaces. We pushed our way to the counter and ordered four glasses of schnapps. A crowd of stoned men were stumbling out of the tavern, singing at the top of their lungs:

We will continue to march,
Even if everything shatters;
Because today Germany hears us,
And tomorrow the whole world!

Their words were barely audible through their laughter and slurred speech. We took their seats, and I tilted my head back, downing the syrupy, sweet liquor. We ordered another glass a moment later, and before I knew what was happening, the schnapps was flowing freely. I was feeling reckless and lost count of how many I had downed. My mind was numb to reality, the liquor coursing through my body and causing me to forget where I was, or who I was. I wiped my mouth with the back of my sleeve and eyed a group of officers sitting a few seats away. Their uniforms were neatly ironed and pressed, their emblems glinting in the tavern lights. I was completely out of myself, doing things I wouldn't dare to do in a state of consciousness. I stood on the wobbly chair with my glass raised, schnapps sloshing from side to side. "Let's sing!"

"Yeah!" Alex shouted, louder than I had ever heard him shout before, which was a considerable feat. "Start it off for us, Hans." His words slurred as he raised his glass. Otto and Dimitri followed his lead, laughing heartily over nothing of consequence. The other soldiers turned as I began to sing off tune.

"When der Führer says we is the master race, we heil, heil right in der Führer's face. Not to love der Führer is a great disgrace, so we heil, heil right in der Führer's face! When Herr Goebbels says we own the world and space, we heil, heil right in Herr Goebbels' face. When Herr Göring says, they'll never bomb this place! We heil—"

Dimitri raised his glass and let out a garbled, "Heil!" Alex and Otto burst out in uncontrollable laughter.

"We bring the world to order! Heil Hitler's world to order! Everyone of foreign race will love der Führer's face, when we bring to the world disorder!" My words mangled together, and I stumbled off the chair, gripping the counter to keep from falling flat on my face. A hearty chuckle flew off my lips.

Someone grabbed the back of my collar and gave it a firm yank. "What the hell was the meaning of that?" An officer bore his eyes into me. I can't define his features, for he was merely a blurred face before me. "Wipe that stupid grin off your face. How dare you insult our Führer!"

The soldiers who had been enjoying the spectacle now began grumbling and throwing anything in their reach at me and my counterparts. I said nothing. I might have been grinning like a fool, but I can't be sure. The officer shoved me into a seat, his voice distant to my ears. Was he on the other side of the room? "I'm letting you off because you're clearly drunk."

I cursed, then looked around for Alex. "Get me some coffee!"

"He's drunk, too," the officer sneered. "Get out of here before you get in real trouble. I could have you court-martialed for this."

homeward

I leaned my chin into my hands and watched as the Russian landscape disappeared. I continued to rehash the events of the evening prior, trying to make sense of my actions. I couldn't find any possible way to justify it. It was plain stupidity. Willi and Hubert had been reassigned to our company for the trip home. They had chastised us when they heard the story. I couldn't blame them.

"Thank God that officer had some pity on us," I muttered. I glared at my reflection in the window. My hair was disheveled, my eyes were bloodshot. "Stoned and singing an anti-Nazi song. That must have been quite the horrific sight."

"It wasn't just you, Hans. I was just as drunk as you." Alex leaned his head against the seat, his eyes closed and a scowl on his face. "I forgot how hellish hangovers are."

The train rattled over the tracks as we neared the Polish border, and it came to a jolting halt once we reached border control. "You are free to unboard," a corporal yelled up the aisle. "It could be a long wait, boys."

I slowly stood up, stretching my hands over my head with a yawn. I had dozed off for the majority of the trip, and now my eyesight was blurry. The autumn breeze felt heavenly as I stepped off the train, and the trees burst with rich yellows, corals, and amber. I squinted into the sunlight that was causing my head to throb.

"What's going on over there?" Willi pointed toward a

large assembly of prisoners shuffling forward, picks and axes slung over their shoulders. "Are they Russians?"

I stepped closer, watching the prisoners being prodded like cattle toward a barbed wire corral. They were gaunt and exhausted. Muddy clothing hung off their slim frames as a group of German soldiers marched alongside them. I reached into my pocket and pulled out my army-issued cigarettes. I glanced at Alex and Willi, and they followed my lead. Without saying a word, we walked to the group of prisoners and began passing out the cigarettes. A few men cast deathly glares at us. Others were stricken with surprise and took the cigarettes with a smile.

"Here. Please, take them," I said to an elderly man who regarded me with bewilderment. His face was slathered with wrinkles, and he was deeply tanned from the sun. He took the cigarette in his trembling, thin fingers, and I lit it for him. A soldier, broad and tall caught us in action.

"What the hell do you think you're doing?" he shouted, marching his way toward us, anger flaming in his eyes.

"Giving them a cigarette," I said evenly.

"These, if you're so stupid as to not notice, are prisoners."

"Yes, I do realize that they are prisoners, but these are our cigarettes, and we may do with them as we like." I began to turn and hand out another one when the soldier violently grabbed my arm.

"You should be right alongside them, you pathetic weakling. You are a disgrace to Germany!"

Alex pushed forward and began rolling up his sleeves. "Shall I knock the teeth out of this bastard, boys?" His fist was raised. The train's wheels screeched against the rails behind us. Alex dropped his fist. "We've got a train to catch, lucky for you."

Our Russian campaign had come to an end. My mind was spinning with all that I had witnessed. I was ready to resume my work again and to erode the Third Reich once and for all.

PART TWO

what have you done with your youth?

I turned over in my bed, watching as the moon cast shafts of eerie light on the floorboards. My mind was darting off in a million directions—recalling Christmas memories from the week prior, mulling over Russia, anxious over the constant air raids that were now plaguing Munich, and thinking over the massive counter attack of the Russians in Stalingrad. And the fact that America, too, was organizing for war against us entertained my thoughts. The Allies would be coming soon. I was certain of it.

"What are you thinking of?" Sophie asked from the room adjacent to mine. She had moved in for the new semester. Her door was wide open, and I could see her face illuminated by the moon beams. Her dark hair was tousled against the white pillow.

"About the leaflets," I said, leaning on my elbow. "I think the time is right to broaden our circle. We need to contact other resistance groups. What time *could* be better than now when the German people know in their hearts that Stalingrad is lost and that we can't win the war?"

Sophie sighed, her bed creaking as she moved into a more comfortable position. "How are you going to find safe connections, Hans? What if someone you thought was a friend ended up betraying us?"

"I'll be careful. Besides, Alex is good at weeding out the betrayers. I already have a safe contact in mind."

"Who?"

"Eugen Grimminger, a friend of father's. Alex and I are going to Stuttgart the day after tomorrow to talk it over with him. We need financial support if we're going to continue with the leaflets."

"Are you sure you can trust him?"

"He's a friend of father's, Sophie."

She smiled softly across the hallway at me.

"What?"

"I'm just glad that you're back from the front, Hans. I'm glad we're in Munich, doing something important."

I grinned. "Me too." Then she started laughing.

"What's so funny?"

"I was just thinking about this evening at the concert." She giggled again.

I sat up, running both hands through my hair. Bartok had swiftly become one of my favorite composers, for his pieces seemed to parallel my exact emotions at the moment ... fear ... restlessness. But I failed to see how Bartok was a laughing matter.

"And why is that so amusing?" I stepped into the hallway and leaned against her door frame, a pillow in my arms.

"Oh, how Gisela melted while you talked of your experiences at the Eastern Front as if your accounts of the destruction were swoon worthy. I don't think she heard a word of it. She was just gazing at you, and you couldn't keep your eyes off her for the entire concert. You two really are a laugh."

"What? I didn't do that." I flung my pillow at her, satisfied when it hit her square in the face.

"Oh, yes you did." She sat up and whipped it back.

"I did not." I threw it harder.

"Hans, you're such a baby. Just admit that you're hopelessly fond of her."

I ran a hand through my hair, not entirely comfortable with where this conversation was going. "Gisela's a sweet girl ..."

"Ha! I knew it." She hurled the pillow, but I dodged it, and it fell beside my feet.

"All I said was that she's sweet." My voice raised indignantly.

An ear-splitting siren filled the air and caused our banter to cease. We stared at each other as the room shook, and an explosion split the night air, brightening the room with white streaks of light. I ran into my room, tripping over a stack of books as I snatched a jacket to put over my flannel pajamas. I grabbed my air raid satchel which held books of poetry, a flashlight, and my army canteen, then pulled open the door and glanced at Sophie. "Ready?"

She was at my side in an instant, bundled up in a thick cable knit sweater over her nightgown. We darted down the corridor, down the stairs, and into the basement where the other tenants were huddled. The landlady was absent. She often fled to the countryside to escape the constant air raids. We separated ourselves from the others and sat in the back corner among cobwebs and dust laden crates. The stone wall was cool against my neck. I cracked open a book of poetry and began to read.

"'The sky above the roof, so blue, so calm! A tree, above the roof, waves its crown. The bell, in the sky I watch, gently rings. A bird, on the tree I watch, plaintively sings. My God, my God, life is there simple and serene. That peaceful murmur there comes from the town. O you, O you, what have you done, weeping without end. Say, O say, what have you done with all your youth?'"

"Beautiful," whispered Sophie, knees pulled to her chest as the sounds of bombing erupted outside the walls. "Who wrote it?"

"A Frenchman by the name of Verlaine," I said quietly, peering around to be sure the others weren't listening. A middle-aged couple was in a heated argument, drowning out any sound we might make. "Our youth will not be in vain. I wouldn't be able to bear living that last line in Verlaine's poem, 'Say, O say, what have you done with all your youth?' We *are* doing something, Sophie."

She lifted her head and grinned. "I know."

"You're not worried then, about what may come?"

She leaned against the wall, biting her lip in a contemplative manner. "If we are acting on our conscience and doing our God-given duty, then why on earth should I be worried? I may be scared, Hans, but I'm not worried. I know we're doing the right thing."

plead for funds

I buried my hands into my pockets as I strolled alongside Eugen Grimminger on the sidewalks of Stuttgart. A crisp winter breeze left icy marks across my face, and I hunched my shoulders against the cold.

"Why couldn't we talk somewhere warm. For instance, a cafe or my office?" Eugen asked, burying his bearded chin into his woolen scarf.

"What I must discuss is confidential," I said. "Let's walk a little further."

We walked in silence, the snow crunching under our boots. In hindsight, perhaps it wasn't the ideal day to plead for funds with the temperature dipping below zero. Perhaps it wasn't the best way to soften a fellow to our cause. We reached the abandoned loading platform meant for transferring companies. It was empty and still, the tracks frozen over. It was a safe distance away from the city, and the land was flat. We would be able to spot someone coming from a mile away.

"How is your father, Hans?" Eugen asked as if that were the sole reason we came to this remote spot in the bitter cold.

"Did you hear the news?" My breath crystallized in the frigid air. He shook his head, his spectacles fogging up. "He was arrested last fall. Someone overheard him stating that the war was already lost and that Hitler is God's scourge on mankind. He was promptly thrown in prison. He finally was released but was recently notified that he can no longer practice tax and accounting because he's 'politically unreliable.'"

"He always was outspoken, but he is a good man," Eugen said, adjusting his spectacles. "That's a dangerous thing to be these days ... outspoken." He seemed to shudder, and I felt a sense of dread fill me. I knew at that moment that he wouldn't assist me. "What is it you wished to discuss?"

I hunted through my pockets until I pulled out my cigarettes. It didn't hurt to bribe him a little. "Want one?" He took it gratefully. "Eugen, you are a good friend of my father's. You always have been. I have reasons to think you are against the Reich and all it stands for. Your wife is Jewish, isn't she?"

Eugen studied me and hesitated before saying, "That is correct."

"You would do anything to see that she is protected and given her inalienable rights back, wouldn't you?"

"Yes, of course I would."

I tapped my cigarette, watching as ashes cascaded onto the icy platform. "My friends and I have written leaflets under the title, *The White Rose*. Perhaps you've heard of it? We wish to grow our resistance, but we can't produce the amount of the leaflets we wish with the sum of money we're making—"

"Resistance?" Eugen uttered the word in a shocked whisper. His eyes were wide in apprehension.

"We have plans, Eugen. We want to organize resistance groups at the universities and combine them together into an *army* of resistance." My heart pounded against my chest. I began pacing and tossed my cigarette on the ground. I ran both hands through my hair. "The Allies can't be far off. With the grim reality of Stalingrad and the United States gearing up for war, the German morale is being obliterated. Now is the time to act. Now is the time to resist. There are more Germans than we realize who would resist if they knew they weren't alone." I glanced over my shoulder and saw Eugen's brow furrowed in deep thought. "The time is coming when we'll all be faced with the question, 'Why did you allow this to happen? Why didn't you do something?'"

"I heartily agree with your principles," Eugen started slowly. "But you must have known that because you wouldn't risk your neck if you thought me a blind follower of Hitler."

"Exactly." I ground the cigarette into the snow with my boot. "We need your support. We need funds to pay for basic materials—ink, paper, stencils, stamps, travel, and more duplicating machines. Without funds, our leaflets will cease, and the resistance will dissolve. We *need* financial support."

"I understand," Eugen scratched his beard. "I sympathize with you completely. I honestly do, but I am a respectable businessman, Hans. I have a family. This is a treasonous enterprise you're involved in. I'm sorry, but I can't risk it. You understand, don't you?"

"Yes." My heart dropped. "I do, Eugen. I'm sorry. I shouldn't have asked so much from you."

"Now Hans, don't think I don't support you, for I wholeheartedly do. I'm just hesitant to jump aboard this sedition. Be careful." He outstretched his gloved hand, and I shook it firmly.

"Don't worry. I will."

long night

"Are you still poring over those account books, Hans?" Sophie asked.

I leaned back in my desk chair and glanced at her as she leaned against my door frame. Her hair was disheveled, and her arms were folded tightly across her chest to ward off the cold. "I thought you were asleep."

"I couldn't sleep. You're being too loud with all your grumbling and shuffling papers. What's wrong, Hans? You look so unsettled."

My chair creaked as I turned to look at her. My eyes felt heavy, and my bones ached from sitting in the same position all evening. "Eugen wouldn't contribute, and I told Professor Huber about our leaflets this evening. He didn't think it was a prudent idea."

Sophie set one hand on the back of my chair and peered over my shoulder at the ledger. "Fritz has contributed."

"Yes, but that's nearly gone already. If we wish to continue with the leaflets and spread them throughout Germany, we need more duplicating machines, and that takes money, Sophie."

"I know that. No need to speak crossly with me." She hit me on the back of my head.

I groaned and rubbed my eyes with the palms of my hands. "I'm sorry. I'm just exhausted."

"Well, if you'd sleep instead of worrying about money, perhaps you wouldn't be so bear-like."

I gave her a scolding look, trying to be the older brother with my firm words, "Go to sleep, Sophie." My older brother authority didn't work half so well on Sophie as it did on Werner. She scowled at me.

"Not until you go to sleep. You'll kill yourself with all this strain. Please, go to sleep. Everything will work out."

"It won't work out unless we get money. Just go to bed and let me figure this out." My voice came out harsher than I intended.

She rolled her eyes with a grumble. "Ugh! Just go to sleep. I hate when you're like this."

I dropped my pen with irritation. "Like *what?*"

"Like this! Moody and horribly mean."

"I'm not moody."

"Yeah," she laughed. "Whatever you say, Hans, but

you're driving me insane."

"Then maybe you should go to bed as I said in the first place."

"And maybe you should get some sleep, so you're not an ogre in the morning."

I pushed away from the desk, resisting the urge to lash out at her with more arguments stating that I *wasn't* moody and that I was *never* mean to her. "All right. I'll go to bed if that'll make you happy."

Sophie smiled and patted my back proudly as if I were a child who had performed a good deed. "What would you do without me, Hans? You'd kill yourself with fretting, that's what would happen."

I mumbled something contrary to her statement, but I knew she was right.

tables turn

Sophie had been right after all. It would all work out in the end. I considered this as I held a check for five hundred marks from Eugen. He had a change of heart was all he said in the letter. In the other hand I held two hundred marks from Eickemeyer who now knew of the treasonous activities happening in his basement and approved in spite of his heated words that the leaflets were "much too literary." We were back in business. I had called a meeting in my apartment to discuss the future of the leaflets. The clock ticked rhythmically as I placed the money in the top drawer of my desk.

"Willi, you haven't told us the results of your resistance mission in your home town," I said, sinking into my desk chair. "Did you make many connections with the university students?"

Willi rubbed his chin and was silent before speaking, mentally evaluating each word to discern which would hold the most weight, then discarding the frivolous ones. He was like that, while I tended to let my words escape before I gave them sufficient thought. "In Bonn I found sympathizers, but none of them were willing to risk their necks. However, I met up with two brothers with whom I grew up. Their names are Heinz and Willi Bollinger. Heinz believes that assassination of Hitler is the only course to take. That reminded me of the Russian machine pistol you brought back from the front, Hans. Is that part of your plan? You've been acting restless since Russia, so I began wondering—"

"No," I scoffed, gazing up at the ceiling. "We fight with our words, Willi. I don't think I could shoot someone. Not even Hitler."

"I could," Sophie stated, sincerity in her eyes. She sat on the floor, tracing the floorboards with her finger. "Then the war would be over, and all these senseless deaths would finally end."

Alex, Christl, Willi, and I all stared at her. "Well! I would never have guessed that a twenty-one-year-old girl would have the guts to kill Hitler, but not her male counterparts who are older, and soldiers on top of that," Alex said with a startled laugh. "You never cease to surprise me, Sophie!"

"Get on with it, Willi. Sophie's not going to kill Hitler right this moment." I tossed her a condescending grin.

Willi nodded. "I gave the Bollingers a duplicating machine and some leaflets to multiply and distribute. They're masters of forging papers and will do it for us if we're in need of them—military passes, railroad tickets, leave papers …"

"Excellent. Good work, Willi." I opened the bottle of wine I had been saving and poured it into a glass. "Have one on me."

Willi took the glass, beaming gratefully.

Christl had been taking in the conversation silently, leaning his chin into his hands. "You've changed, Hans. It's like you're getting ready for something. I don't fully know what's going on, but you better be careful."

"It's restlessness," I said, scratching the back of my neck. "But not the typical kind. It's more like an energized restlessness ... as if something is coming that I can't put my finger on. Something big. And I'm ready for it. 'Lord, it is time. Let the great summer go, lay your long shadows on the sundials, and over harvest piles let the winds blow. Command the last fruits to be ripe; grant them some other southern hour, urge them to completion, and with power drive final sweetness to the heavy grape. Who's homeless now, will for long stay alone. No home will build his weary hands, he'll wake, read, write letters long to friends and will the alleys up and down walk restlessly, when falling leaves dance.'"

"Rilke?" Alex questioned, leaning against the wall.

"Correct."

"Don't I get a glass of wine for being brilliant?"

I nodded and poured a glass for him. "Have one on me for being so well versed in German poets." I lifted my ankle to rest against my thigh as I stared at the moon peeking through the curtains. "Now, back to the matter at hand. We have a restocked treasury, and we'll need someone to monitor it. Sophie?" I looked down at her as she leaned her back against the wall, snacking on a piece of bread. "Will you officially oversee the finance books and dole out cash as needed?"

She tore off a piece of bread and stuffed it in her mouth. "I'd be happy to, especially if it prevents you from staying up at all hours of the night and snapping at me."

Alex set down his glass with a look of astonishment. "Here all this time I thought you two never had a quarrel, even when you were knee high."

Sophie snorted, and I tossed her a smirk. "What siblings never have a quarrel? An incredible breed they must be." I ruffled Sophie's hair playfully.

A rapping sounded at the door moments later. "Ah, must be Traute," I said. Walking across the cold floor, I pulled the door open. Traute stood in the hallway, bundled in a long coat. Her face was ruddy. "Cold out there?" I asked.

"No, it's balmy. I'd like to stay out here all evening."

"Oh, Traute, ever the sarcastic one." I held the door open, and she slipped in, eyeing the others with eyebrows raised.

"A conspiratorial meeting? Hans, won't your landlady begin to grow suspicious with all of us in and out all the time?"

"Nice to see you too. Please, sit down." I motioned to the desk chair, and she sat down, ripping the mittens off her hands.

"I'm sorry. I'm just on edge lately, ever since you all came back from Russia. I knew that when you three returned from the front, the leaflets would start again."

"You are correct, Traute," I said, leaning against the wall opposite her, arms crossed against my chest. "I have big plans for these leaflets. The resistance is going to grow, and the Allies are coming. We must strike now, but in order to do that, we need more supplies. That's why I thought of you and invited you tonight."

Alex handed her his half used up cigarette, and she took it. "Thanks." Then she turned to me. "Why did you think of me?"

"We need a bigger duplicating machine. I recall you telling me that you have an uncle who works in Vienna in the wholesale office supply trade. Is that correct, or am I mistaken?"

"That's correct." She bit her lip. "You want me to get a duplicating machine for you."

"Smart girl."

"I'll do my best. I'm going home to Hamburg soon, to study at a clinic. I'll take along more of the leaflets. Last time I took them, I didn't get favorable responses, but I *know* I'll find sympathetic feelings among the intellectuals this time around, for resistance fever is spreading. Besides, Hamburg never did take to the Nazis quite like Munich did. We can start spreading them in larger numbers there, then who knows how far they'll reach."

"Good work, Traute," I said. "It looks as if the tables are turning in our favor."

a spark of resistance

A meeting had been called the next evening at the Eickemeyer studio by Traute and Gisela. The entire *White Rose* group was assembled, and we sat around the paint stained table, coats and scarves laying haphazardly on the backs of chairs. I leaned my arms across the table while I smoked a cigarette. Traute and Gisela were uptight and restless when they entered, tossing their satchels on the table beside me.

"None of you were at the museum for the Gauleiter speech today, were you?" Traute asked, sinking into a chair beside Alex.

"No. We've made it a rule to never attend any sort of Nazi event." Alex crossed his legs out in front of him.

"Did you hear about it at least?"

We shook our heads.

"It sent off a chain reaction of resistance." Gisela sat beside me, her face ruddy from the cold and her blue eyes bright. She rested a hand on my arm.

"Wait, start at the beginning." I placed a hand over her chilled fingers. "The speech sparked a revolt?"

Traute pushed her dark hair behind her shoulders. "We went to the assembly in honor of the 470th anniversary of the university. Attendance was mandatory, so Gisela, Kate Schuddekopf and I went to avoid getting in trouble. The place was crammed full of students, and the platform was swarming with officials and dignitaries, but the Gauleiter completely overlooked the reason of the assembly and instead led a verbal attack against the students who were ... oh, how did he say it, Gisela?" She leaned forward, a cigarette between her fingers.

"Using their studies to avoid getting drafted," Gisela said, rolling her eyes.

Traute nodded. "He said something to the effect that our country cannot 'pamper' these students who should be doing something profitable for our Führer. He said they should be serving in the army and getting their noses out of books. Oh, but then he went *too* far when addressing the female students. I was ready to drop my books on his bald head." She sat up straight, anger flashing across her face.

I furrowed my brow. "What did he say?"

"'As far as the girls,'" Traute mocked his deep, nasally voice, "'there is no reason why each of them should not make an annual contribution to the Fatherland of a child, preferably a son. Let all girl students with healthy bodies bear children. That is an automatic process, and, once started, continues without requiring the least attention.'" Her face twisted into a scowl. "'If some of you girls lack sufficient charm to find a mate, I will be glad to assign you one of my adjutants.'" Traute's eyes narrowed in contempt.

My fingers tightened over Gisela's. "Did the students just allow him to talk like that?" I peered down at her, and she stared back. I realized how ardently I longed to protect her from everything.

"No, they didn't." Gisela gazed down at our hands. "The crowd grew into an uproar, and the Gauleiter's voice was drowned out completely. No one could stand him smirking at us after such an attack. Female students got up to leave, deeply hurt by the speech, and then a score of male students left as well. It was wonderful to see that many of the male students couldn't stand this attack on the females. They were quite the gentlemen." She smiled.

"The SS guards at the door wouldn't let them out." Traute was on the edge of her chair now, her hands flying this way and that as she spoke. "The male students broke into fists fights with the guards, and veterans who just returned from the front were there, beating the SS to a pulp. Then the students burst through the doors and poured into the streets in a riot, and the students linked arms. They began shouting at the top of their lungs. It was glorious."

I felt a wave of elation travel through me. "A revolt right in the streets? That's the best news I've heard all year!"

"Then the police came." Gisela ran her finger along the grooves in the wood. "The students weren't a match for the police clubs, and it ended quickly. But isn't that grand that the students have begun to rebel?"

"Outstanding," Alex said, his face beaming. "Truly."

"I knew the German people would eventually wake up," I said, grinning with pleasure. "Thank God."

the fifth leaflet

A Call to All Germans!

The war is approaching its destined end. As in the year 1918, the German government is trying to focus attention exclusively on the growing threat of submarine warfare, while in the East the armies are constantly in retreat and invasion is imminent in the West. Mobilization in the United States has not yet reached its climax, but already it exceeds anything that the world has ever seen. It has become a mathematical certainty that Hitler is leading the German people into the abyss. Hitler cannot win the war; he can only prolong it. The guilt of Hitler and his minions goes beyond all measure. Retribution comes closer and closer.

I paused and rubbed my hands together. They were stiff from the cold. My shoulders burned in pain, and I was suffering from a throbbing headache. Alex cranked the duplicating machine as Willi folded the leaflets and slipped them into envelopes. Sophie dipped her finger in a glass of water to apply the stamps. After a hundred were counted, we switched stations, and each took on a new job.

"How many are we up to?" I asked.

"Eighty-eight," said Willi.

I focused my attention on the typewriter once again, willing my fingers to cooperate.

But what are the German people doing? They will not see and will not listen. Blindly they follow their seducers into ruin. Victory at any price! is inscribed on their banner. "I will fight to the last man," says Hitler—but in the meantime the war has already been lost.

Germans! Do you and your children want to suffer the same fate that befell the Jews? Do you want to be judged by the same standards as your traducers? Are we to be forever a nation which is hated and rejected by all mankind? No. Dissociate yourselves from National Socialist gangsters. Prove by your deeds that you think otherwise. A new war of liberation is about to begin. The better part of the nation will fight on our side. Cast off the cloak of indifference you have wrapped around you. Make the decision before it is too late. Do not believe the National Socialist propaganda which has driven the fear of Bolshevism into your bones.

Do not believe that Germany's welfare is linked to the victory of national Socialism for good or ill. A criminal regime cannot achieve a German victory. Separate yourselves in time from everything connected with National Socialism. In the aftermath, a terrible but just judgment will be meted out to those who stayed in hiding, who were cowardly and hesitant.

"What time is it?" Willi asked, breaking the lull of conversation.

I glanced down at my watch. "Three A.M."

"We have to be at the clinic in ... let's see ... four hours? Can I manage to slip a little sleep in I wonder?" Alex's eyes were bloodshot.

"Let's take shifts. Alex, have a rest. I'll wake you up in a half hour," I said.

Alex gratefully sank into a chair and closed his eyes.

What can we learn from the outcome of this war—this war that never was a national war?

The imperialist ideology of force, from whatever side it comes, must be shattered for all time. A one-sided Prussian militarism must never again be allowed to assume power. Only in large-scale cooperation among the nations of Europe can the ground be prepared for reconstruction. Centralized hegemony, such as the Prussian state has tried to exercise in Germany and in Europe, must be cut down at its inception. The Germany of the future must be a federal state. At this juncture, only a sound federal system can imbue a weakened Europe with a new life. The workers must be liberated from their condition of down trodden slavery under National Socialism. The illusory structure of autonomous national industry must disappear. Every nation and each man have a right to the goods of the whole world!

Freedom of speech, freedom of religion, the protection of individual citizens from the arbitrary will of criminal regimes of violence—these will be the bases of the New Europe.

Support the resistance. Distribute the leaflets!

A thick stack of envelopes balanced before Sophie. "All set for tomorrow?" I pushed back my chair and stretched my sore limbs.

"Yes." She walked across the studio to where she had left her suitcase leaning against the wall. She unlatched the buckles and opened it on the table, carefully placing the envelopes in neat stacks along the perimeter of the suitcase.

"You have your identification papers, travel permit, and your Ahnenpass?" I asked as she worked. Dark circles were forming under her eyes from lack of sleep.

"Where's Sophie going?" Willi peered up from his work. His sleeves were rolled to his elbows, and he had unbuttoned his collar.

"Sophie will be taking these leaflets to Stuttgart. Alex has Cologne, and Jürgen agreed to pass them out in Berlin. Willi, you have the Rhineland cities?"

"Yes, Hans."

"Good. I'm going to smuggle them into Austria," I said, lighting a cigarette. I shook the match until the flame was extinguished.

"Austria?" Sophie's head flew up. "Austria?"

Willi's eyes were wide. "What about border control? Hans, that's too fatal. They'll search your bags for sure."

"You worry too much, Willi. Nothing's going to happen, and I'll pay for it with my own money. I won't take it from our treasury. Alex, wake up." I threw a pencil at him. Alex groaned and slowly cracked open one eye.

"What?" he grumbled.

"Sophie's turn to rest. Get on your feet and start cranking the duplicating machine."

Alex stood up, stretching his lanky body. He yawned as he stumbled toward the machine.

we're in this together

I hadn't been able to sleep. I never could when Sophie was

out on a mission. I couldn't calm down even if she was only on an outing with a friend. The threatening danger that stalked us caused me to stay awake for hours pondering what could happen. I had to force myself to stop thinking. I busied myself with Dostoyevsky and attempted to tune out the ticking of the clock that seemed to say: *Your time is running out.*

I shouldn't have let her go to Stuttgart by herself.

I shouldn't have let her get involved.

I'm older. Surely I could have told her "no."

These feelings mingled with my own anxiety over my upcoming trip to Austria. Those things I said to Willi ... did I honestly believe them?

No. I didn't.

But I knew I had to do something other than stuff leaflets in local telephone booths. Those were our resistance efforts of the past. We were now propelling into a more daring future. I had already begun pinning the leaflets to the official Nazi party news bulletins. Willi thought I was getting too risky with my endeavors. I found it rather humorous.

The door creaked open, and I dropped my book. Sophie stepped in, her shoulders hunched from exhaustion. I helped take her coat and hat off, then wrapped her in a tight hug.

"Everything go all right? Sit down, Sophie, you look tired."

"I am tired." She sank into a kitchen chair and closed her eyes for a long moment, her dark lashes brushing against her pale skin. "Everything went fine." I poured her a cup of tea, then joined her at the table. The room was masked in dusky shadows, and the air was frigid, sneaking in through the windowpane. "I distributed all the leaflets, and I'll be ready to go out again whenever we have another few hundred ready."

I rubbed my hands over my face with a groan. "Every time you go out on a mission I get worked up into an anxious mess. I can't stand it any longer."

"But Hans, I want to do this." She pulled the cup toward

herself and breathed in the steam. She grinned over her tea at me. That childlike smile brought me back to days spent hiking in the mountains then returning home to hot chocolate, ruddy faced and dead tired. We hadn't a care in the world then. How I desperately missed that life.

I let my fingers rest on my cup of tea, relishing the warmth seeping through the porcelain. "You're one of the bravest people I know."

She took a long sip of tea with a look of contentment on her face. "I feel completely happy right now."

"I'm rather hungry," I said, pushing my chair back. The legs scratched against the hardwood floor. "Toast?"

"Yes, thanks."

I toasted two thick slices of bread, then smothered them with our rationed butter. "We deserve an extra bit of butter on our toast tonight." I set a slice on a plate and slid it across the table.

"I'll take leaflets to Ulm this week." Sophie bit into her toast. "I have friends who will help me set up a distribution center there."

"Who? Are you *positive* that you can trust them?"

"Yes, I'm positive." She licked the butter off her fingertips. "It's Hans Hirzel, Franz Müller, and Heinrich Guter."

All trustworthy young men, but still ... "Be careful, Sophie."

Our eyes met, and she suddenly became somber. "I will. Nothing's going to happen to us."

I wished I believed that. I began stacking our empty plates atop each other. Crumbs cascading onto the table.

"Hans?"

"Hmm?" I glanced up.

"Have you told Gisela about all this?"

I dusted the crumbs back onto the plates. "No."

"I suppose that's for the best, but I did recruit her to help me the other day. I didn't tell her what I was mailing, but she held the post boxes open for me. She never asked what was in them."

"I'm afraid she might already know." My voice sounded distant to me.

"What?"

I sat back down, leaving the plates on the table. "Gisela stopped by this morning. She was looking for you. I told her you weren't around but that I'd like to visit with her if she had the time. She agreed, and so I went into the kitchen to get us drinks. When I returned to the table, her face was pale, and she seemed distracted for our entire visit. After she left, I … I realized that I forgot to put my knapsack away. It was full of leaflets and easy to spot from where she was standing. She didn't say anything about them, and I hid them as soon as she left, as if that could undo the damage. I was careless."

"You won't be again. I know you. It was just a little mistake—"

My throat tightened. "One careless mistake could cost us our necks."

Sophie grimaced and stared at the table, melancholy washing over her face.

"I'm sorry. I'm so sorry, Sophie. I'll be more careful next time." The room was heavy with silence. I didn't know silence could be so suffocating. I shifted in my seat, eager to talk of something more cheerful than confessing my blunder. "I heard good news this week from Alex. The leaflets have reached the Norwegian underground, and some copies have even reached England."

Sophie lifted her face with a wistful smile and brushed her hair behind her ears. "Can I ask you something?"

"Of course."

"If we got caught," Sophie whispered, as if afraid her words would bring the ceiling crashing in on us, "would you still trust in God?"

I stared at her. She was scared. She wanted answers.

"Yes, because even if I'm caught and killed, I'll be doing it all for Christ. I'll be doing His work ... the work I was given to accomplish during my time on earth. He may call me home sooner than I'd wish, but I'd rather die for what is right, true, and just than to live with a dead soul and conscience. Are you prepared to die in this fight, knowing we might not change things?"

"I'm not planning on getting caught." Her eyes flashed with determination.

"Well, me neither."

She stood up and wrapped her arms around my neck. "We're in this together, Hans. Whatever happens, I'm there with you. And I will cling to Jesus through it all."

down with hitler

Dried flakes of paint scattered to the ground as Willi, Alex, and I stuffed tubes of paint and brushes into our pockets. Alex carried the stencils he had made as I opened the studio door, glancing into the streets to be sure no one was about. I checked my watch. Two minutes past midnight.

"All clear," I said, motioning for Alex and Willi to go ahead. Snowflakes tumbled from the sky, creating a blanket of white across the roads. I pulled out my pistol and checked to be sure it was loaded, then followed behind my comrades. I don't know what I thought I would do if someone caught us. Hadn't I just recently declared that I couldn't shoot anyone in cold blood?

Our boots crunched against the icy brick streets as a gale of wind tried to sneak through our overcoats. We were grinning and stifling our laughter at our daring plan. Alex stopped once we reached the entrance of the university. He glanced at me, his face masked in shadows. "Got us covered, old chap?"

I nodded and withdrew my pistol. It shimmered in the moonlight. Willi held the stencils against the brick wall of the university while Alex moved a paint brush up and down with a roguish smirk. I kept one eye on the graffiti process and the other peeled for any unwanted spectators. The city was still and cloaked in shadows as we worked.

"Well? How does it look?" Alex stepped back, wiping his hands along his trousers.

I slapped him on the shoulder as I admired the black letters that spelled out: *DOWN WITH HITLER!* Next to the words was a swastika with a fat X painted over it. "You never told me that you were such a fine artist, Alex," I grinned.

"You never asked."

We hastened into the night, spreading words all over the city—on street signs, walls, theaters, Nazi shrines, and anywhere that it would be the most visible. Alex painted the words *HITLER THE MASS MURDERER* wherever he felt like it and covered buildings with *FREIHEIT! FREIHEIT!* Alex and Willi's hands were stained from the paint.

"Wash that off before lectures tomorrow," I warned. "It'll give you away in an instant. You have the wine, Willi? Let's go to my place and recount our tales to Sophie."

The three of us, all in good humor and flushed from the cold, ran through the streets, wishing we could scream, whistle, and shout to our hearts' content. We bottled up our energy until we were safe in my apartment where we let out our hearty laughs. Our voices were raised as talked on top of each other, behaving like school boys who were just released for Christmas vacation. We startled Sophie, who was at the table, her head resting in her arms. Willi banged the bottle of wine on the table, and I snatched the glasses from the cupboard.

"A drink, Sophie?" I asked, feeling more alive than I had in weeks as adrenaline coursed through my veins.

She rubbed her eyes, staring at us in a mixture of confusion and relief. "Oh, thank God! I thought you were arrested. Where were you? I've had dinner on the table for the past four hours."

I glanced at the spread of apples, jam, and biscuits. Hunger gnawed at my stomach. "Splendid! Thank you, Sophie. Don't mind if Alex and Willi dig in too, do you?"

"Of course not, but what were you three doing? What's going on?" She slapped her hands onto the table, glancing at each of our bright faces.

"It was Alex's idea," I said, pouring the wine into a glass.

"Yes, it was. A rather good one if I might say so," Alex beamed as he took a bite into an apple.

"But don't worry. Hans was a good lookout. Everything went off without a hitch. No one saw us," said Willi, leaning against the counter with his arms crossed.

"What was his idea?" Sophie's eyes were wide. "What is going on? Are you ever going to tell me?"

I winked mischievously at her. "Are we putting you in too much suspense, Sophie?" I slid the first glass of wine in front of her.

She sipped the crisp wine, then wiped her mouth with the back of her sleeve. "You're all cruel."

"Well, I'll not beat around the bush," said Willi.

Willi, the ever considerate, gentle one. I'd just as soon continue to torture my sister.

"Alex thought we should graffiti buildings and walls with words such as, 'Down with Hitler!' and 'Freiheit!' We took the paints and brushes from the studio. Alex cut out the stencils. Hans came with his pistol, and we painted those words on every blasted public place we could. If you happen to visit any of the Nazi shrines, they now bear crossed out swastikas and the words, 'Hitler is a Murderer.'"

All three of us looked at Sophie to see what she thought of all this.

"Oh," she said, brow furrowed. She sounded disappointed. "Why didn't you take me?"

"Well, you see, Sophie ..." Alex paused, set down his wine glass, then looked at me. "Why didn't we take her along?"

"Take me next time," Sophie pleaded. "I can keep watch and then you can help paint, Hans. Please?" She clasped her hands together like she used to when she longed to tag along with me and my friends back in Ulm.

"Sophie, I don't want you involved in any more dangerous ventures."

"I can be if I want to, and I want to go along next time." Silence.

I risked a glance around. Alex and Willi were smirking behind their wine glasses, and I couldn't help the smile that crept across my face. I was too elated to scold. "Next time we'll take you, Sophie, if that's what you want."

"Thank you." She lifted her wine glass. "To the resistance!"

We raised our glasses and clinked them together. "To the resistance!"

"May we all live to see it bloom," I lifted the glass to my lips and took a long sip.

"You talk dreary. We *will* live to see it bloom, Hans. Just see if we don't," Alex chuckled, propping his feet on the table and sticking his pipe in his mouth. "We are alive and young."

"Which doesn't mean anything to the Nazis," Willi reminded him.

"You all talk rot. We must survive. All of us," he eyed us, sincerity in his gaze. It was at that moment that I realized he really *did* expect us all to come through this. I had my doubts.

"Yes, but some things are out of our control, aren't they?" I lit a cigarette and shook out the match.

stalingrad

I reclined on the sofa near the radio, a cigarette between my thumb and index finger. I flipped the switch on, intending to read a collection of poetry while Bach or Beethoven played in the background. After a moment of humming and static, I caught the end of the announcer's words: "... lost." A long silence. No music. I leaned forward, giving the radio a shake.

"What's lost?" I mumbled under my breath.

As if answering my question, the announcer was back. "The battle of Stalingrad has ended. True to their oath to fight to the last breath, the Sixth Army under the exemplary leadership of Field-Marshal Paulus has been overcome by the superiority of the enemy and by the unfavorable circumstances confronting our forces."

I fell back in my chair, my throat suddenly dry. The sound of drums crackled through the radio, dismal and hollow. Beethoven's fifth symphony sent sorrow spiraling into the German night.

"Sophie!"

Sophie peeked her head out of her bedroom, a pen in hand. "Thought of something to add to Inge's letter?"

I stood up, fingers raking through my hair. "Stalingrad. We've lost." I shook my head as I leaned an arm on the bookshelf, watching the smoke swirl from my cigarette. "Three hundred and thirty thousand of our troops are dead upon the ground that Hitler promised would be a victory."

Sophie leaned against the doorframe, staring at the ceiling. "Three hundred and thirty thousand fathers, sons, brothers, uncles, nephews ..."

"Hitler is an idiot." I paced the floor and peered out the window, scowling as a Nazi flag on a building across the street snapped in the wind. "No. I take that back. Our people are the idiots for allowing an insane man to drive thousands

upon thousands of our boys to a senseless death for him. I've
seen boys die, Sophie, stripped of their childhood and thrown
into the most brutal fighting you can imagine. Set to killing
each other with machine guns and bombs. Boys blown to bits
all over the fields. An arm here, a leg there."

I threw my cigarette in the ashtray as my eyes stung. "All
for what? Our people don't seem to realize that the price for
Hitler's Thousand-Year Reich is their freedom—their very
lives. They followed him blindly to their deaths. 'There is
always such a temptation to shirk the strain of thinking for
oneself, to let oneself be caught up in a great wave of collec-
tive enthusiasm, to embrace some comforting doctrine
because it makes things easy … for it is precisely when his
mind is most beset with doubts that a man is liable, in his desire to find an escape at all costs from perplexity, to clutch at
any ready-made creed that offers reassurance. Any fairly
plausible answer to the problems he has been brooding over,
and cannot solve unaided, will strike him as a heaven-sent
solution—especially if it bears the seeming guarantee of being endorsed by the majority.' *Roger Martin du Gard,
Summer 1914.*'"

Sophie said nothing, but I spotted a tear trickle down her
cheek.

"It'll all be over soon," I said, turning my back to her so
that she couldn't see the tears stinging my eyes. "Go back to
writing, Sophie. I've got some thinking to do."

The following morning Sophie slipped on her coat and went
to purchase a newspaper. When she returned, we sat at the
table with steaming cups of coffee, our hearts heavy. I was
split by the news of Stalingrad. You would think I would only have been elated that Hitler had lost such a substantial
amount of military force. I was. But at what cost? The sorrow of the soldiers' mourning families tore at my heart. So
many had died in vain. The blood is on Hitler's hands. He is

the guilty one—the murderer of millions.

"Look." Sophie slid the newspaper across the table to me. I took a long sip of hot coffee, then picked it up. The entire newspaper was bordered in black. "Three days of national mourning," I read. "Everything has been shut down."

"Read the fallen soldier notices. They're heart wrenching." Sophie leaned her elbows on the table. Her face was flushed from the cold.

My eyes scanned the paper. Black iron crosses were in columns all along the length of the paper. "Our dearly beloved son, in silent pain. My good and loving husband, in deepest sorrow." I flipped to the next page.

More iron crosses.

"You know what this all means, Sophie?" I set the paper down. "The war will end soon. How can Germany go on now? How can our people swallow such a painful loss? The war will end, and Germany will be defeated."

gestapo on my trail

"Good morning, Hans."

Someone acknowledged me, but I didn't glance up to see who it was. I continued walking, eyes fixed on the sidewalk before me. I buried my hands into my pockets and pushed forward against the brisk, February wind. A chill ran up and down my spine. Footsteps sounded behind me. I walked faster.

"Hans, wait up!"

I knew that voice. I glanced over my shoulder to see Gisela saddle up beside me. Her face was rosy, and her golden hair was hidden under a blue knitted cap.

"You're in a hurry," she said, her soft voice soothing my restless heart. "Is something wrong?"

"Wrong?" I asked, staring into her bright, blue eyes.

"Yes. You seem troubled." She touched my arm gently. "Want to pop into a coffeehouse?"

"Yeah, that might be nice," I agreed. She slipped her arm through mine, and we turned, making our way toward the corner coffeehouse. A burst of warmth welcomed us as we entered and found a corner booth near the window. We settled in, breathing in the steam of our ersatz coffee.

I took off my scarf, keeping an eye on the window behind Gisela. Every time a black car drove by, my muscles tensed. She reached over and grabbed my cold hand. My eyes immediately dropped to her fingers covering my calloused ones.

God, I loved her.

My heart compressed. I *knew* this was going to happen. I knew I couldn't suppress my feelings for her no matter how hard I tried. I would either need to walk away from her now, or finally surrender. I made my decision as I leaned forward, placing both hands on her flushed face. She stared into my eyes, and I lost my breath. "Can I kiss you, Gisela?"

Her eyes brightened. "Do you love me?" She was blissfully innocent.

I tried to mask an amused grin. "Yes." I kissed her gently, not caring that others around us were staring in a mixture of surprise and embarrassment.

As we pulled back, I risked a glance to the right of me where a group of students were whispering and peering at us. Gisela followed my gaze and suddenly frowned.

"They're going to tell Traute. She'll hate me."

I raised a brow in confusion. "Traute?"

"I know you two were in love once. I think she still pines over you, and if she finds out that I kissed you—"

"I kissed *you*, remember? Or should I refresh your memory?" I leaned in, kissing her with more passion. "Don't worry over Traute," I whispered in her ear. "I don't love her, Gisela. Are you worried over my sincerity, my loyalty?" I tried to read her countenance.

"No." Her face relaxed. "You are honest, Hans. I don't doubt your loyalty. You are the sincerest person I've ever met. That's why I also believe you'll tell me what's troubling you when you're ready."

I needed someone to help me bear this new burden—that I was being watched. I needed someone to talk it through with, someone who wasn't intimately involved with the leaflet production. "I'm ready."

"Can we talk about it here?" Gisela asked.

"No," I stood up. "Follow me."

My hand found hers as hurried down the streets of Munich toward Eickemeyer's studio. The brisk wind whipped around us, and I pulled Gisela close to keep her warm. When we arrived at the studio, we went downstairs without saying a word. I turned on the light and motioned for Gisela to sit down as I stumbled with the match to light a cigarette.

"Hans, let me help. You're trembling." She grabbed the matchbox from me and lit one, holding it up to my cigarette with a calm hand.

"Thanks," I said, taking a drag.

She stood on her toes and planted a kiss on my cheek. "Tell me what's on your mind. I know it has something to do with those leaflets. I saw them in your apartment." Her hand lingered on my face. I clasped mine over hers.

"I'm being watched, Gisela. By the Gestapo." Those words sounded even more deadly spoken aloud than they did in my mind. "I wrote the leaflets."

Her hand dropped to her side. "Hans ..." she shook her head. "Why?"

I grabbed her hand and pulled her close to me. "Because I had to do something."

"How do you know that you're being watched?" she whispered.

"I have a contact within the Gestapo. He told me to be careful ... that they're watching me." My heart pounded against my chest. It sounded like a death sentence.

"What are you going to do?" Gisela looked up at me. Her face was so pale, so frightened.

"I've been thinking it through. At first I thought I would escape to Switzerland. It would be easy. I've been climbing mountains my entire life, and I could escape by night and apply for asylum there. I'd be completely safe. But—"

"But what?"

"My sudden disappearance would prove to the Gestapo that I am responsible for the leaflets. They'd hunt down my family, my friends, and acquaintances. How in good conscience could I sit in Switzerland safe and sound, all the while knowing that it was my own selfishness to seek asylum that put those I love in danger? I couldn't."

"You don't know how much the Gestapo actually knows. They keep watch on thousands of people who don't get arrested."

I looked down at her. She was trying to make me feel better, so I offered her a reassuring smile. "I won't let this stop me. I'm going to continue on with the leaflets as usual."

Those didn't appear to be the words she wished to hear. She bit her lip as a tear trailed down her cheek. "Hans, please be careful."

"I will." I kissed her forehead.

"I want to marry you once this is all over. You must preserve yourself."

I stepped back, a smirk tugging on my mouth. "Are you proposing to me, Gisela Schertling? Isn't that my job?"

She blushed bright red. "Of course not. I'm not that forward."

I tucked a curl behind her ear. "My father told us that he wants us to live honest, free lives even though it might be difficult. You understand why I'm doing this, don't you?"

"Yes, but why didn't you tell me?"

"Why?" I held her out at arm's length. "Gisela, how could I? And why have I told you everything now? I've endangered you." I released her and stuffed my hands in my pockets, feeling a rush of anger flame inside me at my stupidity. "Gisela, I'm sorry. I ... I shouldn't have told you about all this. You were better off not knowing."

"I don't care about the danger, Hans. Not now. I'm happier knowing, and if anything happens to you, let them take me too."

"Gisela," I shook my head at her naivety, "you *don't* understand."

She furrowed her brow and placed both hands on her hips. "What do you mean by that?"

I stepped closer, gazing into her eyes and willing her to understand. "This may seem like a romantic adventure, Gisela, but it's not. Would you honestly be willing to follow me to death? To the gallows or the guillotine? Lord forgive me, I shouldn't have roped you into this."

"Hans!" Her eyes clouded with tears, and I immediately regretted my words. "Don't say such things."

"Gisela—" I reached out to comfort her, but she covered her face and recoiled as she sank into a chair. Her shoulders were heaving. My heart split open, throbbing like an infected wound as her cries filled the studio. I kneeled in front of her, prying her hands off her face. I brushed the hair from her damp cheeks, then caressed the side of her face. "I'm sorry. I shouldn't have said those things."

She leaned forward, appearing like a little girl who was lost and alone. She wrapped her arms around me and leaned her head onto my shoulder. "I'm scared, Hans. I'm terrified of the future. Why is life so cruel right now? I just want to be your wife and have sons that look just like you. I want a simple life without fear of the government uprooting everything that is good and without fear of them taking away everyone I love. Is that too much to ask?"

I laced my fingers through hers. "We live in a time where we must fight for basic human rights once again. My God, I want us to get married, Gisela. I want to always protect you, but I don't know if I can. I want to say that you can always count on my being there for you, but I don't know if that's true. I'm willing to give up my life for this cause. I want to be your husband and a father someday, but God may not permit that for me."

She lifted her head from my shoulder and stared into my eyes. "You are so brave, Hans Scholl."

"So are you, Gisela." I wiped away a tear from her face, a stanza by Goethe coming to mind as our eyes locked. "'But ah, already at morning light my heart was crushed in parting: in your kisses what delight, in your eyes what suffering. I went, you stood, looked from above, and saw me go with tearful gaze: and yet what joy to be loved. Dear God, to love what happiness.'"

corrections

How is one to correct his own Professor's literary efforts? Kurt Huber had agreed to write the sixth leaflet for us, and I felt rather presumptuous as we sat in the studio, the draft spread out before me. The room was drenched in the scent of cigar smoke and fragrant wine while silence draped over us like a blanket.

"Professor Huber," I started, seeing that Alex wasn't about to say anything. I didn't blame him. Neither of us wished to have this conversation. "We approve of everything you've written in the sixth leaflet except for—"

"Except for what?" Professor Huber leaned forward in his chair, staring evenly at us. Half of his face was cloaked in shadows.

I waved the leaflet at him. "What's this about encouraging German youth to give its support to our 'glorious Wehrmacht?' Do you wish for more German youth to be slaughtered for Hitler?"

"The Wehrmacht ought to be recognized for its discipline and traditions. I do believe that one of these days our glorious Wehrmacht will overthrow Hitler. We need more men to do that."

"What?" I tossed the leaflet on the table with disgust. "It contradicts the other points in the leaflet. We can't keep it."

"It does no such thing." Professor Huber snatched the leaflet from the table protectively. "I will sit here all day and defend my points. I believe every word of what I've written in this leaflet."

"We thank you for writing the leaflet, Professor," Alex said calmly, "but we won't be including that bit about the Wehrmacht under any circumstances. The rest, however, was excellent."

"I don't believe this!" He shot out of his seat, upsetting the wine glasses on the table.

"We apologize," I said. "It honestly *is* a brilliant leaflet, Professor, but we will not encourage any more Germans to enter the Wehrmacht. We're a part of it. Believe what we say."

Professor Huber pressed his lips tightly together, then turned and stalked off. "Goodnight," he called before slamming the door behind him.

Little did I know that it was the last time I'd ever see him. If I had known, I would have made peace at once. I wouldn't have allowed him to leave in such a state of hurt and anger. That wasn't how I wished to part with him. But I didn't know.

I honestly thought we'd be meeting again.

w$ must a$t now

Hindsight can be unbearably painful. When I recall the moments leading up to our undoing, I start to see the mistakes I made and the lack in judgment that led me here. If only I could turn back the clock and warn myself ... no. There's no use whatsoever in thinking of what could have been.

I placed a sheet of paper in the typewriter and began typing the Professor's leaflet, filling the silent studio with rhythmic clicks. I paused and rubbed my arms. The sound of papers sliding off the mimeograph machine mingled with the clicking of Alex's typewriter as he worked across from me.

"Shit!" Alex said between clenched teeth. "Stencil ripped."

I stood, cracked my fingers and walked over. I hit Alex on the back of the head. "Watch your mouth."

Alex glanced sheepishly at Sophie. "Sorry." He ran a hand through his hair.

"It's all right. It's not like I haven't heard curse words before as Hans seems to think." She stopped cranking and sat down, resting her sore feet. "And I might say the same thing if it wouldn't bring all your eyes on me in horror."

She sat there for a long moment, and I ruffled her hair. "Sophie, you could sit near Willi and help him fold leaflets. No sitting around with idle hands."

Sophie smiled smugly and dragged her chair near Willi who sat at the table folding leaflets rhythmically. "Oh, you're such a tyrant."

Alex laughed, getting over his momentary aggravation. "It's rather amusing to hear you two argue."

"It happens under stress," I said, glancing at Sophie. "Apparently we're stressed."

"I know how to get on his nerves," smirked Sophie as she ran her fingers along the crease of the leaflet.

"Please, do it. Willi and I need some amusement," Alex chuckled.

Sophie raised a brow as she slipped a leaflet into an envelope. "Hans, dear, tell us about Gisela."

The little imp.

"Sophie—"

"No, no! Go on, Hans!" Alex said, slapping me on the shoulder as I began typing again. "Are you lovesick?"

"He's smitten," Sophie giggled. "They are inseparable." Her eyes twinkled. Alex and Willi laughed.

I ceased typing, picked up a rag sitting on the counter that was still damp with paint and threw it at her. The laughter grew louder until a siren split through the air. We all grew deathly quiet.

"Air raid," whispered Willi.

"We're safe in the basement, aren't we?" Sophie looked at us, her eyes wide.

"If a bomb doesn't tear off the wall of the studio, exposing our entire operation," I said. The paintings leaning against the walls rattled as an explosion shook the structure. "If only the Allies knew, in the basement of an artist's studio in Munich an underground resistance was at work. Let's just pray they don't kill us before we have a chance to let them know."

Our light-hearted conversation vanished, replaced by hurried work. Sophie folded the leaflets at a rapid pace. I was certain that she could carry out this job in her sleep. Alex sat beside her, addressing the envelopes as he whistled a tune to drown out the bombings. I carried the last thick stack to Sophie and Willi, then sat down and ruffled my hair until it stood on end. My arms and feet burned with pain.

"Where are we distributing the rest of these?" Alex asked, glancing at the large pile.

"I have an idea, but you will think me crazy," I said.

"Yes, we will, but tell us anyway. We could use a laugh."

Alex leaned back in his chair and lit his pipe.

"Suppose we distribute the leaflets at the university on Thursday."

Silence smothered the room. Willi lifted his eyes, shock evident on his face. Alex blinked, and Sophie didn't move.

"Just think! If we can get thousands of leaflets into the hands of the students, an uprising might happen. We need another revolt at the university. The time is right. I think we should do it."

Willi held up his hands with a shake of his head. "It's one thing to sneak into the night and distribute the leaflets, but to do it in broad daylight? Hans, that's ludicrous."

"We must act now!" I pushed back my chair and began pacing the floor. "We have to be bold. The university is one place we haven't yet properly christened with our leaflets. I believe it's time we did so."

"He's crazy." Willi threw his hands in the air. I could see ink stains on his shirt cuffs.

"I'll take full responsibility. I don't expect you to do this, Willi, but I'm going to."

"Sophie, tell your brother he's lost his mind." Willi turned to her, his eyes wide.

Sophie was quiet as she studied me. "I don't think he's crazy. I think we should do it. I'll help you, Hans."

I grinned. Dear little Sophie, always so daring.

Willi shook his head again, adamant against it. "Hans, you can't make your sister do this, too. It's too dangerous."

"He's not making me do anything, Willi. I volunteered, and I never volunteer for things I don't have a passion for." Sophie bore her eyes into him.

Willi looked at Alex for help. "Talk some sense into them!"

Alex threw his hands up in surrender. "When a Scholl makes up their mind, it's set in stone, Willi, and when two Scholls set their mind on the same cause, no one can talk them out of it."

Willi sat down with a sigh, casting a nervous glance from me to Sophie. "Are you sure about this? It'll be broad daylight. There will be students everywhere."

"We'll go when everyone's at lectures. The corridors are empty then. I've already thought it through." I glanced at my friend. "The university will be ignited on Thursday, Willi. Mark my words."

christl

Christl and his oldest son, Michael, came for a visit the following morning. I was at once taken aback by how much the boy resembled him. Christl was in uniform while Michael wore a suit and tie. He had both arms wrapped around his father's neck and pressed his face against Christl's cheek.

Sophie was seated at the table poring over her studies, and she leaped up when they walked in. "Christl, we haven't seen you in ages! Just look at how big Michael has grown." She ruffled the boy's hair. "Why didn't you tell us you were in Munich?"

"I never know when I can get home," he said. "I'm stationed with my Luftwaffe unit in Innsbruck and only come to Munich when I can get leave."

"Sophie, would you put on the tea? There's also a bit of rum in the bottom cupboard that you might add to it," I said, sinking into a chair. "Oh, and some cookies for Michael. You don't like cookies, do you, Michael? Awful things, aren't they?" I winked at the boy.

Two and half year-old Michael grinned coyly, his dark brown eyes studying me. It seemed to me that he was trying to decide if I was a complete lunatic or just another dumb adult who didn't understand children. "I like cookies."

I ruffled the boy's head of brown curls. "I thought so."

"Aren't you sleeping at night?" Christl asked, sitting across from me with Michael perched on his knee.

I laughed and buried my face into my arms. "No." I had been up all last night trying to formulate the next leaflet but was constantly distracted by thoughts of Gisela. My hair stood on end, and I couldn't stop my constant yawning.

"Why not?"

I squinted up at him. The morning light shining through the windows was too much for my tired eyes. "Leaflet production, leaflet writing, can't stop thinking of the future and … Gisela."

"Hans, you need to get some rest," he said in his fatherly tone. I imagined it was the same voice he used when telling Michael it was bed time.

"I know, but there's so much to do."

"Look," Christl said, slapping his hand on the table. "I fully agree with your convictions and aims, but I saw Alex today, and he told me about the graffiti. What were you thinking? Not only is that foolish and dangerous, Hans, but it's completely adolescent."

"Think what you like." I shrugged, staring at the empty papers in front of me. I couldn't think of anything intelligent to write.

"Sorry." Christl leaned back in his chair. "I didn't come here to play father to you, although I am good at it." He cradled his son in his arms. "At least, I try to be."

"We're trying to create a better world for your boys to grow up in. We're doing what we think is right."

He nodded and tapped his fingers along the table. "And I thank you for it."

I motioned for Michael to come over to me. The toddler jumped off Christl's knee and hurried over, allowing me to lift him onto my lap. I pushed a piece of scrap paper in front of him and placed a pencil in his hand. Michael gripped the pencil and began scribbling lines all over my unreadable, mangled attempt at a leaflet. I glanced up at Christl with a sudden thought. "Christl?"

"Hmm?"

"We haven't included you in the leaflets out of safety for your family. But would you be willing to do something for the cause that wouldn't put you in immediate danger?"

He hesitated, staring at me with a perplexed visage. "What are you asking me, Hans?"

"To write an outline for the seventh leaflet ... something regarding the situation in Germany after our defeat at Stalingrad. You won't be involved in producing the leaflets or distributing them. Just the outline."

Christl heaved a sigh and ran a hand through his hair.

"Why me?"

"Because you have passion and the ability to change the world."

He shook his head with a modest grin. "Well, I'm not certain about that."

"You're too humble to even think it," I said over Michael's curly head.

"Just the outline?"

"Just the outline. You can pass it to my friend at the bookstore. I'll pick it up there. We won't be in contact. All would be completely safe for you."

The clock filled the momentary void of noise.

"I'll do it." His voice was firm with conviction. "It'll be good for me. It's been hard, Hans, not doing anything about all this." He leaned his chin into his hands. "I need an outlet."

I grinned, feeling certain that this leaflet was in the right hands. "Thank you. Germany thanks you." I paused a moment, then said, "Will you tell Herta?"

Christl peered out the window. "No. I can't worry her. She's in the final stages of her pregnancy and is so frail."

Sophie entered the room and set tea and cookies in front

of us. She joined us at the table and stole Michael off my lap. She pecked a kiss on his cheek as he swiped a cookie.

"What do you say, Michael?" Christl admonished.

Michael stuffed the cookie in his mouth. "I like cookies."

I met Sophie's gaze, and we suppressed our laughter as Christl remained stoic. Perhaps I wouldn't have made a good father. I'd have laughed at my children's every antic.

"Say thank you to Sophie." Christl urged him on. Michael just grinned sheepishly. Christl took a sip of tea, then picked up where we had left off in our conversation. "She's had enough worry over this sort of thing. Both her brothers had to escape Germany a few years past because the Gestapo was on to them. She doesn't know where they're living, or *if* they're living. She doesn't want our children to grow up with this corrupt regime, but to let her know … it would be too much on her."

"What's going on?" Sophie looked from Christl to me. "He's involved now?" She gaped at me. "Hans, he has a family."

Christl set a hand on her arm and cut in before I could say anything. "I'm not one to let others sway my decision, Sophie. If I honestly felt I shouldn't do this, I'd tell Hans no. We're old friends. I don't beat around the bush, and anyway, it's not as dangerous a job as you think. I'm simply writing the outline. That's all. I won't get caught." He stared across the table at Michael, love for his son burning in his eyes. "I can't."

beginning of the end

I pulled on my trousers, not bothering to slip my arms through the suspender straps. I glanced at my watch. Eight thirty. I had overslept. Blissful sleep was the only escape from the lurking fears and dangers ever present in the corners of my mind. I ran a hand over my eyes and breathed in deeply.

"Are you awake?" Sophie called from the kitchen.

I set my bare feet on the cold, wooden floorboards and shivered. "Barely." I stretched my arms over my head, yawned, and glanced at the calendar hanging on my wall. *Thursday, February 18th.*

I pulled back the blackout curtains and squinted as morning light warmed my face. It cast itself on my bookshelf and brought out the vivid colors of the French Impressionist paintings tacked to my walls. I kneeled beside my bed and searched for my briefcase and suitcase, which homed the leaflets. I carried both into the kitchen where Sophie was sitting at the table, spreading jam over a slice of toast. She was still in her nightclothes, and her dark hair was pulled back haphazardly.

"Your hair," she laughed when I stumbled in. "Hans, run a comb through it."

I mumbled something inaudible as I set the bags down, then sank into a chair across from her. My stomach flipped with hunger, yet the thought of eating made me sick.

"Didn't you sleep?" Sophie asked.

"Yeah, I did." I rubbed my face. "I just wish I could have stayed asleep longer. I'm safe then."

"Do you think we shouldn't do this?" Sophie questioned, placing the butter knife atop the jam jar.

"No, I didn't say that. I wholeheartedly think we should do this, but I suppose I'm more nervous this morning than I was last night about the whole ordeal." I smiled sheepishly.

She smiled back, pushing a strand of hair behind her ear. "Hungry?"

"Not really." I began unrolling my shirt sleeves and buttoning the cuffs. "We need to get to the university. Are you almost ready?"

She sliced through the toast with a butter knife and handed half to me. "You can't carry out treasonous acts without having your breakfast."

I hesitated, then gave in and grabbed the toast. "I suppose you're right." It tasted bland to me, and I wished I hadn't taken it.

"I had a dream last night, Hans," Sophie said as she brushed the toast crumbs onto her plate. "I dreamt that the Gestapo caught us."

"It was just a bad dream," I consoled her, tossing the remainder of toast on her plate. "Do you know how many times I've dreamt that same thing? Try not to worry."

"I won't. I'm more worried about you. Since when don't you eat breakfast?"

"I just don't feel like eating."

She shrugged her shoulders as she disappeared into her room to get dressed. I slipped my arms through the suspender straps and combed my hair back with Brylcreem. My hands were trembling as I raised a damp cloth to my face. I swallowed, took a shaking breath, then set the cloth back down.

Have a strong spirit and a gentle heart.

I buried my hands into my pockets to keep the trembling at bay as I sauntered into the hallway. We got ready in complete silence. I plunged my arms through my overcoat, then wrapped a black scarf around my neck a bit too tightly. I quickly loosened it.

It felt like a noose.

The clock sounded behind us, reminding me that time wouldn't wait for us. I adjusted the collar of my tan overcoat as I cleared my throat. The suitcase full of leaflets sat at my feet. Sophie yanked on a pair of red mittens and glanced up at me. We stood there in silence, staring at each other. Sophie's brown eyes were wide and alert, but no hint of fear was evident in them. She grinned at me, her eyes crinkling.

"Well, how do we look? Like treasonous criminals?" Her face beamed. "Hans, I thought I told you to comb your hair."

"I did."

She shook her head as if I were a hopeless case, swiping a hand over my hair. I felt a wave of nauseating fear pass over me, eating away at my insides until I felt I might be ill. I wrapped my arms around her as she linked her arms around my neck. We embraced for a long moment, our hearts pounding. There had been a moment in our past when I had felt an equally overwhelming fear for her safety.

The snow crunched under our feet. We knew the pathways that led to the mountain pass—could make it in good time. We charged up the mountain, legs burning from the exertion.

"Sophie?"

She had disappeared, vanished off into the snow-laden twilight. "Sophie, you better come out now or you'll be sorry. Sophie!"

I continued calling her name as I hiked along a path of thick pine trees. I wouldn't admit to anyone how frightened I was when I noted her absence. The mountains had been known to consume people in their large embrace. She could be lost for days. That's when I spotted her footprints in the snow to the left of me, leading all the way to a thick tree trunk.

"Sophie," I dragged her name out threateningly. The tree branches were frosted with thick snow, and snowflakes tumbled from the sky. When I looked up, she was peering down at me with a broad smile spread across her face.

"You're impossible." I said, trying to sound annoyed, but only coming across as amused.

"I know." Sophie swung down from the tree limb and landed in a heap beside me. She let out a little sigh. "Hans, I think I twisted my ankle," she said matter-of-factly.

"Sophie." I was scolding her now. "Mother will be furious."

"It's not my fault."

"Yes, it is."

"I'll be all right. We can still hike. I'll just lean against a stick. Can you find me one?"

"No. I'm carrying you home." *I leaned down and lifted her small frame into my arms. Her legs dangled off my forearms, and her arms were linked around my neck.*

"I can walk, Hans. Let me walk."

"No."

"I'm not a damsel in distress. I can do things myself, you know."

"Yes, I know." *But I didn't let her down. I carried her all the way back down the mountain, through the roads leading into town, then back toward the Ulm Cathedral which was adjacent to our home. I pushed open the door, the warmth seizing us. I gently set Sophie down and helped take off her snow-covered coat.*

"You didn't have to carry me all that way," *she said. I could sense that her pride was wounded.*

"No, I didn't, but I'm your brother. I have to take care of you, no matter how stubborn you are."

I wasn't taking care of her now. I was allowing her to dive head first into danger with me. The thought struck me like a bullet to the heart.

"Are you scared, Sophie?" I whispered into her ear.

"No, Hans. Jesus is with us."

I pulled back and looked into her face. She was calm and collected. I picked up my briefcase and ruffled her hair like I used to when we were younger. "Well, let's go."

She nodded, suitcase clasped in her red mittens.

danger

Sophie and I walked alongside each other, saying nothing as

we headed down the familiar tree-canopied streets to the university. Our footfalls sounded against the gritty brick road as a cool breeze stroked our faces. I tucked my chin into my scarf and watched my feet move involuntarily. I was in a dreamlike state. Buildings hovered over us on all sides, each bearing swastika flags that snapped in the wind. Bells jingled from the door of the apothecary shop as someone stepped in, while the sign in the butcher shop flipped to *open*. The sight of skeletal remains of houses intermixed with businesses was an everyday occurrence now, along with the weeping women who searched the rubble with soot and tears covering their faces. Life went on all around us. People shopped and tried to forget what was happening, to block out the realities of war.

I lifted my eyes to the sun and squinted. How strange that the sun could go on shining with all its brilliance while humans were in bondage and despair under its cheerful rays. Civilians passed us on bikes, ringing their bells to warn us to get out of their way. We passed the medieval structures of the university and passed the fountains, water bubbling from them in a peaceful cadence. The steady flow was an antithesis to my restless heart. We hastened through the broad pillars which stood like sentries outside the glass doors. I held the door open for Sophie, then we climbed up the stairs, eyes alert as we entered the main hall. It was empty, just as I had planned. The expansive arches gave me a clear view of the second floor which was basked in morning light from the skylight. I nodded my head toward the staircase to our right. Sophie followed, composed and silent.

My heart gave a chilling leap when I heard footsteps above me. My eyes flashed forward and met with Willi's. Next to him stood Traute with a stack of books cradled in her arms.

"Good morning," she said, eyeing our bags.

I willed my mind to focus and stay alert. I inclined my

head. "Good morning. Where are you two going? Aren't you supposed to be at your lectures?"

"We left early, so we could reach the nerve clinic in time." Willi pulled on Traute's arm. "We better be off, or we'll be late." Our eyes met. "See you both later."

I climbed on, glancing over my shoulder. Willi and Traute had slipped out of the glass doors and were dashing across the street, their coats billowing in the wind. We were on the second floor now, beams of sunlight illuminating the white pillars and statues below us which seemed to be watching our every move. The wooden doors to the lecture rooms were closed, and I could hear the muffled voices of Professors lecturing to their students. I stopped walking, clenched my jaw, and cast a cautious look around.

Fellow Fighters in the Resistance!

Shaken and broken, our people behold the loss of the men of Stalingrad. Three hundred and thirty thousand German men have been senselessly and irresponsibly driven to death and destruction by the inspired strategy of our World War I Private First Class. Führer, we thank you! The German people are in ferment. Will we continue to entrust the fate of our armies to a dilettante? Do we want to sacrifice the rest of German youth to the base ambitions of a Party clique? No, never! The day of reckoning has come—the reckoning of German youth with the most abominable tyrant our people have ever been forced to endure. In the name of German youth we demand restitution by Adolf Hitler's state of our personal freedom, the most precious treasure we have, out of which he has swindled us in the most miserable way.

I was on my knees in the next instant, unlatching the suitcase and withdrawing a stack of leaflets. I handed a batch to Sophie without saying a word, then we separated.

We grew up in a state in which all free expression of opinion is unscrupulously suppressed. The Hitler Youth, the SA, the SS have tried to drug us, to revolutionize us, to regiment us in the most promising young years of our lives. "Philosophical training" is the name given to the despicable method by which our budding intellectual development is muffled in a fog of empty phrases. A system of selection of leaders at once unimaginably devilish and narrow-minded trains up its future party bigwigs in the "Castles of the Knightly Order" to become Godless, impudent, and conscienceless exploiters and executioners—blind, stupid hangers-on of the Führer. We "Intellectual Workers" are the ones who should put obstacles in the path of this caste of overlords.

I tossed piles of leaflets along the perimeter of the walls and outside the lecture doors, each pile situated few feet away from the next. My throat went dry as I set a handful on a windowsill, then darted down a flight of stairs where I met Sophie. She stooped down and opened her suitcase as I kept watch, my knee bouncing as I anxiously peered around. We placed stacks of leaflets across the stairs. *Keep moving, keep moving, keep moving.* My nerves were on edge.

For us there is but one slogan: fight against the party! Get out of the party organization, which are used to keep our mouths sealed and hold us in political bondage! Get out of the lecture rooms of the SS corporals and sergeants and the party bootlickers! We want genuine learning and real freedom of opinion. No threat can terrorize us, not even the shutting down of the institutions of higher learning. This is the struggle of each and every one of us for our future, our freedom, and our honor under a regime conscious of its moral responsibility.
Freedom and honor! For ten long years Hitler and his

coadjutor have manhandled, squeezed, twisted, and debased these two splendid German words to the point of nausea, as only dilettantes can, casting the highest values of a nation before swine. They have sufficiently demonstrated in the ten years of destruction of all material and intellectual freedom, of all moral substance among the German people, what they understand by freedom and honor. The frightful bloodbath has opened the eyes of even the stupidest German—it is a slaughter which they arranged in the name of "freedom and honor of the German nation" throughout Europe, and which they daily start anew.

Working across from each other on the ground floor, Sophie and I set leaflets before each pillar. We met in the middle of the entryway and shared a silent glance before adorning the foot of the statues.

"Let's go." The hem of my trench coat rippled as I turned toward the door. Sophie grabbed my arm.

"There's still more, Hans."

"What?"

She looked down at the suitcase in her hands. My heart was pounding hard, sending pain racking throughout my entire body. I glanced at my watch, then swept my eyes over the entryway. I hesitated, then gave in.

"We have a few minutes before lectures end." I ran up the staircase toward the high gallery, Sophie on my heels.

The name of Germany is dishonored for all time if German youth does not finally rise, take revenge, and atone, smash its tormentors, and set up a new Europe of the spirit. Students! The German people look to us. As in 1813 the people expected us to shake off the Napoleonic yoke, so in 1943 they look to us to break the National Socialist terror through the power of the spirit. Beresina and Stalingrad are burning in the East. The dead of Stalingrad implore us to take action.

"Up, up, my people, let smoke and flame be our sign!"

Through the archways I could see the large corridor below, polished and bright. Sophie unlatched her suitcase behind the cover of a pillar. I shifted from one foot to the other. Sophie handed me a bundle, and I placed them on the marble surface of the banister, then again on the floors outside lecture doors.

Our people stand ready to rebel against the National Socialist enslavement of Europe in a fervent new breakthrough of freedom and honor.

The bell rang throughout the university, vibrating in my bones. I picked up the suitcase, brushing against Sophie's shoulder. "We need to go."

She looked at me, then at the lecture doors that would soon open and release a sea of students. Her hand landed on the stack of leaflets sitting on the banister. What was she doing? I was just about to grab her arm when she slid her palm across the stack, sprawling the papers throughout the air. I watched as they fluttered down to the corridor floor, a tempest of truth. Sophie hooked a tendril of hair behind her ears calmly, then strolled down the stairs. We lost ourselves in the mass of students bustling out of lectures. Their chatter drowned out the pulse pounding in my ears. I felt a shiver of satisfaction travel through me when the students paused and began picking up the leaflets that were strewn across the floor. I gave Sophie a small grin.

I had just begun to relax and breath normally again when one of the students up ahead shouted, "The doors are all locked. What's going on?" Students gathered around, peering at each other curiously. Dread marred my momentary calm.

"You are under arrest!"

Those four words sliced into my chest like a knife. I continued down the stairs, now understanding why the doors had been hastily locked. I pretended that I didn't hear. Sophie saddled up beside me, our arms brushing against each other.

"Stop them!" Someone grabbed my sleeve and viciously tugged me back. The man was stout and short with a bulldog face and anger-inflamed eyes. "You're under arrest." Spit flew from his mouth as he yanked on my arm again. His breath smelled sour.

I didn't attempt to escape from his grasp. It would only make me appear guilty. I wasn't about to confess anything. I would fight this with all I had in me.

"What's going on? Get your hands off me." I challenged his stare.

"I saw you." The man was trembling with nervous excitement. The reward money for napping "traitors" causes neighbors to turn against each other and not care about their fellow man anymore, only money. I don't understand how they can live with themselves.

The man held a leaflet in his burly hands and waved it in my face. "You threw them."

"I threw them," Sophie pushed forward, her confession crushing my heart.

This can't be happening.

"You're both coming with me." He gripped Sophie's arm in his other hand and prodded us upstairs, cursing and rambling on about disgusting traitors in his midst. He threw the door open to the office of Dr. Walther Wüst. It smelled of cigar smoke and paper. The man shoved us in and slammed the door behind us. He wiped his hands on his shirt as if we were contaminated.

"Well done, Schmid. You have notified the Gestapo?" Dr. Wüst stood up to his full height. His SS pin with the death's head insignia glinted in the afternoon light.

"They're on their way," Schmid said, his face red with outrage as he stared at us.

Along with your reward, you bastard.

"Sit," Dr. Wüst ordered us. His soulless eyes studied us from across the room. I sat on the wooden bench, Sophie close at my side. Our shoes grazed against each other's. The only sound was the ticking of the clock behind Dr. Wüst's desk. I stared out the window that overlooked the busy streets of Munich. People went on with their day. How could life be seemingly normal outside the window while my life had been suddenly thrown into a deadly upheaval? It seemed strange to me.

A sharp pain traveled through my chest, weighing on me like a heavy stone. Christl's draft of the seventh leaflet was in the inside pocket of my overcoat. I started to reach for it, then caught the hawk-like glares coming from the doctor and Schmid. I dropped my hands and glanced out of the corner of my eye at Sophie. Her back was straight as a rod, her eyes forward. She clasped her hands together tightly in her lap in a prim and proper air. She didn't appear frightened or even a slight bit upset. She held herself with grace. I beamed at her fortitude.

"What are you grinning about?" Schmid's grating voice filled the room.

"Nothing."

Schmid sniffed indignantly and pointed a fat finger at me. "It's people like you who threaten our glorious Reich. We'll be better off without you."

I shrugged my shoulders, feigning indifference.

Perhaps they won't believe Schmid ... we might have a chance ... Christl's leaflet must be destroyed before ...

The office door flew open, bringing in the Gestapo agents clothed in black trench coats and fedoras. The sound of their boots thumping across the floor brought my wandering thoughts to an abrupt halt. A tall, middle-aged man with dark hair and a clean-shaven face towered over us, arms behind his back. He eyed us for a long moment. I stared back.

I heard Dr. Wüst whisper to Schmid, "It's Robert Mohr, head of Secret State Police. He'll take care of the traitors. They'll be sorry."

"Papers," Mohr's deep, commanding voice was a contrast to Schmid's irritating tone.

I reached into my coat pocket and withdrew my identification. I held it out, and Mohr snatched it with a condescending glare at me. Sophie presented hers, and Mohr held them both, looking from one to the other.

"Hans Fritz Scholl. Born September 22nd, 1918. Sophie Magdalena Scholl. Born May 9th, 1921." He lifted his eyes.

"Are you brother and sister?"

"Yes," Sophie and I said in unison.

Robert Mohr turned to converse with the others gathered. *Now or never.*

I leaned forward and twined my arms around my middle. The doctor and Schmid were going over papers with the agents and speaking in hushed tones. My fingers searched inside my pocket and landed on the handwritten leaflet. I dug my fingernails into the top. Slowly I began ripping the leaflet into tiny shreds and littering them on the floor. I ground them under my boot and pushed the pieces underneath the bench.

My throat tightened as Robert Mohr glanced over his shoulder. He nodded to his agents who stormed over and gripped both my arms, pulling me to my feet. Three fourths of the leaflet were still in my pocket. I had to dispose of it.

Now.

In one quick motion I seized the leaflet and began tearing it to bits. The open window was only a foot away. I flicked my arm away from one tall agent and made a move to throw it out onto the street below. The agent grabbed my wrist with a curse. My mind was racing, adrenaline coursing through my body. If this leaflet wasn't disposed of, it would be the end of not only Sophie and myself, but Christl. I viciously wrenched my other arm away from the distracted agent and grabbed the leaflet from my other hand. I stuffed it in my mouth. The taste of ink and paper nearly caused me to gag.

"Spit it out!" An agent slapped my back with so much force that I stumbled forward. The second agent grabbed my face between his thick hands while the third wrenched open my mouth and pulled the leaflet out. Schmid was on the floor, scooping up the pieces of the leaflet in a frantic whirlwind.

"It was given to me by a student. I don't know what its contents are, but I was afraid they may be incriminating." I said with as much calmness as I could muster.

Robert Mohr motioned for his agents to handcuff us, while his steel eyes studied me. I cringed as the cold iron clasps cinched around my wrists. I turned my head to look at Sophie. Her countenance was composed and peaceful as they handcuffed her. I offered her a reassuring smile, for what could we do now except be calm and confident?

It was our only hope of surviving.

The image of my fellow students all meshed together as I descended the steps, arms wrenched backward and arms held firmly by the two Gestapo agents. I willed my eyes to stay focused on the door ahead of us, to not look at any of the students. But there were a pair of eyes I longed to gaze into.

Gisela.

I could see her out of the corner of my eyes. Her head was bent down, and she was staring intently at the floor. Her hands were clasped together in front of her. As I was whisked by, I leaned down to her. "Tell Alex not to wait for me." That earned me a painful shove from the agents.

I earnestly hoped that Sophie and I had somehow inspired the students who were witnessing this. Maybe they would see how ludicrous a state we lived in where an individual couldn't even share his opinions without being arrested. The Gestapo was hoping an entirely different thing, I'm certain. They hoped they were breeding fear into the minds of these young people. But I wouldn't let them conquer me. I kept my gait and countenance calm and confident as if nothing was wrong in the least. As if being arrested was an easy task. But as soon as I was pushed through the large entrance doors and out into the street, fear seized me. Alex, Willi, Christl, Professor Huber—they all must be warned. But how? The sun warmed my face and soothed my troubling thoughts for a blissful second.

There is always hope. There is always God.

A black Gestapo car was parked outside the university. It was polished so carefully that I could see my reflection. An agent threw open the door and pushed my head down as he shoved me in. Sophie was stuffed in after me followed by the tall, husky agent. We were packed in so tightly that our arms and legs were pressed against each other. The instant the door was shut, the driver slammed on the gas pedal, and the car went speeding down the street. I swallowed against a pain that gripped my throat as we passed the street along which Sophie and I had just recently walked.

How fast our circumstances had changed.

I could hear Sophie's uneven breathing, but when I looked at her, she was gazing out of the side window with an indifferent air, as if she were taking a Sunday drive. She didn't seem as affected by the handcuffs as I was. My arms ached, and I couldn't find a comfortable position to sit in. I laughed bitterly to myself.

That's my biggest concern?

"Sophie—" I began to whisper.

The agent beside her leaned forward. "Silence!"

Sophie turned her face toward me. Her eyes conveyed peace.

I breathed deeply as the car turned a corner, and the Wittelsbach Palace—the dreaded Gestapo headquarters—came into view.

interrogation

Panic racked me as I realized that Sophie and I were being separated. She was dragged toward a doorway ahead of me, but she turned one last time to meet my gaze. For the first time that day I caught a longing in her eyes that seemed to beg, *Help me.* But what could I do? *Investigator Anton Mahler.* I read the nameplate on the door as I was shoved inside an office.

"Sit." The agent motioned toward a bench. I sat down and leaned forward, keeping my eyes fixed on the window opposite me. The sky continued to beam a brilliant blue, and I spotted a bird diving through the sky. Free. Not a care in the world. There was a door leading into another office to my right. A red light suddenly flickered on beside it, and the agent clasped my arm once again and led me into the adjoining room. It was wrapped in dark shadows. If the Gestapo was trying to depress its prisoners by sheer lack of light, they were doing an exceptionally good job. A mahogany desk stood in the center of a maroon rug. A small window was smothered with thick black curtains. Behind the desk sat a man with a narrow face and callous eyes staring back at me behind round spectacles. His fingers were arched under his chin.

He nodded toward the chair then at the agent, giving him permission to take his leave. I sat down, resolving to be calm and collected and to mislead the investigator by my complete ease. That was easier said than done.

Mahler shuffled through his papers. He grabbed a pen, tested it, then set his eyes on me. "Name?"

"Hans Fritz Scholl." My voice sounded gravelly. I cleared my throat.

"Occupation?"

"I'm a medical student at the University of Munich." I sat

straight in the chair.

"Date of birth?

"September 22nd, 1918."

"Residence?"

"I reside in Munich on Franz-Josef-Strasse."

"Citizenship?"

"I'm a citizen of the German Reich."

Mahler paused from his writing and studied me. I exhaled and let my eyes wander on the curtained window as if I was entirely bored of this conversation.

"Religion?" Mahler went on.

"I'm Lutheran."

"Are your parents of German blood?"

"Of course."

"Are your grandparents of German blood?"

"Yes."

"Marital status?"

"I'm single."

"First and last name of your father?"

"Robert Scholl."

"His occupation?"

"He's a business adviser in Ulm."

"First name and maiden name of your mother?" "Magdalena Scholl. Her maiden name is Müller."

"You served in the Reich Labor Service?

"Yes, I joined the Reich Labor Service in the spring of '37. I served for seven months."

Mahler took another pause and lit a cigarette while I let my eyes wander about the room again.

"Am I boring you, Scholl?" Mahler snapped.

I tore my eyes from the ceiling and back to the face of my investigator.

Stay calm.

"I find this all unnecessary. While I'm sitting here, the person who distributed those leaflets could be crossing the border by now."

"So, you deny any involvement with the leaflets?"

"Yes, I deny it."

Mahler cleared his throat and continued with his questions, ignoring my statement. He didn't believe me. "How long have you been a member of the National Socialist German Workers' Party?"

"I joined the Hitler Youth in March of '33. I was promoted to squad leader a few years later. My brother was also a member of the Hitler Youth, and my sisters were members of the League of German Girls, but I am not currently a member of the National Socialist German Workers' Party."

"Not currently a member?" Mahler scoffed as he penned my answer down. "Military service?"

"In November of '37, I volunteered and joined a cavalry regiment. I was then furloughed to the school of the medical corps for six months. In April of '41, I was drafted into the student company in Munich. I have the rank of Sergeant."

"Prior convictions?"

"I have no prior convictions."

"Tell me who else was involved with these leaflets, Scholl."

I stared at him. "I deny any involvement with the leaflets."

Mahler set his pencil down and bore his eyes into me, as if his sharp look could bring the truth out of my mouth. "You were caught with a draft of a leaflet in your possession and attempted to destroy the evidence."

"A student thrust it on me, and I suspected it to be dangerous. That's why I tried to destroy it. My sister and I had nothing to do with the leaflets." I leaned back into the leather chair and ran my fingers along the arms.

"You are required to tell the truth, Scholl," Mahler slammed his fist onto the table. "Tell the truth."

"I just did."

I risked a glance up, wondering how Mahler was taking this. He took out a cigarette, lit it, and took a drag. "Recount your morning to me."

"I woke up, ate breakfast, then left my apartment around, oh, half past ten. My sister walked with me to the university, and I'm not sure of the exact time we got there. I wasn't planning on attending lectures because I'm studying for my boards."

"Why were you at the university if you weren't attending any lectures?" Mahler positioned his cigarette between his thumb and index finger, running his thumb nail across his lips.

"I was meeting my girlfriend there."

"What's her name?"

I swallowed hard. "Gisela Schertling."

Mahler's pen moved furiously. "What are her political views?"

I had to keep her safe. I dropped my gaze. "Her father is the editor of a National Socialist newspaper. I'm sure you've heard of it. If I recall correctly, it's called *Pössnecker Newspaper*, but I wouldn't know because I don't read it. Gisela is sympathetic to National Socialism."

"Who do you associate with on a daily basis, Scholl?"

To feign that I didn't know Alex, Willi, or Christl could be dangerous. The Gestapo undoubtedly knew who I associated with if they had been watching me, and trying to cover it up would be a telltale sign of guilt. I was certain that the most prudent course of action was to be open and honest ... to a point.

"I'm acquainted with many people in the student company. Alexander Schmorell for instance."

"Another man by the name of 'Willi' also associates with you. Isn't that true?"

"Wilhelm Graf? I only see him very rarely."

"When did you last see him?"

"We accidentally ran into each other on Ludwig Street the other day." That was true. No need to mention I saw him a mere hour ago.

"What did the suitcase contain that you were carrying today, Scholl?" Mahler tapped the pen on the table.

"It was empty."

"Why on earth were you dragging an empty suitcase around the university?" He raised a brow questioningly.

"My sister wanted to catch the express train that left around 12:28. She was going to visit our parents in Ulm."

"Why was your sister traveling with an *empty* suitcase?"

"Sophie should answer this. I wasn't the one traveling."

"You are required to give an explanation"

I leaned forward. "She most likely intended to fetch clean towels, sheets, jam—maybe even a half a liter of schnapps to bring back with her. I don't know."

Mahler stared at me. "Schnapps?"

I shrugged.

"What was in your briefcase?"

The lies were springing from my mouth without much thought. "My briefcase was empty. I was planning on buying clay pipes today."

"Where did you go inside the university?"

"My sister and I walked around the corridors, and we also went to the third floor."

"Did you see leaflets in the university?"

"We went to the second floor where I saw cleaning ladies gathering up leaflets."

Mahler paused and took another drag on his cigarette, eyeing me as if he knew all. His stare unsettled me. "It is well-known that you have expressed to numerous people that National Socialism should be replaced by Christian Democracy. Is this a true statement?"

What had this to do with the leaflets? I shifted in my seat.

"I don't have to answer. That has nothing to do with the

matter at hand."

Mahler tensed, anger flashing across his face. "Schmid said that he encountered you and your sister immediately after the leaflets were thrown from the third floor, but you claimed to have seen them for the first time on the *second* floor."

"After I saw the leaflets on the stairs to the second floor, my sister and I strolled around the university. We were bored, so we went up to the third floor as we waited until the lectures in the philosophical institute lecture hall finished. I was waiting for my girlfriend, as you recall me stating before."

"Where else did you see the leaflets inside the university?"

"As I was walking along the third floor, I noticed a pile of leaflets. Then I heard a loud noise as they fell. Someone must have tossed a stack of leaflets over the banister at that exact moment, but I didn't do it. I'm not sure if my sister threw them. If Sophie was the one who did this, I could understand that for practical jokes are typical of her. I didn't have a chance to ask her about it because Schmid detained us and put us under arrest moments later."

"There is reason to believe that *you* brought the leaflets to the university in the suitcase and threw them from the third floor. Do you not wish to make a true statement, Scholl?" Mahler challenged.

"I carried this suitcase from my apartment until I was apprehended by Schmid. It was empty the entire time."

Mahler leaned back, his eyes still fixed on me as he picked up the phone and mumbled, "We're finished for now." An agent arrived promptly and escorted me out of the room.

prison

"I'm here, so you don't kill yourself."

Those were the first words I heard as I was shoved into the Gestapo prison. Two cots leaned against the walls, one on each side of the room. A small desk was situated at the foot of the left cot where a teenaged boy sat. He pulled off his reading glasses.

I stared at him blankly. "And why would I kill myself?"

The boy shrugged. "All I know is that they don't want you dead ... yet. They want to squeeze a confession out of you. I have to keep an eye on you and see to it that you don't kill yourself first."

He didn't have to worry about that. That was the furthest thing from my mind. "That would be an insult to God." I sank onto my cot with a heavy sigh. I was overcome by exhaustion.

The boy nodded. "Well, that makes my job considerably easier then." He was tan and thin—a farmer most likely.

"What's your name?" I asked.

"Helmut Fietz. You're Hans Scholl, or so they tell me."

"That's me. Why are you here?" I began taking off my boots.

"So you don't—"

"Yeah, I know." I held up a hand. "I mean, are you a prisoner yourself? What have you done?"

"Oh," Helmut straightened his shoulders. "I was arrested because someone heard me comparing Hitler to a brainless, ugly pig I have back home. In my defense, it was a good comparison. The man who reported me to the Gestapo didn't think so."

I smiled as I fell back onto my cot. "I'm glad to have you for company, Helmut."

"Yeah? Well, that's good I guess, seeing as we haven't

much choice. So, why are you in here?"

"Charged with writing and distributing anti-Nazi leaflets."

Helmut gave a low whistle. "Dangerous stuff. Did you do it?"

I closed my eyes. The coldness seeping through the walls seemed to penetrate my bones, making them ache. Or was it fear that caused my limbs to freeze?

"Never mind. You don't have to tell me. How was the first interrogation?" He said it so matter-of-factly, as if he were asking me how my first day of university went.

"I had a coherent, reasonable answer for everything they asked me." I folded my arms behind my head.

"They have a way of finding things out, you know."

I opened my eyes and squinted over at him. "What an encouraging statement."

"Sorry," Helmut shrugged. "I suppose that wasn't the right thing to say."

The cell was lit up by a bright white light above us even though night had fallen. I could see the moon through the small window. "Why don't they turn off the lights?" I asked.

Helmut didn't look at me as he answered. He was writing something in a notebook. "The light means that the prisoner in this cell is a death candidate."

I turned over and covered my face with the lumpy pillow to block out the condemning light. I wondered how Sophie was doing … if she was scared … if she regretted what she had done. I tried not to think, just pray as I stared at the wall. Isolation and despair washed over me. There was no way to contact anyone outside these prison walls.

No way to warn them.

second interrogation

"Have you purchased large quantities of postage stamps recently? If so, where and how many did you purchase?"

I blinked, trying to stay awake and coherent so as not to succumb to stupidity and give everything away. It was early, not even sunrise yet. Or was it? I couldn't be sure. The curtains were drawn, and the room was cloaked in dismal hues of black and grey. I hadn't slept. Between the cold, the condemning light, Helmut's snoring, and my own thoughts, I estimated I slept for only an hour or two.

"I've never purchased large quantities of postage stamps, except for a few days ago when I purchased ten stamps at the post office near Danziger Freiheit Plaza. I used these stamps to mail letters to friends and my mother. The rest of the stamps must have been used by my sister, or perhaps are still in my apartment."

"Can you use a typewriter?"

I rubbed at a wrinkle in my trousers. "I can ... somewhat. My father has always owned typewriters, which I have been using here and there for the past ten years, and I also have access to my landlady's typewriter. I type on that typewriter very rarely and use it mainly for impersonal letters. The letters I mentioned previously I wrote by hand."

"Do you own or have you owned large quantities of paper?"

I noticed that a woman sat in the corner of the room now, typing my statements. "No. My parents send me the amount of paper I need."

"In the last couple of years, have you purchased or acquired large quantities of envelopes?"

"I receive envelopes from home as well. My father has connections to a stationery store in Ulm and gives me a folder of such things at Christmastime."

"Do you own a duplicating machine or have use of one?"

"No, I don't own a duplicating machine. I've never duplicated any documents before."

"Today after having been taken into custody, have you spoken with any of your acquaintances? If so, what did you talk about?"

I remembered Gisela's downcast eyes. "Yes, as I was being taken out of the university, I saw my girlfriend, Gisela Schertling. Like all the other students, she had to wait in the university until it was unlocked. I told her to tell Alexander Schmorell not to wait for me. I was sure he would be waiting in my apartment. He comes over nearly every day around noon, but there was no particular purpose for our meeting today. I just didn't want him waiting around."

"Does Alexander Schmorell own a typewriter or has he ever brought a typewriter to your apartment?" Mahler narrowed his eyes at me.

"Not to my knowledge. I can't remember a time when he brought a typewriter to my apartment."

"Have you used a typewriter to type any reports or essays?" "No."

Mahler's eyes flashed with pleasure, as if he hit on something. He did. "Your sister made a different statement. Which one of you is lying?"

My throat tightened. "I won't believe Sophie made that statement without hearing her say it."

A door in the corner of the room near the typist opened, and I turned my attention toward the sudden streak of light. I could see into the next interrogation room where Sophie sat. Our eyes met for a split second before the door closed.

"Mohr," Mahler breathed. "He's too soft." I realized then that Robert Mohr had opened the door so that Sophie and I could see with our own eyes that the other was all right. Mahler leaned back in his chair, taking another puff of his cigarette when the door opened from behind me. Mahler nodded at the secretary who handed him a sheet of paper. I watched as Mahler's eyes followed the words across the page, and his anger began to morph into something else—satisfaction. He glanced up at the secretary. "We're finished for now."

I stood as an agent entered the room and gripped my arm, leading me out of the office and back into the hallway. I tried to keep my eyes fixed ahead, to not stare at the others who were detained, but I couldn't help myself when another agent brushed past me, Gisela's arm in his grasp. I searched her face. She was pale, her blue eyes wide and her lips pressed tightly together. Regret coursed through me.

I should never have told her.

I tried not to think about what could happen—tried not to remember the satisfaction on Mahler's face. Something had been brought to the surface, and I had a painful hunch of what it was.

Gisela and I shared one last glance.

oh life! oh living!

"What happened?" Helmut met me at the cell door. I sank onto the cot, covering my face with my trembling hands.

"He's getting so close. I don't know how much longer this can go on." I had given up hiding the truth from Helmut when I was certain he wasn't set there as a trap. I trusted him.

"Maybe they won't find out. Just stay calm, and you'll mislead them."

"But for how long, Helmut? I'm afraid he's broken through. His face today after he got that paper ..." I felt exhaustion press against me. "I need to sleep."

I drifted off into a deep sleep. My thoughts and cares momentarily vanished, but they were brought to the surface

again as the sound of a prison cell clanking open jolted me
from my sleep. I leaned on my elbow, listening. I heard the
guards shouting something, heard feet dragging against the
floor outside my cell. A grown man was crying, screaming,
pleading. I glanced at the cot across the room. Helmut was
staring at the ceiling. "Someone's being taken for execution."
He said. "They all cry like that."

I could still hear the man's screams echoing in the hallway. It made my stomach turn with dread. I covered my
body with a blanket, turning over to stare at the wall, resolving not to be led to my execution like that.

If I must die, I'll do it with dignity.

I couldn't drift back to sleep then. The sounds replayed in
my mind over and over again until I finally threw off my
blanket and sat up. I ran both hands through my hair as I
thought of Sophie. I wished I could see her again and tell her
that everything would be all right. I took quiet steps to the
chair leaning against the wall and climbed up on it. Grabbing
the two iron bars on the window, I pulled myself up to get a
glimpse of the evening scene. Clouds slowly drifted over the
full moon.

"'Is it still I, who there past all recognition burn? Memories I do not seize and bring inside. O life! O living! O to be
outside! And I in flames. And no one here who knows me.'"

Poetry helped me sort out my wandering thoughts. It was
a warm compress for my restless heart. I soaked it in—the
peaceful night, the poetry, knowing that I was still alive and
breathing. I began to feel better.

"What's that?" Helmut asked.

"Rilke."

Helmut didn't respond, and I thought he must have fallen
asleep again. I turned my gaze toward the stars, wondering
how they could bear to shine down on such a cruel world.

"'Do you remember still the falling stars that like swift
horses through the heavens raced and suddenly leaped across

the hurdles of our wishes—do you recall? And we did make so many! For there were countless numbers of stars: each time we looked above we were astounded by the swiftness of their daring play, while in our hearts we felt safe and secure watching these brilliant bodies disintegrate, knowing somehow we had survived their fall.'"

evidence

I rubbed my hands together, watching as Mahler tapped his pen on the table's surface. He knew something.

"Are you ready to tell the truth, Scholl?"

"I have told the truth." I waited.

Mahler sighed. "Why don't you just admit your fault? You committed treason against the Reich."

"I deny it."

"You deny it?" Mahler laughed.

I met his gaze. "That's correct."

Mahler took his time lighting a cigarette. He took a drag, then exhaled the smoke toward me. It stung my eyes, but still I remained stoic. Mahler opened the desk drawer and pulled out an envelope and a letter. A cold burst filled my stomach.

"One hundred forty stamps," declared Mahler, "were found in your apartment. Now, what would you be doing with that many stamps, Scholl?"

All the things I had told myself came crashing down around me. *They won't find out. Everything will be fine.* They were lies I had told myself to keep sane.

"This letter was also found in your apartment. It's from Christoph Probst. The writing matches the leaflet you tried to destroy. Why don't you give up and tell me the truth?"

My body felt numb, and I couldn't breathe. Nothing seemed real, tangible. What was there left to do now? The evidence was there. I could continue to deny it, but it would be futile. I suddenly felt weak, as if all my life and energy had been stolen from me.

A strong spirit and a gentle heart.

"Are you ready to confess?" Mahler's voice brought me back to reality.

I dropped my eyes to my hands, blinking back stinging tears when I realized what this meant. "Yes."

"Did you write and distribute these leaflets, Hans Scholl?"

A rush of pride and honor overtook me, and I lifted my gaze defiantly. "Yes, and I have no regrets. I knew what I took upon myself. I was prepared to lose my life by doing so."

another arrest

"There's been another arrest," Helmut said.

I was sitting on the cot, staring at the wide, blue sky. I dropped my gaze and turned to Helmut. "Do you know who it is?" My mind raced. "Is it Alex?"

"Christoph Probst. Do you know him?"

"Christl?" My voice broke, and I gripped the edge of my cot. I knew this was coming, but it still hurt like hell.

"You do know him, then. Was he involved with the leaflets, Hans?"

I swallowed and watched the shadows move across the floor. "It wasn't supposed to end like this, and yet, I suppose I always knew it would."

"Are you sorry you did it?"

The cot creaked as I covered my forehead with my hand.

"No, I'm not sorry. I took it upon myself, knowing the consequences. I don't regret it, but that doesn't make it easy … especially the arrest of Christl. He's a husband and a father. I've never seen a man more in love with his family—the way he shows off his boys and carries them on his shoulders for us to admire. His wife just gave birth to a daughter. Herta's still in the hospital and she's very ill." I swallowed hard. "I never wanted to get Christl involved, but we needed his ideas and words. To think we should all die because of our convictions and morals. It's not right, Helmut."

"How'd they find out he was involved?"

"It was a lapse in my memory. I had placed the outline of his leaflet in my coat pocket, intending to reproduce it at the studio as soon as I had the chance. Then I would destroy the handwritten leaflet. I didn't think about it when I put my coat on that morning. It wasn't until I sat in the office after Schmid turned us in that I remembered. The Gestapo found letters from Christl in my apartment. The handwriting was identical, and his identity was established instantly."

"Don't blame yourself, Hans."

"But I do!" I brought a fist down onto my cot. "I'm having trouble forgiving myself, Helmut."

"Maybe you should recite some of that poetry you're always saying in the evenings."

I glanced at Helmut. "Am I so loud?"

"It's all right. Remember, Hans, your friends didn't have to join you in this. You're all brave souls. I admire you each greatly."

"I admire them, too. I couldn't have done this without them … each of them. Christl won't be sentenced to death. He only wrote the outline, and there's no proof that we reproduced it. Alex and I were the only ones who ever saw it. I'm certain he'll get imprisonment, but then the war will be over soon. The Allies will be here in no more than eight weeks."

"You believe the invasion will be that soon?"

"Yes, but I don't expect to see it."

Silence hovered over us as the weight of my words struck me. The lock suddenly turned, and the cell door opened slowly. I sat up on my elbows, watching as a guard stepped in with food in his hands. "From your sister," he said, placing sausage, butter, rolls, cookies, and a few cigarettes on the table.

My eyes widened. "What? Where did Sophie come across this? And why—"

"Some of the prisoners and guards wanted to do something for your sister. She's become a favorite around here. She wanted to share it with you." The guard left the spread of food, then closed the door.

Helmut and I stared at the feast in awe. "Is your sister a queen or something?"

I laughed. "Something like that." I picked up a roll, ripped it apart and placed a piece of sausage in between the pieces. I took a bite, savoring the spices. "Go on, Helmut. There's enough for us both." "I wish I had a sister. I'm an only child," Helmut said, smothering butter on the roll.

"I have three."

"Three?" Helmut whistled. "That's a lot of sisters. Do you ever argue?"

I shrugged. "Not much. Though, Inge and I are only a year apart, and sometimes we'd snap at each other over stupid things when we were younger. Sophie and I got on fine most days, but it wasn't until she came to Munich that I realized how much we're alike."

"How did she find out about the leaflets?" Helmut asked between the roll in his mouth.

"She came across an underlined passage in a book I own. Those passages were in the leaflets which she had read that day. I kept it all a secret from her because I knew how dangerous this whole thing was. The thought of her getting involved was unthinkable … until she confronted me about it. She wanted to be a part of it. She's like that—determined and stubborn."

"Then it must be hard, having her this deeply involved."

I grabbed a cigarette as my eyes burned. "I didn't want this for her, Helmut. I wanted to protect her. I keep thinking about her as a little girl climbing trees, getting into trouble." I laughed to hide my emotions, but it wasn't working. I clenched my jaw to keep my tears at bay. "Damn this war."

"Maybe she'll only be given a prison sentence. Don't think the worst," Helmut said.

I lit the cigarette and shook my head. "I can't believe that, Helmut. I just can't."

indictment

"The Reich must be scared." My voice wavered as I held the indictment paper. I sank onto my cot, reading the verdict aloud to Helmut.

"'I herewith charge the following persons: Hans Fritz Scholl from Munich, born September 22, 1918 in Ingersheim, single, no prior convictions ... Sophie Magdalena Scholl from Munich, born May 9, 1921 in Forchtenberg, single, no prior convictions ... Christoph Hermann Probst from Aldrans near Innsbruck, born November 6, 1919 in Murnau, married, no prior convictions ... All are currently held in the prison located at State Police Headquarters in Munich. All are currently without defense counsel.

I herewith indict the above for jointly undertaking the following actions in Munich, Augsburg, Salzburg, Vienna, Stuttgart, and Linz in 1942 and 1943: Preliminary actions of high treason with intention of changing the constitution of the Reich by force. Actions included: Creating an organization for purposes of high treason. Attempting to render the army unfit for fulfillment of its duty to protect the German Reich against attacks from domestic or foreign elements. Influencing the masses by production and distribution of documents. Aiding and abetting the enemies of the Reich here at home and inflicting damage on the ability of the Reich to wage war, this during a time of crisis in the Reich. Seeking to publicly cripple and destroy the will of the German people for militaristic self-determination ...'"

I glanced up at Helmut. My skin went cold. "They must be scared if they accuse three young citizens of all these crimes against the Reich. I didn't realize that Hitler found me so dangerous." I tried to make light of it, if only to hide the pain I felt when reading 'high treason.' "This supposedly solid Third Reich who claims they will last one thousand years, the Reich who has taken over Europe, is quaking in their boots over *us*. Quite the tribute." My hands trembled as I folded the paper, swallowing hard. I set the indictment paper beside me. I buried my hands inside my pockets to stop the tremors.

"Maybe they'll only impose a prison sentence." But Helmut's face was pale, as if he had been the one to receive the indictment.

"No," I said, shaking my head with firm conviction. I brought my hands out, seeing that I had lost complete control over them. They trembled of their own free will. "We committed high treason, and they will treat us accordingly. They won't give us a way out. I think this will be hardest on my mother, harder even than it is for Sophie and myself. How can a woman bear to lose two children at once? And with my little brother off on the Russian front, my mother ... I just can't fathom what this will do to her." I ran my hand over the scratchy wool blanket, swallowing back the pain tearing at my throat.

"What about your father?"

"He'll understand, I think, more than mother."

"How?" Helmut stared at me, shaking his head. "How do you stay so calm, Hans?"

I lifted my gaze, feeling tears burn behind my eyes. "I could have been killed while on the Eastern Front, Helmut.

At least I'll be dying for a righteous cause this way."

"You're a soldier of the Wehrmacht. Perhaps you'll at least be granted death by firing squad." Helmut sank into his cot across the cell, raking a hand through his hair.

I leaned forward, staring at my shoes. "I don't think they'd even grant me that."

"Just listen to us!" Helmut scoffed, throwing his hands in the air. "You haven't been sentenced to death. There's still hope."

But I knew.

We all knew that death was coming.

dear mother and father

I opened my eyes, surprised to find myself strangely well rested. All those hours of interrogations had caught up with me, and I had slept them off with considerable ease. I felt alert and steady as I pulled back the blanket, my eyes searching for the sun outside the window. It sent streaks of light in, casting shadows of the iron bars across the floor. I jumped when the cell door clanged open and squinted up as a man stepped in. I recognized his face, which was a strange mixture of sternness and compassion, as if he hadn't quite made up his mind whether he was enraged or sympathetic toward us. It was Mohr.

"I've advised your sister to write her farewell letters now. You might as well do the same," he said.

"Now?" I stared at him. "But what about the trial?"

Mohr didn't answer me as he placed a few sheets of paper and a pencil on the desk.

I clenched my jaw as a deadly chill ran over me. "The entire trial, the defense lawyers … it's all a charade, isn't it? It doesn't mean anything. Our fate is already sealed."

"Get writing," was all that Mohr said. He turned and

walked off as the guards promptly closed the cell door behind him. I stared at the door for a long moment. Surely someone was strangling me. Why else was I battling for my breath?

"I told you," I said finally. "I told you, Helmut, that they want to kill us. They wanted to from the moment they arrested us, and they always get what they want. They murder those who get in their way."

Helmut didn't speak. He stared down at his hands. I felt a hot tear trail down my face.

Weakling.

I brought my sleeve across my eyes and leaned forward with a strangled gasp. "Oh, God!" I buried my face into my hands, trying to grasp what this all meant.

Death.

It hit me.

I was approaching my last moments on this earth. The realization tore through me then. The tears racked against my ribs, strangled my throat, burned my eyes. I scolded myself brutally. I wouldn't wallow away the precious moments left of my life in tears. I stood up, feeling the cell shift under my feet. I gripped the back of the chair and sank into it, running my fingers along the desk until they grasped the pencil. The blank paper stared back at me. How could I express everything that burned in my heart in a single letter?

I ran both hands over my face, finding them trembling once more. I wanted to scream, to let everything I was feeling out into the open. If Helmut hadn't been there, I might have, but I didn't want to scare the boy. I cleared my throat and took the pencil in my shaking hand.

Dear Mother and Father,

I beg for your forgiveness. I know my actions have caused you such pain that no parents should be forced to endure. I can't comprehend how hard this must be for you. Please know that Sophie and I didn't intend for our actions to wound you. We are considered traitors and condemned as such, but I believe that the future will justify our actions. Perhaps what we did will be approved of in the future. One can hope. Mother, father, how can I express my thanks for all the love I've received from you? You are ever patient, loving, full of goodness even when my younger self defied you and rebelled. Thank you for giving me life, and please don't be too grieved that I have to leave this earth so soon. What is death but coming home, being born anew? When I consider it that way, knowing that God is with me, I don't fear. Please know that Sophie and I couldn't have acted in any other way. I'm sure you understand.

Your loving son,

Hans

I folded the letter, slipped it into the envelope provided for me, and scribbled my parents address on the front ... the home I had spent my boyhood in ... the home I would never set foot in again.

"Prisoners are often given six to eight weeks before execution at Stadelheim. Perhaps a last-minute appeal can still be granted." Helmut offered me a scrap of hope.

"Perhaps."

He stood up and outstretched his hand to me. "I'm sorry it has to be like this," his voice broke. His eyes were red.

I shook his hand firmly. "That's why I did it, Helmut. To stop this."

I heard footsteps shuffling in the hall. They were coming back for me to take me to the trial. In a split second, I grabbed the pencil, leaned over the surface of the desk and wrote: *Allen gewalten zum trotz, sich erhalten*—despite all the powers, maintain yourself—on the white-washed wall. The message stirred something in my heart, caused me to feel an overpowering sense of courage and steadiness.

"To help those who come in after me," I explained to Helmut as he looked at the words. "And to help myself." I stared at the wall until the cell door opened.

the people's court

The sunlight burned my eyes as I was prodded outside. I tilted my face upward, soaking in its warmth. The streets hadn't changed. Nothing had changed. I had expected something to be different, years to have gone by. I couldn't understand how the world looked just the same after all I had been through. An agent yanked open the Gestapo car door, and I was shoved inside, Christl behind me. His face was drawn, pale, and his eyes bloodshot.

"I'm sorry, Christl," I whispered.

The agent between us viciously jabbed his elbow into me. "Be quiet."

I gritted my teeth. They couldn't extend even a small measure of mercy and allow us to speak to each other? I turned my face to the window, watching as the civilians hurried along the streets, eyeing the loathed Gestapo vehicle as it turned a corner.

"It's all right, Hans." I heard Christl's voice fill the car. "What we did was right."

A mile passed too swiftly as we neared the Palace of Justice. I inwardly scoffed. *Justice. The Nazis don't know the meaning of the word.*

"Out," ordered the agent.

I ducked and climbed out of the car, gazing up at the castle-like structure with a large dome extruding from its top. Sculptures were arched above the long windows and adorned the roof. I felt a sense of dread as the doors to the Palace of Justice opened, and I was escorted inside. Sophie was brought in behind us. Our eyes met for a split second. I hadn't seen her since that glimpse through the interrogation doors. She was erect and calm, her eyes ever alert. Her eyebrows were furrowed, the telltale sign that she was thinking. I knew the look well. Her lips were pressed together, but when our eyes met, they tipped up into a small grin. I hoped I looked as well as she did, but I couldn't be sure. I felt beaten, but still I tried to hold myself with dignity. We were handed over to guards now, who escorted us into the courtroom. I found it laughable that we were each flanked by two guards, as if we were dangerous criminals who would lash out at any given moment.

As the door opened into the courtroom, my eyes swept over the walnut paneled room. Hundreds of Nazi officers were seated, their eyes fixed on us. We were prodded toward a bench where we were released of the handcuffs. I rubbed my wrists that ached from the iron clasps. I glanced to my right, seeing Sophie lost in the bulk of her assigned guards. I leaned forward.

"How are you?" I asked her.

She looked at me, our eyes connecting. "Fine. Are you all right, Hans?"

"Of course."

"Silence!" The guards yanked us back.

I scanned the room, taking in the charade. Everyone in this room knew what our fate was, and yet, to make everything appear legal, they put on a grand show. Nazi banners were draped from the ceiling, and a portrait of Adolf Hitler hung on the wall to my left. I felt myself being pulled upward to stand as a door flew open, and the President of the People's court—Roland Freisler—entered, his scarlet robe billowing as he strode to his place in the front of the room.

He raised his right arm sharply. "Heil Hitler!"

Hundreds of arms rose in unison. "Heil Hitler!"

I refused to raise my arm, to cheer and praise a man who was corrupt and self-serving. As I watched the devotion these men had for Adolf Hitler, I saw the root of this problem. They were making him their god. Roland Freisler tossed a glare our way when we didn't salute. A sea of noise filled the courtroom as everyone took a seat.

"I hereby begin the proceedings of the people's court in the case against Hans Fritz Scholl of Munich, Sophie Magdalena Scholl of Munich, and Christoph Hermann Probst of Aldrans, charged with high treason, aiding and abetting the enemy, and troop demoralization." Roland Freisler turned his head toward us, his countenance hard as stone. I studied him. The man had the greyest eyes I'd ever seen, stripped of color and life and replaced by such cruelty that I almost felt sorry for him. "Probst, Christoph," Roland Freisler ordered.

I moved my feet under the bench as Christl and his escorts brushed past me. I peered up, meeting my friend's gaze. "Fight for yourself, Christl."

That earned me a sharp kick in the leg by the guard on my left. I rubbed my sore hands together and leaned forward, watching as he was prodded forward to stand before Freisler. Christl's face was haggard and wan, save for his red, swollen eyes. His shoulders were hunched, and he slowly raised his eyes to Freisler.

"Probst," Freisler spat his name out in disgust, as if it tasted bad on his tongue. "You are married?"

"Yes, Herr President."

"You have children?"

"Three, the third was just born. My wife is ill with childbed fever. Please," his voice broke, and he turned to me. I nodded, urging him to go on. "They need me. My wife and my children—"

"How can an idiot like you raise three children to be loyal citizens of the Third Reich? No, they don't need a failure like you in their life, Probst."

I fought back the urge to shout out a retort. My palms grew sweaty.

Freisler held a paper and read a section aloud, "'Hitler and his regime must fall so that Germany can live. Make your decision, Stalingrad and downfall, or Tripoli and a hopeful future. And once you have decided, act.'" He stared at Christl. "This is your handwriting, Probst?" Freisler held the discriminating leaflet in his hand, waving it in disdain.

Christl was quiet, then nodded. "Yes, Herr President, but it was only a rough draft. I'm apolitical, Herr President, and I didn't pay for supplies or help reproduce the leaflets." Freisler wrinkled his nose and tossed the leaflet down.

"Apolitical?" He laughed, and the judges to his right and left joined in. "You, Probst, are a traitor."

I could hear Sophie breathing hard. Her face was flushed, and her lips pressed together tightly.

"You were asked to write this leaflet by Scholl, and yet, the fact that the Reich was paying for your education and allowing you to have a family while studying didn't hinder you from helping the weakling?"

I found it strange that they thought their onslaught of insults would move us to repentance.

"Herr President, please, my wife is gravely ill and—"

"Stopping wailing, you blundering dimwit. You are dishonorable and unworthy of life in our glorious Reich. Any questions from the defense?"

"None, Herr President."

"Take him away." Freisler waved his hand, as if Christl were an annoying gnat.

I couldn't bear the look of despair that swept over Christl's face as he was brought back to the bench.

"Scholl, Sophie." Freisler's voice broke through my thoughts, bringing my full attention upon my younger sister, who was being brought to stand in front of Freisler. She managed good posture and held her head high. I ran a hand across the back of my neck, taking deep breaths to keep my emotions in check. She was so small and delicate in a sea of military men. It wasn't supposed to end like this.

Not for her.

"What caused you to help with this treasonous business?" Freisler's voice vibrated throughout the courtroom. "My brother and I wished to help enlighten our people on the horrors our state is carrying out ... the slaughter of Jews for instance. I don't want our nation to be cast aside. I wished to take a stand for the very things our nation is destroying— human dignity, goodness, conscience, morals, and God."

"There is no God," Freisler taunted.

"Yes, there is, and He will judge us each accordingly."

Freisler looked as if he had gotten a whiff of something rotten. "Your leaflets are products of uneducated minds. You could have had so much, and yet you didn't take what our nation offered you. Aren't you ashamed, Scholl?"

"No, the war is lost, Herr President, and I don't understand why you can't all face that with courage."

I felt a grin tug at my lips.

"The war is not lost, you little swine! You have been misguided by your half-witted brother. He dragged you into this, didn't he?"

"No, he didn't. I wanted to help, and I would do it again."

"You are a disgrace to Germany! What can we expect from this sub-human, the weaker sex?" Freisler raised his hands in disgust. "Questions from the defense?"

"No, Herr President."

"Then take the blight away."

"Somebody had to make a start." Sophie's voice split through the courtroom as the guards took her arms. "What we wrote and said is believed by many others. They just don't dare express themselves as we have."

Then I smiled—a full, broad smile—and nodded my head in approval as Sophie was brought back to the bench. I was so proud of her. Prouder than I could express.

"Scholl, Hans."

As I brushed past Sophie, she reached out to me, trying to grab my arm. The guards tugged me forward, the pain from their grip shooting through my veins. The only sound filling the courtroom was their boots against the hardwood floor. I watched as Freisler took a long sip of water, banging the glass down before picking up his pencil. "You are a medical student, thanks to the support of the Reich?"

I let my arms rest at my side in a relaxed position and chose my words with consideration. "I am a medical student, that is correct."

No thanks to the Reich.

"At the expense of the Reich, you had the privilege of studying medicine in time of war, a profession which requires you to carry out your duty for your fellow Germans.

A privilege you have abused, you parasite."

A wave of nods filled the courtroom, everyone confirming that I was, in fact, a parasite.

"You served on the Eastern Front as a medical aid?" Freisler continued.

"Yes, but—"

"Shut up! Don't speak unless spoken to." The veins in Freisler's neck bulged.

I clenched my jaw, a missile of words building inside me.

"Am I correct in saying that after all the support you received from the Reich regarding your future in a medical profession, you deliberately went against our Führer and Fatherland by publishing these leaflets of *The White Rose?*"

"I—"

"Yes or no, Scholl? Why can't you grasp that simple concept, you floundering fool?" Freisler shouted, his fists slamming against the desk. The water in his glass sloshed against the sides.

"Yes, I published the leaflets out of belief that—"

"These treasonous leaflets," Freisler shouted above my words, "called for resistance, predicted the defeat of Germany, called our Führer a political imposter, and tried to strip the people of our National Socialist way of life. Is this true, Scholl?"

I lifted my head, meeting Freisler's hostile glare. "That is correct. The blame is on me alone."

A chorus of horrified shouts filled the courtroom. I looked down at my hands. They were gripped in tight fists.

"Traitor! Kill this bastard!" someone shouted.

I closed my eyes to regain my composure. My limbs felt weak.

"Traitors like you must be swept off this earth. You don't deserve to live in our Reich, Scholl. You are a stupid, brainless dog who deserves nothing but death. But why, Scholl, did you stoop so low and involve your sister? Are you so cowardly as to have a woman carry out your filthy treachery?"

I could bear the insults directed at me, but Freisler now had struck a nerve.

Sophie.

"I told you that I wanted to help!" Sophie's voice tore through the silence, bringing my eyes upon her. She was leaning forward in the bench, her eyebrows furrowed in her thoughtful way. "He didn't drag me into it. I joined of my own free will."

"Spare us your droning comments, defendant!" Freisler yelled. "Or I'll have you thrown out of the courtroom." He turned to me and sneered. "Did you write the leaflets because you honestly believed you could influence us to think that Germany would lose the war?"

I was beginning to feel light headed. I planted my feet firmly, willing myself to stay clear and composed. "The war—"

"Germany will not lose this fight, Scholl, and you are an idiot to believe otherwise."

"Germany doesn't stand a chance," I shouted, my heart

racing. "The Allies—"

"The Allies don't stand a chance against the Third Reich!" Freisler shouted above me again, banging his fist on the table. "The Allies will perish under our boots just as your white rose has."

I quoted from *The White Rose* leaflet, perhaps for the last time in my life: "'It has become a mathematical certainty that Hitler is leading the German people into the abyss. Hitler cannot win the war; he can only prolong it. The guilt of Hitler and his minions goes beyond all measure. Retribution comes closer and closer.'"

Freisler's face was bright red, and his eyes flashed with rage. "Your treasonous aid to the enemy will cause the death of more of our soldiers!"

"No, only the war will do that. The only way to stop this unending bloodshed is the end of the war."

"Ah! I see, and how do you propose to do that?"

"Germany—"

"Germany wants this war!" Freisler screamed, jumping up from his chair.

"No, Germany doesn't want this war. Hitler does. Germany wants peace! Hitler has caused the death of millions upon millions. He is to blame for all this bloodshed and so are they who follow him, yourself included, Herr President, and all those gathered here."

"Who on earth do you think you are? How dare you insult the Führer! He is bringing glory back to Germany." Freisler pointed his finger at me, fury racking his body.

"Glory?" I scoffed. "You've never been to the Eastern Front, Herr President. I found no glory in the endless bloodshed. I found no glory in watching women and children being murdered by our soldiers. I found no glory in the atrocities our people are committing in occupied countries."

"We will not stand here and listen to your infernal, treacherous talk. How can you possibly think we believe a word you're saying? You are mistaken, Scholl, gravely mistaken!"

"I am not mistaken, Herr President. You are frightened of our opinions because you know they hold truth. We would not be standing here if that weren't so."

"The lies flooding from this parasite's mouth are unforgivable!" Freisler collapsed in his seat. "Questions from the defense?"

"No, Herr President."

"Take him away!"

I met Sophie's gaze as I walked past her to my seat. Once again she tried reaching for me, but the guards prevented any bit of comfort. A door at the back of the courtroom burst open, and everyone's heads turned. My eyes widened, and my heart thudded wildly as they fell on the form of my mother, father, and Werner pushing their way into the courtroom. Guards had seized them the moment they entered.

"I'm the mother of two of the accused!" Mother's voice caused my heart to drop to the pit of my stomach.

Dear mother, how can she bear this?

"You should have raised them better," a guard shouted at her.

I longed to run to my mother's arms, comfort her and tell her I was sorry. Werner was holding tightly to mother's arm, upholding her through this. His youthful face was ashen and scared. Father pushed his way to the desk where my defense attorney sat, the attorney who sat idly by for the entire trial. Father whispered something to him as Freisler scowled at the disruption.

"What is this?"

My attorney stood up, took long strides to Freisler and said something in his ear. Freisler's face twisted into mock pleasure. "Aha! So the father has come to defend his children? Remove him from this courtroom now!"

Guards immediately seized father, dragging him toward

the door. My breath caught in my throat as father passed me, sorrow in his dark brown eyes. "There is a higher justice than this." Father's voice filled every crevice of the courtroom. "My children will go down in history. My children are heroes!"

"Get him out of my sight." Freisler's anger was written all over his face. "Stand up, accused," he ordered.

The three of us stood in unison, looking at each other. We now were free from guards blocking our view of one another.

"In the Name of the German People in the action against Hans Fritz Scholl, of Munich, Sophie Magdalena Scholl, of Munich, and Christoph Hermann Probst, of Aldrans, now in investigative custody regarding treasonous assistance to the enemy, preparing to commit high treason, and weakening of the nation's armed security, the People's Court find that the accused have in time of war by means of leaflets called for the sabotage of the war effort and armaments and for the overthrow of the National Socialist way of life of our people, have propagated defeatist ideas, and have most vulgarly defamed the Führer, thereby giving aid to the enemy of the Reich and weakening the armed security of the nation. On this account they are to be punished by death by guillotine. Their honor and rights as citizens are forfeited for all time."

My throat closed. Christl swayed and gripped the dock. Sophie didn't move. Freisler gave us a bored look, as if he wished to have us convicted and executed as soon as humanly possible, so he could go on with his day. "Last statements from the defendants." Freisler leaned across his desk. "Probst?"

Christl raised his head, gripping his hands together. "I only acted out of the best interest for our country … to end this bloodshed and to spare more defeats such as Stalingrad."

"Yes, and you support Roosevelt's fight for unconditional surrender, labeling him the most powerful man in the world. I don't find that to be in our country's best interest."

A roar of indignation rose from the crowd, and they began shouting, cursing, and insulting Christl.

"Please, my children need me. They need their father." Christl's voice was strained with emotion.

When Freisler finally raised a hand to hush the crowd, the courtroom grew deathly silent.

"I ask the court to spare this man for the sake of his family," I said. "He had nothing to do with the leaflet production. Leniency should be given to him because of his situation."

"If you don't have anything to say for yourself, then kindly shut up and spare us your wallowing statements." Freisler bore his eyes into me.

"I do have something to say." I stood up, gripping the dock. "You will soon be where we stand now." The crowd shifted in their seats.

"You are an impertinent fool, Scholl." Freisler turned to Sophie, ignoring my statement. "Scholl, Sophie? Do you have anything to say?"

Sophie shook her head.

"This case is closed, take the traitors away." Freisler stood up in a wave of scarlet red. I couldn't leave it like this, Freisler getting the last word in.

I pointed my finger at him, passion for our cause burning in my soul. "You may kill us today, but tomorrow it will be your turn."

don't yield to them

I raised my head as the three of us were taken out of the courtroom. I blinked back tears. I wouldn't let them see I was slowly breaking.

Werner was pushing his way through the officers, fresh from the front. His brown hair was mussed, and his face was blotched and raw. His brown eyes searched mine, and I could see tears pooling in them. Werner thrust out his hand to me, pumping it with brotherly warmth. The despair I saw in his eyes tore through me, ripping me apart.

"Hans ..." Werner couldn't speak. A tear trailed down his boyish cheek. He sucked in a breath.

"Stay strong, Werner. Don't yield to them." My hand slipped from my brother's as I was pushed forward toward the staircase. I looked back as Werner and Sophie exchanged a quick embrace.

"My God, Sophie what will I do without you both?" My throat tightened at the sound of tears in my brother's voice.

"Werner, have courage. God is with us," I heard Sophie say.

We were brought outside to where the cars waited to take us to death row. My breathing quickened as I realized I might never see Sophie again in this life. She was being taken to a separate car from me and Christl. Tears had slipped from my eyes without warning. I kept my gaze fixed on her as a guard shoved my head down into the car. I whipped around, looking out the back window. Her face was pale as they pushed her into the car.

Our eyes met one last time.

stadelheim

"Hans Scholl."

I stood up as my prison cell in Stadelheim opened, sending a blinding white light into my pitch-black quarters.

This is it.

I was frozen in place, not wishing to stay in the dark inferno but also resisting walking toward that lighted hallway. The one that would lead me to my death.

"You have visitors," said the guard. He roughly grabbed my arm. "Come with me."

I breathed a little easier now as I stepped into the light. *There's still time. Still time to breathe. To live.*

He led me to a holding cell, shoving me inside. I stood there for a long moment taking in the faces of my parents. Mother's eyes were warm and loving, and tears glistened on her wrinkled face. Father was holding her in his arms, calm as Sophie had been during court. I smiled at them as I closed the space between us. I reached out my hand, and mother grabbed it, bringing it to her lips.

A cold fist closed over my heart, twisting it until the pain was nearly unbearable. "Thank you for the love and warmth you've given me. I love you both ... so much."

Mother's smooth hand caressed my face. "My little boy." Her voice broke, and tears spilled down her cheeks. "What have they done? How can they do this?"

All I wanted to do at that moment was rest my head on mother's shoulder like a child, and hear her tell me everything would be all right. "I hold no hate for anyone. That's all in the past."

I turned to father, a million words of thanks burning in my heart that I wished to express to him. "Father, you stood with me even when I was a trial for you. I'm sorry for our arguments and not heeding your advice when I should have."

"Hans." Father bit his lip to keep back his tears. "My son, I am proud of you."

Love swelled in my heart for the two who had given me life. "Please give my love and warmth to Inge and Elisabeth." My sisters. How I longed to see them just one last time. To hug them close. To tell them to be brave and take care of mother and father. "And to Jürgen, Traute, and ... Gisela if you see her." I couldn't blink back the tears now. They tore at my eyes, demanding to be set free. I turned my head, not wishing for my parents to see them. I cleared my throat and wiped my eyes with the back of my sleeve.

I leaned down and kissed mother on the cheek, then

wrapped her in a hug. She held me close. "Oh, Hans, to think I'll never hug you again. To think ... you'll never come home again." Cries racked her small frame, and she clung to me tighter.

"We took it upon ourselves knowing the consequences. I just wish I could spare you the pain."

She held my face between her hands, searching my eyes. "God is with you, son. Remember, Jesus."

"Yes, mother. We'll see each other again." I wiped a tear from her wrinkled cheek with my thumb.

She kissed my cheek, then released me, giving me over to my father. He gathered me in his arms, patting my back tenderly. "You both are so brave," he whispered. "I'm proud of you and Sophie. So proud."

I nodded my thanks as the guard stepped into the room. Our time was up. I stepped back, not breaking the connection with my parents until the last moment. They were holding each other upright as I was taken from the room. That was the last time I saw them—brave love upon their faces in the midst of overwhelming sorrow. It was a balm to my weary soul.

blessed

This confession has run full circle, bringing me to this moment. I sit here with my back against the stone wall, nearly choking on all the emotions that are overpowering me as I remember. My helpless cries are the only sound in my ears. I hate hearing them. Tears are foreign to me, and I don't know how to stop them once they've started.

I've just had a visitor. My last visitor. The cell door opened not long ago, bringing in the pastor. I stepped forward to greet him, outstretching my hand.

"I'm Hans Scholl. Thank you for coming."

"I'm Karl Alt," the pastor said. "Shall we sit?"

I nodded, sinking into a hard-backed chair as I rubbed my hands together. "I would like to read a Psalm together."

"Do you have one in mind?" Karl asked, opening his ancient Bible.

"The ninetieth."

I watched as Karl opened the Bible, leafing through the fragile pages until he came upon the selected verse. I closed my eyes and bowed my head as Karl began reading: "'Lord, you have been our dwelling place throughout all generations. Before the mountains were born or you brought forth the whole world, from everlasting to everlasting you are God. You turn people back to dust, saying, 'Return to dust, you mortals.' A thousand years in your sight are like a day that has just gone by, or like a watch in the night. Yet, you sweep people away in the sleep of death—they are like the new grass of the morning: In the morning it springs up new, but by evening it is dry and withered. We are consumed by your anger and terrified by your indignation. You have set our iniquities before you, our secret sins in the light of your presence. All our days pass away under your wrath; we finish our years with a moan. Our days may come to seventy years, or eighty, if our strength endures; yet the best of them are but trouble and sorrow, for they quickly pass, and we fly away...

"'Teach us to number our days, that we may gain a heart of wisdom. Relent, Lord! How long will it be? Have compassion on your servants. Satisfy us in the morning with your unfailing love, that we may sing for joy and be glad all our days. Make us glad for as many days as you have afflicted us, for as many years as we have seen trouble. May your deeds be shown to your servants, your splendor to their children. May the favor of the Lord our God rest on us; establish the work of our hands for us—yes, establish the work of our hands.'"

My eyes flew open. Peace washed over me like a summer

breeze. "These words cause my concerns to feel insignificant in the face of eternity."

Karl seemed taken aback, but smiled warmly. "This is strange for me, Hans Scholl. I'm usually the one administering to the needs of lost souls."

"I would like to read a few more verses," I said, knowing my time was running out. Death was lingering outside the door. "My childhood favorite was first Corinthians thirteen."

As Karl began to read, I joined in, recalling it all from memory and feeling a fountain of joy flow through me as I recited it. "'If I speak in the tongues of men or of angels, but do not have love, I am only a resounding gong or a clanging cymbal. If I have the gift of prophecy and can fathom all mysteries and all knowledge, and if I have a faith that can move mountains, but do not have love, I am nothing. If I give all I possess to the poor and give over my body to hardship that I may boast, but do not have love, I gain nothing.

"'Love is patient, love is kind. It does not envy, it does not boast, it is not proud. It does not dishonor others, it is not self-seeking, it is not easily angered, it keeps no record of wrongs. Love does not delight in evil but rejoices with the truth. It always protects, always trusts, always hopes, always perseveres. Love never fails. But where there are prophecies, they will cease; where there are tongues, they will be stilled; where there is knowledge, it will pass away. For we know in part and we prophesy in part, but when completeness comes, what is in part disappears. When I was a child, I talked like a child, I thought like a child, I reasoned like a child. When I became a man, I put the ways of childhood behind me." I prepared to soak in the last verse, for it struck my soul. "'For now we see only a reflection as in a mirror; then we shall see face to face. Now I know in part; then I shall know fully, even as I am fully known.'"

Karl closed the Bible, and I felt his stare. "No greater love than this; to lay down one's life for one's friends. You may rest in peace knowing that you have done just that and knowing that Christ has done this for you. Scholl, you may have to die at the hands of an executioner, but to die with such love and faith in your heart is to die a good, honorable death. You are blessed."

epilogue

"This way."

Hans was led out of his cell. The guard seemed uneasy, glancing to the right and left of him with a cautious eye. He stepped across the hall and unlocked another cell, releasing Christl.

"It's against the rules," the young guard said, his eyes dodging around the halls. "But I thought you three should be allowed to say goodbye. Your sister is coming, Scholl."

Hans exchanged a look of surprise with Christl. For the first time in days, they could speak freely.

"I've just become Catholic," Christl said. "Father Speer admitted me into the Church. I received my first—and my last—communion in the cell. Hans, I feel so free! Peace and joy have banished any fears. I'm ready."

Hans smiled, clasping his friend's arm. "We are free, Christl."

The sound of footsteps shuffling up the narrow hallway brought their eyes on Sophie being led by a female guard. They all grinned at each other, feeling in awe that the time had come, and yet, they didn't feel any fear.

"Here," the female guard said, handing Sophie a cigarette and lighting it. "Hurry."

Sophie put the cigarette to her dry lips, her fingers shaking slightly. She took a long drag, then slowly handed it to Hans, their eyes meeting. He took it from her, puffing out a stream of smoke into the dimly lit hall. Finally, he gave it to

Christl, who closed his eyes as he exhaled. The three of them stood closely to each other, Sophie appearing so small and childlike in the midst of Hans' and Christl's tall forms. She wrapped an arm around each of them, pulling her comrades close to herself. Hans wrapped an arm around her and the other around Christl's shoulder. He rested his head against Sophie's hair. The trio held each other for a long, silent moment before calmly pulling away. They stood close, their arms brushing against each other.

"What we did was right," Sophie said, gazing up at them with a content smile. "Don't think it was in vain, for it wasn't. I'd do it all over again in an instant."

"And we shouldn't mourn over losing each other," Christl said. "For in just a few short minutes, we'll be meeting again in eternity."

"Until then," Hans smiled.

"You have to go now," the female guard said. They were taken to a large holding cell. There was a door at the end of the cell which led into an open yard. Two men in black suits entered and seized Sophie, clamping handcuffs around her small wrists.

Hans watched in peaceful awe as his sister allowed them to take her prisoner once more and lead her toward her death. He swallowed, knowing that it would be only a few short moments without her, and yet, how much he would miss her.

"I love you, Sophie," he said. "A strong spirit—"

She glanced over her shoulder at him, her brown eyes bright with joy. "And a gentle heart."

The door opened, and Sophie was led out into the courtyard. It slammed shut. Hans and Christl had only to wait a few painful moments until the same men returned. Without Sophie.

"Probst," they ordered.

Christl stepped forward, nodding to Hans with a smile. "I didn't know that dying was so easy."

The tall, good natured friend Hans had come to regard as a brother was taken through the door, his posture erect and his gait quick. Now Hans stood by himself in the holding cell, awaiting the men to come back for him. He was grateful that Sophie had gone first, for the thought of her being in his place now—all alone while the others were dead—was the worst punishment of all.

The door opened, bringing in two dark silhouettes against the bright sunny sky. Without a word, they pinned Hans to the wall, handcuffed him, then prodded him outside and down the stairs that led into the courtyard. Hans lifted his eyes to the sun which warmed his face with its glorious rays. The wind was brisk, but he relished the sensation of it running through his hair. *O Life! O Living!* His stride was light. He didn't resist as he was led closer to the unmarked shed on the opposite end of the courtyard.

"'For now we see only a reflection as in a mirror; then we shall see face to face.'"

The door of the shed was thrust open, and he entered a room which was divided by a black curtain. In front of this curtain sat a man behind a table, papers before him.

"In accordance with the sentence given by the People's Court on this day, February 22nd, 1943, the Reich has disregarded any appeals for clemency as justice must be served. The execution will take place now—5:10 P.M."

Hans clenched his jaw and stood tall as the curtain was pulled back, revealing the guillotine in all its filth and terror. He remembered the wailing man he had heard from his cell days before. *If I must die, I'll do it with dignity.*

The guillotine blade glinted in the light, its edges sharp and savage. The concrete floor beneath it was stained with fresh blood. A guard lifted Hans' chest, the other his legs, and they slid him onto the block, securing his head through the hole. He heard the death machine clink. In one last burst of life, he screamed, "Long live freedom!"

"Such a fine, sunny day,
and I have to go, but what
does my death matter, if
through us, thousands of
people are awakened and
stirred to action?"

—*Sophie Scholl*

note from the author

For Hans, Sophie, and Christl, it was a deadly whirlwind of four days from the time of their arrest to their execution. In reality, there wouldn't have been time for Hans to write his confession, nor would he have given away the names of his fellow resisters, but for the sake of the story, I granted myself poetic license.

Willi, Alex, and Professor Huber each faced their deaths with great courage and faith in God. Alexander Schmorell and Professor Huber were executed on July 13th, 1943. Willi Graf was executed on October 12th, 1943. The Gestapo held him longer to attempt to gain more information on *The White Rose* operation. Although the Nazis had put the leaders of this resistance group to their deaths, *The White Rose* lived on. Shortly after Hans, Sophie, and Christl were in their graves, the seventh leaflet circulated with the words: *Despite everything, their spirit lives on!*

These words were also painted on walls and sidewalks after their execution. In the same year, the Royal Air Force got ahold of the leaflets and renamed them: *A German Leaflet—Manifesto of The Munich Students.* The RAF dropped the leaflets from their planes into cities across Germany.

The White Rose may not have overthrown the Nazi regime or put an immediate end to the terror, but they proved to the world that there was still goodness, humanity, and faith in God abounding in the hearts of people throughout Nazi occupied Europe. They will forever inspire and challenge us to do what is right in the midst of overwhelming evil.

Remember the brave souls of *The White Rose*, and share their story. It deserves to be told.

acknowledgments

I'd first like to thank my wonderful editors Maria Putzke, Emily Chapman, and Meghan Gorecki. Thank you for your time and effort getting this manuscript ready for publication. I'd also like to thank my historical editor, Steve Appleby, director of the Eldred WWII Museum. Thank you so much for looking over the manuscript and for your enthusiasm in *The White Rose* and WWII in general. You bring history to life! A thank you also goes to my family and advance readers for their encouragement and support in this project. Most of all, I'd like to thank my Heavenly Father for giving me the gift of writing to bless and encourage others. May I always use it to bring Him glory.

bibliography

Bamm, Peter. *The Invisible Flag.* Faber; First edition, 1956.

Dumbach, Annette, and Jud Newborn. *Sophie Scholl and the White Rose.* Oneworld Publications: Second Edition, June 2, 2007.

Hanser, Richard. *A Noble Treason.* Ignatius Press: Reprint edition, October 19, 2012.

Hermann Vinke. *The Short Life of Sophie Scholl.* Harper & Row, 1984.

Jens, Inge. *At the Heart of The White Rose—Diaries and Letters of Hans and Sophie Scholl.* Harper & Row: First edition, August 1987.

Melon, Ruth. *Journey to the White Rose in Germany.* Dog Ear Publishing LLC, January 10, 2007.

Scholl, Inge. *The White Rose: Munich, 1942-1943.* Wesleyan: Second edition. (Originally published as Students Against Tyranny). Translated from the German edition, June 15, 1983.

films

Sophie Scholl: The Final Days. Dir. Marc Rothemund. Zeitgeist Films, 2005.

websites

Lisciotto, Carmelo. 2007. *The White Rose* Leaflets: Translations of The Six Printed Leaflets. Holocaust Education and Archive Research Team.

about the author

Emily Ann Putzke is a young novelist, historical reen-actor, and history lover. She's the author of *It Took a War*, *Sweet Remembrance*, *Resist*, and co-author of *Ain't We Got Fun*. You can learn more about Emily and her books at:

www.authoremilyannputzke.com

Made in the USA
Middletown, DE
22 March 2020

87067108R10151